PAIN

Also by Arturo Pérez-Reverte

THE FLANDERS PANEL
THE CLUB DUMAS
THE SEVILLE COMMUNION
THE FENCING MASTER
THE NAUTICAL CHART
THE QUEEN OF THE SOUTH

Captain Alatriste Series

CAPTAIN ALATRISTE
PURITY OF BLOOD
THE SUN OVER BREDA

THE PAINTER *of* BATTLES

A Novel

ARTURO PÉREZ-REVERTE

Translated from the Spanish
by Margaret Sayers Peden

RANDOM HOUSE / NEW YORK

Published in the United States by Random House, an imprint of The Random House Publishing Group, a division of Random House, Inc., New York.

LIBRARY OF CONGRESS CATALOGING-IN-PUBLICATION DATA
Pérez-Reverte, Arturo.
[Pintor de batallas. English]
The painter of battles: a novel/Arturo Pérez-Reverte; translated from the Spanish by Margaret Sayers Peden.
p. cm.
ISBN 978-0-8129-7938-1
I. Peden, Margaret Sayers. II. Title.
PQ6666.E765P5613 2008
863'.64—dc22 2007016997

Printed in the United States of America

www.atrandom.com

OPM 9 8 7 6 5 4 3 2 1

Saint Augustine has seen that one
labors in uncertainty at sea
and in battles and in all the rest,
but he has not seen the rules of the game.

—*Blaise Pascal,* PENSÉES, 234

1.

HE SWAM ONE HUNDRED AND fifty strokes out to sea and the same number back, as he did each morning, until he felt the round pebbles of the shore beneath his feet. He dried himself, using the towel he'd hung on a tree trunk that had been swept in by the sea, put on his shirt and sneakers, and went up the narrow path leading from the cove to the watchtower. There he made coffee and began, mixing blues and grays that would lend his work the proper atmosphere. During the night—each night he slept less and less, and that only a restless dozing—he had decided that cold tones would be needed to delineate the melancholy line of the horizon, where a veiled light outlined the silhouettes of warriors walking beside the sea. Those tones would envelop them in reflections from the waves washing onto the beach that he had spent four days creating with light touches of Titian white, applied pure. So in a glass jar he mixed white, blue, and a minimal amount of natural sienna, until they were transformed into a luminous blue. Then he daubed some of the paint on the oven tray he used as a palette, dirtied the mixture with a little yellow, and worked without stopping the rest of the morning. Finally he clamped the handle of the brush between his teeth and stepped back to judge the effect. Sky and sea were now harmoniously combined in the mural that circled the interior of the tower, and although there was still a lot to be done, the horizon was now a smooth, slightly hazy line that accentuated the loneliness of the men—dark strokes splashed with metallic sparks—dispersed and moving away beneath the rain.

He rinsed the brushes with soap and water and set them to dry. From the foot of the cliff below came the sound of the motors and music of the tourist boat that ran along the coast every day at the same hour. With no need to look, Andrés Faulques knew that it was one o'clock. He heard the usual woman's voice, amplified by the loudspeaker system, and it seemed even stronger and clearer when the boat drew even with the inlet, for then the sound reached the tower with no obstacle other than the few pines and bushes that despite erosion and slides were still clinging to the cliff face.

This place is known as Cala del Arráez. *It was once the refuge of Berber pirates. Up there on the top of the cliff you can see an old watchtower that was constructed at the beginning of the eighteenth century as a part of the coastal defense, with the specific purpose of warning nearby villages of Saracen incursions . . .*

It was the same voice every day: educated, with good diction. Faulques imagined the woman to be young; no doubt a local guide who accompanied the tourists on the three-hour tour the boat—a sixty-five-foot tender painted blue and white that docked in Puerto Umbría—made between Ahorcados Island

and Cabo Malo. In the last two months, from atop the cliff, Faulques had watched it pass, its deck filled with people armed with film and video cameras as summertime music thundered over the loudspeakers, so loud that the interruptions of the woman's voice came as a relief.

A well-known painter lives in that tower, which stood abandoned for a long time, and he is embellishing the entire interior wall with a large mural. Unfortunately, it is private property and no visitors are allowed . . .

This time the woman was speaking Spanish, but on other occasions it might be English, Italian, or German. Only when the tickets were bought with francs—four or five times that summer—did a masculine voice relieve her, in French. At any rate, Faulques thought, the season was almost over; with every trip there were fewer tourists on board the tender, and soon those daily visits would become weekly, until they were interrupted by the harsh gray mistrals that blew in the winter, funneling in through the straits called Bocas de Poniente, darkening sea and sky.

He turned his attention back to the painting, where new cracks had appeared. The large circular panorama was not as yet continuous; some zones were blank except for strokes of charcoal, simple black lines sketched on the white primer of the wall. The whole formed an immense and disquieting landscape, no title, no specific time, where the shield half buried in the sand, the medieval helmet splashed with blood, the shadow of an assault rifle falling over a forest of wood crosses, the ancient walled city and modern concrete-and-glass towers coexisted less as anachronisms than as evidence.

Faulques went back to his painting, laboriously, patiently. Although the technical execution was correct, it was not an outstanding work, and he knew it. He had a good hand for drawing, but he was a mediocre painter. He knew that as well. In truth, he had always known it; however, the mural was not destined to be seen by anyone but him. That had little to do with artistic ability and much to do with his memory. With an eye guided by thirty years of hearing the sound of a camera shutter. Hence the framing—that was as good a name to give it as any other—of all those straight lines and angles traced with a singular, vaguely Cubist severity that lent beings and objects contours as impossible to breach as barbed wire or moats. The mural took up the wall of the ground floor of the watchtower in a continuous panorama twenty-five meters in circumference and almost three meters in height, interrupted only by the openings of two narrow, facing windows, the door that led outside, and the spiral staircase that led to the upper floor that Faulques had arranged as his living quarters: a gas ring, a small refrigerator, a canvas cot, a table and chairs, a rug, and a trunk. He had lived there for seven months, and had spent the first two making it habitable: a temporary waterproof wood roof for the tower, concrete beams to reinforce the walls, shutters at the windows, and the drain that emptied out over the cliff from the small lower-level latrine carved out of the rock. He also had an outdoor water tank installed atop a board-and-tile shed that served both as a shower and as a garage for the motorcycle he rode down to the village each week to buy food.

The cracks worried Faulques. Too soon, he told himself. And too many. They would not actually affect the future of his work—it was a work *without* a future from the minute he discovered the abandoned tower and conceived his plan—only the time he needed to execute it. With that in mind, he nervously passed the tips of his fingers over the crazing that fanned out across the part of the mural that was closest to being finished, over the black and red strokes that represented the asymmetrical, polyhedral backlighting of the walls of the ancient city burning in the distance—Bosch, Goya, and Dr. Atl, among others: the hand of man, nature, and destiny fused in the magma of a single horizon. There would be more cracks. These weren't the first. The structural reinforcing of the tower, the plastering, the white acrylic primer, were not enough to counteract the deterioration of the three-hundred-year-old building, the damage that had been caused by harsh weather, erosion, and salt from the nearby sea while it was abandoned. It was also, in a certain way, a struggle against time; its tranquil passing could not disguise its inexorable victory. Although not even that, Faulques concluded with a familiar professional fatalism—he'd seen a few cracks in his lifetime—was of major importance.

The pain—a sharp stab in his side over his right hip—arrived every eight or ten hours with reliable punctuality, faithful to their tryst, though this time it came with no warning. Faulques held his breath and didn't move, to allow time for the first whiplash of pain to end; then he picked up a jar from the table and swallowed two tablets with a sip of water. In recent weeks he'd had to double the dose. After a moment, calmer now—it was worse when the pain came at night, and although it was eased by the tablets, it kept him awake till dawn—he reviewed the panorama with a slow look around the entire circle: the distant, modern city and the other city, closer and in flames, the abject silhouettes fleeing from it, the somber, foreshortened, armed men in the foreground, the reddish reflection of the fire—fine brushstrokes, vermilion over yellow—sliding along the metal of their guns, with the peculiar brilliance that catches the eye of an unfortunate protagonist, uneasy the minute the door opens—*cloc, cloc, cloc*—the nightly sound of boots, iron, and guns, precise as a musical score, before they make him come outside, barefoot, and cut off—in the updated version, lop off—his head. Faulques' idea was to extend the light of the burning city as far as the gray dawn of the beach, where the rainy landscape and the sea in the background were fading into an eternal twilight, a prelude to that same night, or another identical to it, an interminable helix that brought the point of the wheel, the swinging pendulum of history, to the top of the arc, again and again, and sent it back the other way.

A well-known painter, the voice had announced. She always used the same words, while Faulques, imagining the tourists aiming their cameras toward the tower, wondered where the woman—the man who spoke in French never mentioned the tower's resident—had acquired such inexact information. Maybe, he concluded, it was merely a way of adding more interest to the tour. If Faulques was known in certain places and professional circles, it was not for his painting. After a few youthful cracks at it, and for the rest of his professional life, drawing and brushes had been set aside, far—at least so he had thought until only recently—from the situations, landscapes, and people recorded through the viewfinder of his camera: the stuff of the world of colors, sensations, and faces that constituted his search for the definitive image; the both fleeting and eternal moment that would explain all things. The hidden rule that made order out of the implacable geometry of chaos. Paradoxically, only since he had put away his cameras and taken up his brushes anew, in search of the—reassuring?—perspective he had never been able to capture through a lens, had Faulques felt closer to what he had sought for so long without finding. Maybe, he now thought, the scene had never been in front of his eyes, in the soft green of a rice field, in the motley anthill of a souk, in the tears of a child or the mud of a trench, but inside him, in the backwash of his own memory and the ghosts that lined its shores like markers. In the tracing of sketch and color, slow, meticulous, thoughtful, that is possible only when the pulse is already beating slowly. When old, mean-spirited gods, and their consequences, cease to harass man with their hatreds and their favors.

Battle painting. The concept was daunting to anyone, whether or not he was expert, and Faulques had approached the subject with all the circumspection and technical humility possible. Before he'd bought the tower and moved into it, he had spent years collecting documentation, visiting museums, studying the execution of a genre that hadn't interested him in the least during the days of his youthful studies and tastes. Faulques had trekked through galleries of battles from the Escorial and Versailles to certain Rivera or Orozco murals, from Greek vessels to the mill of Los Frailes, from specialized books to works exhibited in museums throughout Europe and America, observing everything with the unique eye that three decades of capturing war images had given him: in all, twenty-six centuries of the iconography of war. The mural was the end result of all these sources: warriors strapping on armor in terra-cotta reds and black; legionnaires sculpted on Trajan's column; the Bayeux tapestry; Carducho's victory at Fleurus; Saint-Quentin, Spain's victory over France, as seen by Luca Giordano; slaughters painted by Antonio Tempesta; Leonardo's studies of the battle of Anghiari; Callot's engravings; the burning of Troy interpreted by Collantes; Goya's *Second of May* and *Disasters of War;* the *Suicide of Saul* by Bruegel the Elder; the sacking and conflagrations depicted by Brueghel the Younger, or by Falcone; the Burgundy wars; Fortuny's *Battle of Tetuan;* the Napoleonic grenadiers and horsemen of Meissonier and Detaille; the cavalry charges of Lin, Meulen, and Roda; an assault on a convent by Pandolfo Reschi; a night conflict by Matteo Stom; Paolo Uccello's medieval clashes; and so many other works studied for hours and days and months, searching for a key, a secret, an explanation or a useful tool. Hundreds of notes and books, thousands of images, piled everywhere, around and inside Faulques, in the tower, and in his memory.

But not only battles. The technical execution, the

resolution of difficulties such a painting posed, were also indebted to the study of paintings with motifs other than those of war. In some disturbing paintings or engravings by Goya, in certain frescoes or canvases by Giotto, Bellini, and Piero della Francesca, in the Mexican muralists and modern artists like Léger, de Chirico, Chagall, or the early Cubists, Faulques had found practical solutions. In the same way that a photographer approaches problems of focus, light, and framing posed by the image he intends to appropriate, painting, too, supposed confronting problems that could be solved by means of the rigorous application of a system based on formulas, examples, experience, intuition, and genius—should there be genius. Faulques was familiar with style, he had mastered technique, but he lacked the essential characteristic that separates enthusiasm from talent. Aware of this, his early attempts to devote himself to painting had been quickly abandoned. Now, however, he possessed the required knowledge and the vital experience needed to meet the challenge: a project discovered through the viewfinder of a camera and forged in recent years. A panoramic mural that before the eyes of an attentive observer would unfurl the implacable rules that held war—chaos made apparent—to be the mirror of life. There was no ambition to achieve a masterwork; the mural did not even pretend to be original, although in reality it was the sum and combination of countless images taken from painting and photography that would be impossible without the existence and the eye of the man who was painting in the tower. And the mural was not destined to be conserved indefinitely, or to be exhibited to the public.

Once it was finished, the painter would abandon his tower studio and the mural would be left to its fate. From there on, the only agents to continue the work would be time and chance, using brushes dipped in their own complex and mathematical combinations. That was a part of the very nature of the work.

Faulques lingered in his appraisal of the large circular landscape created mostly from recollections, situations, and old images brought into the present in acrylics after years of rambling through the thousands of kilometers, the infinite geography, of the circumvolutions, neurons, folds, and veins that constituted his brain and that would be extinguished, along with him, at the hour of his death. The first time, now years ago, that Olvido Ferrara and he had talked about painting battles had been in the gallery of the Alberti Palace in Prato, standing before the canvas of Giuseppe Pinacci entitled *After the Battle,* one of those spectacular historical paintings with perfect composition, balanced and unrealistic, one that no lucid artist, despite all the intervening technical advances, experience, and modernity, would ever dare discuss. How curious, she had said—among pillaged and dying bodies a warrior was using the butt of his harquebus to club to death a fallen enemy who looked for all the world like a crustacean, completely encased in helmet and armor—that nearly all the interesting painters of battle scenes lived prior to the seventeenth century. Since that time, no one, except Goya, was bold enough to contemplate a human being realistically touched by death, with authentic blood instead of the syrup of heroes in his veins. Patrons who commissioned paintings from the rear guard thought that was not entirely practical. Then photography took the place of painting. Your photos, Faulques. And those of others. But even that has lost its integrity, right? Placing horror in the foreground is now politically incorrect. Today, even the face and the eyes of the boy with upraised arms in the famous war photo taken in Warsaw would be covered, to comply with laws concerning the protection of minors. Besides, that whole thing about how you really have to work hard to force a camera to lie is a long way behind us. Now every photo in which you see people lies or is suspect, whether or not it is accompanied by a text. A photograph is no longer a witness, it has become a part of the scene around us. Anyone can comfortably choose the parcel of horror he wishes to be moved by. You don't agree? Don't ever forget how far we are from those painted portraits from days past in which the human face was surrounded with a silence that rested the eyes and awakened the conscience. Now our official sympathy toward all kinds of victims frees us from responsibility. Or remorse.

Olvido could not imagine it then—they hadn't at that time traveled together through wars and museums for very long—but her words, like those spoken later in Florence before a painting by Paolo Uccello, were prophetic. Or it could be that what happened was that those words, and others that followed later, awakened in Faulques something that had been germinating for some time. Perhaps from the day when one of his photos—a very young Angolan guerrilla fighter crying beside a friend's body—was bought to promote a brand of clothing, or maybe it was another, no less exceptional day, when after carefully scrutinizing a photo of a dead Spanish militiaman immortalized by the camera of Robert Capa—indisputably an icon of honest battle photography—Faulques had concluded that in the countless wars he himself had covered, he had never seen anyone die in combat with the knees of his trousers and his shirt so spotlessly clean. Those details, and many others, minimal or major, including the disappearance of Olvido Ferrara in the Balkans and the passing of time in the heart and head of the photographer, were remote motifs, pieces of the complex framework of coincidences and causalities that had led him to the place where he was standing: before a mural in a tower.

There was still much to be done—he had covered a little more than half of the painting sketched in charcoal on the white wall—but the painter of battles was satisfied. As for the morning's work, the beach beneath the rain and the ships sailing away from the burning city, that recently applied misty blue on the melancholy of the horizon, nearly gray between sea and sky, oriented the spectator's gaze toward hidden converging lines that connected the distant silhouettes bristling with metallic sparks to the column of fleeing soldiers, and especially to the face of a woman with African features—large eyes, strong line of brow and chin, hand about to cover those eyes—positioned in the foreground in warm tones that accentuated her proximity. But nothing comes out of you that you don't have inside, Faulques believed. Painting, like photography, love, or conversation, was like those rooms in bombed-out hotels—all the window glass broken, all the contents stripped—that can be furnished only with things you take from your own backpack. There were scenes of war, situations, faces, the obligatory photos that belonged to a different order of things: Paris, the Taj Mahal, the Brooklyn Bridge. Nine of every ten recent photographs observed the ritual, looking for the quick shot that would inscribe them in the select club of tourists of horror. But that had never been the case with Faulques. He didn't try to justify the predatory character of his photographs, like some who claimed they traveled to wars because they hated wars and went with the goal of bringing an end to them. Neither did he aspire to collect the world, nor to explain it. He wanted only to understand the code of the blueprint, the key to the cryptogram, so that his pain and all pains might become bearable. From the beginning, he had sought something different: the point from which he could become aware of, or at least intuit, the tangle of straight and curved lines, the chess-like scheme upon which the mechanisms of life and death were formulated, chaos in all its forms, war as structure, as fleshless skeleton . . . the gigantic cosmic paradox. The man who was painting that enormous circular painting, the battle of all battles, had spent many hours of his life seeking such a structure, like a patient sniper, whether on a terrace in Beirut, on the shore of an African river, or on a street corner in Mostar, waiting for the miracle that would suddenly, through his lens, sketch on the rigorously Platonic camera obscura of his camera and his retina the secret of that surpassingly complex warp and woof that returned life to what it really was: a perilous excursion toward death and nothingness. To reach these kinds of conclusions through their work, many photographers and artists tended to isolate themselves in a studio. In Faulques' case, his had been special. After abandoning a series of classes in architecture and art, he had at the age of twenty thrown himself into war, observant, lucid, with the caution of one exploring a woman's body for the first time. And until Olvido Ferrara walked into and out of his life, he had believed he would survive both war and women.

Intently, he studied that other face, or rather, the stylized representation on the wall. She had been on the cover of several magazines after he had captured her face, almost by chance—the chance, he smiled crookedly, of the randomly precise moment—in a refugee camp in the south of Sudan. One day of routine work, of a tense and silent ballet, subtle dance steps among enervated children dying before the lenses of his cameras, bone-thin women with blank gazes, skeletal old men whose memories were their only future. And as he listened to the whirring of his Nikon F3 as it rewound, Faulques saw the girl out of the corner of one eye. She was lying on the ground on a rush mat, clutching a chipped jug to her stomach; she had put one hand to her face with a gesture of incalculable weariness. It was the gesture that caught his attention. With an automatic reflex he checked the film remaining in the camera slung around his neck, an old but solid Leica M3 with its 50-mm lens. Three exposures would be enough, he thought, as he began quietly to move toward the girl, attempting not to do anything that might cause her to alter the pose—an indirect approach Olvido would later call it, fond of applying cynical military terminology to their work. But just as Faulques got the viewfinder of the camera to his eye and was focusing, the girl noticed his shadow on the ground, moved her hand slightly, raised her head, and looked at him. He had snapped two quick exposures, pressing the shutter release as his instinct told him not to miss a look that might never be repeated. Then, aware that he had only one more chance to capture her face on the gelatin silver bromide of the film before it vanished forever, with his forefinger he brushed the ring that regulated the aperture, set it at the 5.6 he calculated for the ambient light, varied the angle of his camera a few centimeters, and snapped his last shot one second before the girl turned her face away and covered it with one hand. After that there was nothing more he could do, and five minutes later, when he came back with his two cameras loaded and ready, the girl's look was not the same and the moment had passed. Faulques traveled back with those three photographs in his thoughts, wondering if the developer would bring them out just as he thought he'd seen them, or remembered them. And later, in the red dusk of the darkroom, he anxiously awaited the emergence of lines and colors, the slow configuration of the face whose eyes stared up at him from the depths of the developer tray. Once the prints were dry, Faulques spent a long time in front of them, aware that he had been very close to the enigma and its physical formulation. The first two were less than perfect, a slight problem of focus, but the third was clean and sharp. The girl was young and ethereally beautiful despite the horizontal scar that marred her forehead and the lips cracked—like the cracks in the mural—by illness and thirst. And all of it—scar, lips, the fine, bony fingers of the hand just touching her face, the line of her chin and faint suggestion of eyebrows, the background of the mat's rhomboidal braiding—seemed to flow together in the brightness of her eyes, the reflection of light in the black irises, her unflinching and hopeless resignation. A moving, very ancient and eternal mask on which all lines and angles converged. The geometry of chaos in the serene face of a dying girl.

2.

WHEN FAULQUES GLANCED OUT the window on the landward side of the tower, he saw the stranger standing among the pines, looking toward the tower. Cars could come only halfway up the road, which meant another half hour on foot by way of the path that snaked up from the bridge. An uncomfortable hike at that hour, with the sun still high in the sky and without a breath of air to cool the small smooth rocks of the slope. Fine physical shape, he thought. Or a strong desire to call. Faulques stretched his arms to ease the kinks in his long skeleton—he was tall, heavy-boned, and his short gray hair gave him a vaguely military air—rinsed his hands in a basin of water, and went outside. The two men stared at each other a few instants amid the monotonous shrill of the cicadas in the undergrowth. The stranger had a knapsack over his shoulder and was wearing a white shirt, jeans, and hiking boots. He was regarding the tower, and its resident, with tranquil curiosity, as if he were trying to assure himself that this was the place he was looking for.

"Hello there," he said.

An accent that could be from anywhere. The

painter's response was an expression of extreme annoyance. He did not like callers, and to discourage them he had put up very visible signs along the path—one warned *Vicious Dogs,* though there were none—making it clear that this was private property. No one ever came this way. His only relations were the superficial contacts he maintained when he went down to Puerto Umbría: the clerks in the post office and city hall, the waiter in the bar where he sometimes sat on the terrace beside the little fishing dock, the shopkeepers from whom he bought food and supplies for his work, the director of the branch bank he'd transferred money to from Barcelona. He nipped in the bud any attempt at closer ties, and anyone who breached that line of defense was dispatched with surly inhospitality, for he knew that intruders are not discouraged by a simple, courteous dismissal. For extreme cases—that term included unsettling, though remote, possibilities—he kept a sportsman's pump shotgun that until then he'd had no occasion to take from its case; it was in the trunk on the second floor, cleaned and oiled, along with two boxes of buckshot shells.

"This is private property," he said shortly.

The stranger nodded phlegmatically. He kept studying Faulques from a distance of ten or twelve steps. He was heavyset, of medium height. His straw-colored hair was long. And he wore glasses.

"Are you the photographer?"

Faulques' discomfort grew stronger. This individual had said photographer, not painter. He was referring to a previous life, and that did not please Faulques at all. Least of all from the mouth of a stranger. That other life had nothing to do with this place, or with this moment. At least in any official way.

"I don't know you," he said, irritated.

"You may not remember me, but you do know me."

He spoke with such aplomb that Faulques could do nothing but stare at the man as he moved a little closer, narrowing the distance between them to facilitate communication. The painter had seen many faces in his life, most of them through the viewfinder of a camera. Some he remembered and others he had forgotten: a fleeting look, a click of the shutter, a negative on the contact sheet that only sometimes merited the circle of the marker that would save it from being assigned to the archives. Most of the people who appeared in those photos evaporated among a multitude of indistinguishable features and a succession of scenes impossible to identify without a major effort of memory: Cyprus, Vietnam, Lebanon, Cambodia, Eritrea, El Salvador, Nicaragua, Angola, Mozambique, Iraq, the Balkans . . . Solitary hunts, trips with no beginning and no end, devastated landscapes of a vast geography of disaster, wars that blended into other wars, people who blended into other people, dead that blended into other dead. Countless negatives among which he remembered one in every hundred, in every five hundred, in every thousand. And that precise, unremitting horror that extended through the centuries, through history, prolonged like an avenue between two incredibly long, desolate, parallel straight lines. The graphic evidence that summed up all horrors—perhaps because there was only one horror, immutable and eternal.

"You really don't remember me?"

The stranger seemed disappointed. But nothing about him was familiar to Faulques. European, he concluded, studying him more closely. Husky, light eyes, strong hands. Vertical scar through the left eyebrow. A rather rough appearance, softened by the glasses. And that slight accent. Slavic, perhaps? The Balkans, or somewhere around there?

"You photographed me."

"I've taken a lot of photographs in my lifetime."

"This one was special."

Faulques knew he was bested. He stuck his hands in his pants pockets, and shrugged his shoulders. Sorry, he said. I don't remember. The visitor smiled an encouraging half smile.

"Try and remember, señor. That photograph earned you a lot of money." He pointed to the tower with a quick gesture. "You may owe all this to it."

"This isn't much."

The intruder's smile widened. He was missing one tooth on the left side of his mouth; an upper bicuspid. None of his teeth seemed to be in very good shape.

"Depends on your point of view. For some it's quite a bit."

He had a rather stiff, formal way of speaking. As if he were pulling words and phrases from a grammar manual. Faulques made another effort to recognize his face, without success.

"That important prize you won," said the stranger. "They awarded you the International Press prize for taking my photograph . . . Have you forgotten that, too?"

Faulques looked at him with misgivings. He remembered that photograph very well, as well as everyone who appeared in it. He remembered them all, one by one: the three Druse militiamen, all on their feet, eyes blindfolded—two about to drop, one proud and erect—and the six Maronite Kataeb who were executing them at nearly point-blank range. Victims and executioners, mountains of the Chouf. Cover of a dozen magazines. His consecration as war photographer five years after having taken up the profession.

"You couldn't have been there. The militiamen died, and the ones who shot them were Lebanese Phalangists."

The stranger wavered, disconcerted, never taking his eyes off Faulques. He stood absolutely still a few seconds, then shook his head.

"I'm talking about a different photograph. The one at Vukovar, in Croatia. I always thought they gave you the prize for that one."

"No." Now Faulques studied him with renewed interest. "The Vukovar photo was a different one."

"Was it important, too?"

"More or less."

"Well, I'm the soldier in that one."

Faulques stood very quiet, hands still in his pants pockets, with his head tilted slightly to the right, again scrutinizing the face before him. And now, at last, as in the gradual process of developing a print, the image he carried in his memory slowly began to impose itself upon the features of the stranger. Then he cursed himself for being so slow. The eyes, of course. Less fatigued, brighter, but they were the same. As were the curve of the lips, the chin with a slight cleft, the strong jaw, now recently shaved, whereas in the old image it had been covered with a two-days' growth of beard. His recognition of that face was based almost exclusively on observation of the photograph he had taken one autumn day in Vukovar, in the former Yugoslavia, when Croatian troops, battered by Serbian artillery and Serbian ships bombarding from the Danube, were battling hard to hold the narrow defensive perimeter of the walled city. The battle was intense in the suburbs, and on the Petrovci road. Faulques and Olvido Ferrara—they had slipped in a week earlier by the only possible route, a hidden path through cornfields—had come upon the survivors of a Croatian unit that was falling back, defeated, after fighting with light arms against armored enemies. They were scattered, at the limit of their strength, dressed in a motley mixture of military uniforms and civilian clothing. They were farmers, officials, students mobilized for the recently formed Croatian national army, faces bathed in sweat, mouths open, eyes crazed with fatigue, weapons hanging from their straps or being dragged along the ground. They had just run four kilometers with enemy tanks right at their heels; now, under the reverberating sun, they were moving along the road at a lethargic, nearly ghostly, pace, and the only sound was the muffled rumble of distant explosions and the scraping of their feet over the ground.

Olvido hadn't taken any photographs—she almost never photographed people, only things—but as they passed Faulques, he had decided to record this image of total exhaustion. He put the camera to his face, and while he fiddled with the focus, f-stops, and composition he let a couple of faces go by, then captured the third in his viewfinder, almost randomly: bright, extremely vacant eyes, features distorted by weariness, skin covered with drops of the same sweat that plastered his dirty, tangled hair to his forehead. He had an old AK-47 carelessly slung over his right shoulder and held by a hand wrapped in a dark, stained bandage. After the shutter clicked, Faulques had gone on his way, and that was all there was to it. The photograph was published four weeks later, coinciding with the fall of Vukovar and the extermination of all its defenders, and the image became a symbol of the war. Or, as the professional jury that awarded him the prestigious Europa Focus for that year concluded, the symbol of all soldiers of all wars.

"Oh, my God! I thought you were dead."

"I nearly was."

They stood not speaking, looking at each other as if neither of them knew what to say or do.

"Well," Faulques murmured finally. "I admit that I owe you a drink."

"A drink?"

"A glass of something. Alcohol, if you like. A beer."

He smiled for the first time, somewhat forced, and the stranger returned Faulques' smile, as before revealing the missing tooth. He seemed to be reflecting on something.

"Yes," he concluded. "Maybe you do owe me that drink."

"Come in."

They went inside the tower. Faulques' unexpected guest looked around, surprised, and slowly turned in place to take in the enormous circular painting, while the painter of battles searched beneath the table piled with brushes, jars, and tubes of paint, then, on the floor, among cardboard boxes, sheets of sketches, ladders, frames and planks for scaffolding, two halogen 120-watt lightbulbs that, placed on a mobile structure with a shelf and wheels and connected to the generator outside, illuminated the wall when Faulques was working at night. Spanish cognac and warm beer, he said. That's all I can offer you. And there's no ice. The refrigerator runs only briefly, when I turn on the generator.

His eyes still on the mural, the visitor gave an indifferent wave of his hand. Either, it was all the same to him.

"I would never have recognized you," commented the painter of battles. "You were thinner then. In the photo."

"I got even thinner."

"I imagine that those were bad times."

"You got that right."

Faulques walked toward him with two glasses half filled with cognac. Bad times for everyone, he repeated aloud. He was thinking of what had happened three days later, near the place where he'd taken the photo: a ditch along the Borovo Naselje road, on the outskirts of Vukovar. He handed the visitor a glass and took a sip from his own. It wasn't the most suitable choice for that hour, but he'd said a drink and this was a drink. The stranger—that wasn't a strictly applicable term by then, he thought suddenly—had taken his eyes from the mural and was holding the glass rather apathetically. Behind the lens of his spectacles, his light eyes, a very pale gray, were now focused on the painter.

"I know what you're referring to . . . I saw the woman die."

Faulques was not given to showing his stupor, or to revealing emotions. But something must have been reflected in his face, for again he saw the black hole in the visitor's mouth.

"It was days after you took my photograph," the man continued. "You weren't aware that I was there, but I was on the Borovo Naselje road that afternoon. When I heard the explosion I thought it was one of ours . . . As I went by I saw you kneeling in the ditch, beside the . . . body."

He had hesitated an instant before that last word, as if pondering whether to choose "corpse" or "body" . . . and had chosen the latter. Well, that was interesting, Faulques decided, that half courteous, half old-fashioned way of searching for a word, pausing as he weighed their relative merits. Now, finally, the visitor held the glass to his lips, still with his eyes on his host. They both stood a little longer in silence.

"I'm sorry," said Faulques. "That I didn't remember you."

"Only natural. You seemed deeply affected."

"I'm not talking about the incident on the Borovo Naselje road, but about the photo I took several days before that. Your face was on the cover of several magazines, and since then I have seen it hundreds of times. I do now, of course. Now that I know it was you, it's easier. But you've changed a lot."

"Well, you said it earlier, eh? Bad times . . . And then a lot of years have gone by."

"How did you find me?"

Asking around, the visitor replied, again focusing on the painting. Here and there. You are a well-known man, señor Faulques, even famous, he added, distractedly wetting his lips with the cognac. And even though you've been retired for some time, a lot of people remember you. I can assure you of that.

"How did you get out of there?"

The visitor shot him a strange look. I suppose you're referring to Vukovar, he replied. I was wounded two weeks after you shot the photograph. Not the wound in the hand that you see in the image, of course—look, I still have that scar—a different one, more serious. It happened when the Chetniks hadn't as yet cut off the path through the cornfields. I was evacuated to a hospital in Osijek.

He touched his left side, indicating the exact spot. Not with a finger, but with his open hand, from which Faulques deduced that the wound had been serious. He nodded with faint sympathy.

"Shrapnel?"

"A 12.7 bullet."

"You were very lucky."

He didn't mean lucky that his visitor hadn't died of the wound, but that it had happened while it was still possible to get the wounded out of Vukovar. When the Serbs had also sealed that path, no one could get out of the walled city. And when it fell, all the prisoners of combat age were killed. That included the wounded, who were dragged out of the hospital, shot dead, and thrown into huge common graves.

When he heard the word "lucky," the visitor looked at Faulques with a strange expression. For some time. At last he set the glass on the table and his eyes again made the slow circuit of the room.

"A curious place you have here. But I don't see any mementos of other times."

Faulques pointed to the painting: the shadowy citadel backlighted against a fire that suggested the eruption of a volcano, the metallic reflections off modern weapons, the steel-clad troops spilling through the breached wall, the faces of women and children, the hanged men swinging like clusters of fruit from the trees, the ships sailing away on the gray horizon.

"These are my mementos."

"I'm talking about photos. You're a photographer."

"I was."

"You were, that's true. And photographers tend to hang photos on their walls. Photos they've taken. Especially when they've won important prizes. You're not ashamed of your photos, are you?"

"They just don't interest me anymore. That's all."

"Of course." The visitor smiled his strange smile. "That's all."

Now he was studying the images of the mural close up, frowning.

"So ancient wars also form part of your memories? Troy and places like that?"

Now it was Faulques' turn to half smile.

"That's what it's about. Places like that are always the same place."

That must have interested the visitor because he said nothing, his eyes fixed on the mural, pondering what he had just heard. The same place, he replied in a low voice. He stepped closer, examining the details. Suddenly he seemed uncomfortable.

"I don't understand painting," he said.

Then he went over to the knapsack he'd set beside the door and pulled out a notebook, from which he took a sheet of paper folded in half. Old paper that bore signs of frequent handling: the page of a magazine. The cover of *Newszoom,* the photograph taken ten years before. He brought it back to the table, laid it beside the brushes and paint jars, and both men contemplated it in silence. It truly was a unique photo, Faulques told himself. Cold, objective. Perfect. He had seen it many times, but he never failed to take pleasure from the invisible—visible to an attentive viewer—geometric lines that supported it as if on a coarse canvas: foreground, the exhausted soldier, the lost gaze that seemed to form part of the lines of that road that led nowhere, the nearly polyhedral walls of the ruined house peppered with the pox of shrapnel, the distant smoke of the fire, vertical as a black, baroque column, without a breath of a breeze. All of that, framed through a viewfinder and imprinted on a 24 x 36 millimeter negative, was more the fruit of instinct than of calculation, although the jury that awarded the prize to the image emphasized that what seemed random was relative. It is not only its perfection, one member of the Europa Focus committee had declared, it is our certainty that the point of view, the eye of the man who took it, has been formed by intense experience, and that the image is the final sediment, the culmination, of a long personal, professional, and artistic process.

"I was twenty-seven," said the visitor, smoothing the page with the palm of his hand.

He said it in a neutral tone, without nostalgia or melancholy, but Faulques was not paying attention. The word "artistic" was vibrating in his memory, producing a retrospective malaise. In our profession, Olvido had once said—sitting in a gutted chair, cameras in her lap, rewinding film before the body of a headless man whose shoes were the only thing she had photographed—the word "art" has always suggested hoax and half measures. Better to be amoral than immoral. Don't you think? And now, please, kiss me.

"It's a good photograph," the visitor continued. "I look tired, don't I? And I was. I suppose that exhaustion is what gives my face that dramatic flair. Did you choose the title?"

It was precisely the opposite of art, thought Faulques. The harmony of lines and forms had no object other than to reach the innermost keys to the problem. Nothing to do with aesthetics, nor with the ethics other photographers used—or said they used—to filter their objectives and their work. For him, everything had been reduced to moving about the fascinating grid of the problem of living and its collateral damage. His photographs were like chess: where others saw struggle, pain, beauty, or harmony, Faulques saw only coalescing enigmas. The same was true of the vast painting he was working on now. Everything he was trying to resolve on that circular wall was located at the antipodes of what people ordinarily called art. Or maybe what was happening was that once he had passed a certain ambiguous point of no return where ethic and aesthetic were dispassionately left behind, art would be converted—and perhaps the operative words were "once again"—into a cold and possibly effective formula. An unemotional tool for contemplating life.

He was slow to realize that his guest was waiting for him to answer. He made an effort to remember. The title, that was it. He had asked about the title of the photo.

"No," he said. "The magazines did that, the newspapers and agencies, on their own. It didn't come from me."

"*The Face of Defeat.* Very appropriate. What do you remember about that day, señor Faulques? About that defeat?"

He was observing Faulques with curiosity. Perhaps a too formal curiosity, as if the question were motivated less by interest than by courtesy. The painter of battles shook his head.

"I remember that houses were burning and your squad was retreating. Little else."

That wasn't entirely true. He remembered other things, but didn't say so. He remembered Olvido walking in silence along the other side of the road, camera resting on her chest and her small pack on her back, her wheat-colored hair combed into two braids, her long, slim legs sheathed in jeans, her white tennis shoes crunching over the gravel of the road chewed up by mortar shells. As they neared the front, and the combat sounded close by, her step seemed livelier and firmer, as if without realizing it she was pushing herself to be on time for the inescapable rendezvous that awaited her three days later on the Borovo Naselje road. As they climbed a slope that left them in the open, when the curved lines became tangential to hostile straight lines and the *ziaang, ziaang* of two stray bullets passed over their heads, at the limit of their range, Faulques had watched her stop, crouch slightly, and look around with the caution of a hunter close to his prey, before she turned toward him and smiled with an almost ferocious tenderness, slightly distracted and absorbed, nostrils flared, eyes shining as if they were on the verge of weeping adrenaline.

The visitor picked up his glass from the table, and, after holding it a moment, set it down where it had been, without tasting it.

"Well, I remember very well when you took the photo.

Although our circumstances were different, he added. For Faulques it was just another job, of course. Professional routine. But for him it was the first time he'd been involved in anything like that. He'd been recruited only a few days before, and had ended up among comrades as frightened as he was, facing Serbian tanks with a rifle in his hands.

"Listen, they wiped us out. Literally. Of the forty-eight of us who started, fifteen came back. The ones you saw along the road."

"They didn't look too good."

"I wonder why. We'd run like rabbits across the fields until we regrouped on the outskirts of Petrovci. We were so scared that our officers ordered us to fall back toward Vukovar . . . That was when you and the woman came across us. I remember that I was surprised to see her. She's a photographer, I thought. A correspondent. She passed us on our side of the road, walking rapidly, as if she didn't see us. I stood looking at her, and when I turned I found you right in front of me. You were focusing on me, or framing, or whatever you say, taking the photograph. Yes. Your camera clicked and you kept right on going, without a wave or a hello. Nothing. I think you'd already stopped thinking about me; you didn't even see me once you'd lowered your camera."

"That's possible," Faulques conceded uncomfortably.

The visitor waved vaguely toward the photograph. You can't imagine, he said then, the number of things I've thought about through the years, looking at it. All I've learned about myself, about others. From studying my face for so long, or rather the face I had then, I've come to see myself from the outside. Do you understand that? You might say that the person looking is a different man. Though the truth, I suppose, is actually that the person looking *now* is a different man.

"But you," he concluded, slowly turning toward the painter, "you haven't changed much."

His tone was strange. Faulques gave him a suspicious, questioning look and watched as the man lifted a hand slightly, as if that unformulated question lacked meaning. Nothing in particular. I was passing by and I wanted to say hello, the gesture said. What else do you want me to want?

"No," the visitor continued after a long pause. "The fact is that you haven't changed. Not much at all. The gray hair, maybe. And more wrinkles on your face. Even so, it hasn't been easy to find you. I went to a lot of places, asking about you. I went to your photography agencies, to magazines. I knew a few things about you but, as I found out a little more, I learned that you were a famous photographer. One of the best, they say. That you almost always worked in war zones and won a lot of prizes . . . That one day you left everything and disappeared. At first I thought that the woman's death had something to do with it, but then I found that you continued to work a few years after that. You didn't retire until after the business of Bosnia and Sarajevo. Isn't that right? And something in Africa."

"What do you want from me?"

Impossible to know whether his visitor smiled or not. The eyes seemed to be doing their own thing, cold and detached from the benevolent curve of his lips.

"You made me famous. I decided I wanted to meet the person who had made me famous."

"What is your name?"

"That's funny, isn't it?" The unwelcome guest's eyes were still cold and staring, but his smile widened. "You took a photograph of a soldier you crossed paths with for a couple of seconds. A soldier you knew nothing about, not even his name. And that photograph traveled around the world. Then you forgot that anonymous soldier and took other photos. Of other people whose names you also didn't know, I imagine. Maybe you made them famous the way you did me. It's a strange profession, yours."

He fell silent, perhaps reflecting on the uncommon aspects of Faulques' former profession. He stared absently at the glass of cognac, which was sitting beside the photograph. Then he seemed to notice it, and picked it up and took a sip.

"My name? Ivo Markovic."

"Why have you come looking for me?"

The visitor had put the glass down and was wiping his mouth with the back of his hand.

"Because I'm going to kill you."

For a moment the only sound was the whirring of the cicadas outside in the brush. Faulques closed his mouth—it had dropped open when he heard those words—and looked around. His heart was beating slowly and arrhythmically. He felt it jumping in his chest.

"Why?" he asked.

He moved, slowly, only a few centimeters. With great caution. Now he was turned to one side, with his left shoulder to the visitor. The closest thing to hand was a wide palette knife ending in a point; its handle jutted up among the cans and glass jars. He reached toward it but Markovic made no comment, and showed no alarm.

"Yours is a difficult question to answer." The visitor was looking, thoughtfully, at the palette knife in Faulques' hand. "After so many years of turning it over and over in my mind, planning each step and each situation, the matter is more complex than it appears."

Giving Markovic his full attention, the painter of battles calculated lines, angles, and volumes: open spaces, distance to the door, physical qualities. To his profound surprise, he didn't feel alarmed. It remained to be seen whether that was because of the visitor's tone and attitude, or whether it was his own way of looking at things.

"Is that right. More? It already seems extremely complex to me. Provided that you are actually sane."

"Pardon?"

"That you're not out of your mind. Crazy."

The other nodded, almost solicitously. I understand perfectly your reservations, he said in a completely normal voice. But what I mean to say is that earlier, at the beginning, I fancied that everything would be extremely simple. At that point I would have been able to kill you without saying a word. With no explanation. But time doesn't go by for nothing. You think and think. I've had time to think. And to kill you straight off no longer seems enough.

"Do you intend to do it here? Now?"

"No. I've just come to talk with you about it. I've already told you that I can't just kill you. I need for us to talk first; I need to know you better, to be sure that you realize certain things. I want you to learn and understand . . . After that, I'll be able to kill you."

After his amazing pronouncement, the man stood staring at Faulques with an almost timid air, as if he wasn't sure he'd been courteous enough in explaining himself, or if he had used the proper syntax. Faulques let out the air he'd been holding in his lungs.

"What is it you want me to understand?"

"Your photograph. Or, better put, my photograph."

Both men were looking at the palette knife in Faulques' right hand. Suddenly the tool seemed ridiculous to the painter. He put it back in its place. When he looked up, he read sober approval in the visitor's eyes. Then the painter of battles smiled a slight, crooked smile.

"Has it occurred to you that I can defend myself?"

Markovic blinked. He seemed disturbed that this man he was talking with would think he hadn't considered that. Of course it has, he replied. We all deserve a chance. You, as well. Naturally.

"Or that I might . . ." Faulques hesitated a second, for the words seemed absurd, "run?"

His visitor was slow to answer. He had raised both hands, as if to show that he had nothing hidden, or that he was not ready to wield a weapon, before going to his pack and taking out a dog-eared book of photographs. As he walked toward him, Faulques recognized the English edition of one of his collected works: *The Eye of War.* Markovic laid the open book on the table, beside the cover of *Newszoom.*

"I don't think you'll run away." He leafed through pages, indifferent to the fact that Faulques wasn't looking at the album, but at him. "I've been studying your work for years, señor. Your photographs. I know them so well that sometimes I think I've come to know *you.* That's why I know that you won't run, or do anything for the moment. You will stay here while we have our conversations. One day, several . . . I still don't know. There are answers you need as much as I do."

3.

IN THE BLACK DOME OF the sky, the stars were slowly wheeling to the left, around the fixed point of the Pole. Sitting at the tower door, back against stone eroded by three hundred years of wind, sun, and rain, Faulques didn't have a view of the sea, but he could see the flashes from the distant Cabo Malo lighthouse and hear the roar of the high tide hammering the rocks below, at the foot of the cleft on which canted pines, leaning out like indecisive suicides, were silhouetted against a waning yellow moon.

In his hands he held the glass of cognac he had refilled after his visitor had marched off without saying good-bye, as if his leaving were an insignificant pause, a technical displacement of no consequence in the complex affair that both—Faulques himself recognized now that this was something that affected them both, no question about that—would have to deal with. At one moment in the conversation that had lasted beyond nightfall, his singular visitor had interrupted himself in the middle of a sentence, when he was describing a landscape: a fenced area and a rocky, barren mountain that the fence defined like an ironic and perverse frame, or a photograph. And with that word, "photograph," on his lips, the visitor had stood up in the dark—Faulques and he had been talking a long time, two dark shapes sitting face-to-face with no light but the moon at the window—and after groping to find his knapsack had stood stock-still at the open door for a moment, as if hesitating between leaving without a word or saying something first. Then, unhurriedly, he had walked to the path that wound down to the village. Faulques got up and went outside after him, in time to see the white blotch of his shirt moving away through the shadows of the pine grove.

Ivo Markovic, for that was his name—Faulques had no reason to doubt it—had forgotten to take the cover of *Newszoom* that featured his photograph. The painter had realized this when he turned on the portable gas lamp. He looked for his empty glass in order to fill it again, and saw the page spread out among the cans of paint, dirty rags, and preserve jars filled with brushes. Although it was more likely that it hadn't been an oversight, but something as deliberate as leaving the worn copy of *The Eye of War*, which was on the seat the visitor had occupied as they talked. I need for you to understand a few things, he'd said. Then I will be ready to kill you. And on, and on.

Maybe it was the cognac, the painter of battles thought, its effect on the heart and the head, that had mitigated the sensation of unreality. The unexpected visit, the conversation, the recollections and images unfolded with evidence as strong as the cover photo and the book of his images of war, seemed to have taken their place, with no undue discord, in the familiar landscape. Even the vast concave painting—Faulques was at that moment sitting with his back against its exterior wall—and the night that was enveloping everything, had reserved appropriate locations, corners, perspectives in which to position—like a prestidigitator before his rapt audience—the things the visitor had taken from his pack as the fading light turned first crimson, then a deeper shade, until finally darkness erased their surroundings. To the surprise of the erstwhile photographer, nothing of what the other man had said, or left unsaid, including the announcement of his death, less a presentiment than a promise, seemed incompatible with the presence of the painter of battles in that place, with his labor on the immense fresco on the tower wall. If, as art theoreticians maintained, the photograph reminded painting of what it should never do, Faulques was sure that his work in the tower reminded photography of what it was capable of suggesting, but not achieving: a vast, continuous, circular vision of a chaotic chess game, the implacable rule that governed perverse randomness—the ambiguity of which governed things that were absolutely not fortuitous—of the world and of life. This point of view confirmed the geometric character of that perversity, the norm of chaos, the lines and forms hidden to the uninformed eye, so like the wrinkles on the brow and the eyelids of a man he had photographed once as he squatted for an hour or so beside a common grave, smoking and rubbing his face as his brother and nephew were being disinterred. No one would gift anyone with the dubious privilege of seeing that kind of thing in objects, or landscapes, or in human beings. For some time, Faulques had suspected that it was possible only after a certain class of travel or journey: Troy, with a return ticket, for example. The loneliness of a hotel room, captioning photos and cleaning cameras with ghosts still fresh on your retina; or later, once home, studying the prints spread across the table, shuffling and discarding them like someone playing a complicated game of solitaire. Ulysses with gray in his hair and blood on his hands, and the rain scattering the ashes of the smoking city as his ships sail away. Until then, you could look again and again, focus, *clic, clic, clic,* dark room, print, International Press Photo, Europa Focus, and still fail throughout a lifetime. Faulques, now a painter of battles, had been led to that tower by a dead woman and a certainty: that no one could capture all that on film in 1/125 of a second.

The man who had just marched away confirmed it. He was yet another sketch on the enormous circular fresco. One question more directed to the silence of the Sphinx. No doubt but that the man deserved a place of honor on the wall, assigned by the paradoxes and pirouettes of a world tenacious in demonstrating that, despite the fact that the straight line is absent from the animal world, and far from lavish in nature in general—except perhaps when the law of gravity tightened the ropes of the hanged—chaos did possess impeccably straight shortcuts to precise sites in place and time. Despite himself, Faulques was impressed. That afternoon, after he had laid the book of photographs on the table, Ivo Markovic had turned to the circular wall, giving it all his attention for a long time.

"So that's how you see it, then," he murmured finally.

It wasn't a question, nor was it a conclusion. It was the confirmation of an old thought. Impossible to separate that, Faulques decided, from the dog-eared book on the table, opened—by chance was impossible—to one of his first professional photos, black and white, taken after the impact of a rocket fired by the Khmer Rouge in Pochetong, the market of Phnom Penh. A wounded boy, half sitting on the ground, his eyes clouded from the trauma of the explosion, was looking at his mother, who lay on her back, stretched on a diagonal to the frame of the camera, her head blown open by shrapnel, her blood tracing long and intricate streams across the ground. It doesn't seem possible, Olvido Ferrara would say much later—years later—in Mogadishu, at another scene identical to the one in Pochetong, identical to many others. It doesn't seem possible that we can have all that blood in our bodies, she'd said. A little more than five liters, I think. Amazing how easy it is to spill, and to lose it all. Have you thought about that? And Faulques would remember those words and those photos later, right eye glued to the viewfinder of the camera in the market in Sarajevo, which was still smoking after being battered by projectiles fired from Serbian mortars. Five liters multiplied by fifty or sixty bleeding bodies; that was a lot of blood: streams, spirals, crisscrossing lines, glossy red dulled to a matte finish, coagulating as the minutes went by and the moans faded. Children staring at their mothers as if mesmerized, and vice versa; bodies oblique, perpendicular, parallel to other bodies, and beneath them liquids in capricious patterns, all flowing into an enormous red grid. Olvido was right: we have an astounding quantity of blood inside us. After centuries of being drained, it continues to flow. But she wasn't there to appreciate the analogy. Her five liters had already been spilled, at a point in time and space located between the market in Phnom Penh and the one in Sarajevo: a ditch beside the Borovo Naselje road.

"That's how you see it without cameras," Ivo Markovic insisted.

He had walked right up to the wall, hands clasped behind his back; he'd adjusted his glasses with a finger, and bent close to inspect a part of the painting, where bold strokes, a bit of color applied over the charcoal sketch, depicted a female body. An odd perspective, a face as yet not defined, naked thighs open toward the foreground, a red trickle of blood between them, and the silhouette of a child squatting beside her, turned toward the woman, or the mother. A curious evolution, man's, Faulques thought: fish, crocodile, killer, with his own corpse interposed between each stage. Today's children, tomorrow's executioners. The same partially painted features of the child reserved for one of the soldiers who, at the right of that scene, guns in hand, were driving the fleeing multitude from the city, resolved pictorially—the old Flemish masters were not only to be admired—on the basis of repeated squares of windows and crenellated lines of black ruins sharply delineated against the red of the fires and explosions crowning the distant hill.

"I'm no good when it comes to appreciating art," Markovic commented.

"In fact it isn't art. Art lives on faith."

"I don't understand much about that, either."

He hadn't moved, or unclasped the hands behind his back as he studied every section of the mural. Like a peaceful visitor in a museum.

"I'm going to tell you a story," he said without turning.

"Yours?"

"What does it matter? A story."

Then he slowly turned toward Faulques and began. He talked for a long time, interrupting himself with long pauses as he searched for a specific word. He meant to tell his story in detail, with the greatest precision possible, sometimes judging that his way of speaking, the mounting heat of the tale itself, was no longer impersonal but had become impassioned. When he noticed this, he immediately stopped, shook his head by way of apology, asked for his listener's understanding, and then after a brief silence, began again at the same point, his tone more objective. More discreet.

And this was how the amazed painter of battles, listening closely, reconfirmed his certainty that there was a hidden network that trapped the world and its events, where nothing that happened was innocent or without consequences. He learned about a young family in a small town in a country that in another time had been called Yugoslavia: the husband an agricultural engineer, the wife dedicated to the home and to cultivating the family garden, a young child. He also learned, once again, what he already knew: that politics, religion, old hatreds, and stupidity combined with a lack of refinement and the infamous human condition, had demolished that place with a war that set relatives, friends, and neighbors against one another. Massacred by the Nazis and their Croatian allies during World War II, this time the Serbs took the lead role, which could be summarized in two words: "ethnic cleansing." The Markovics were one of those mixed marriages encouraged by Marshal Tito's policy of integration; but the aged marshal was dead, and things had changed. The husband was Croatian, the wife Serbian. The partition separated them. When bands of Chetnik militiamen began killing their neighbors, the wife and child were lucky; they were living in a zone with a Serbian majority, and they stayed there while the husband, a fugitive, enrolled in the Croatian national militia.

"In regard to his family, the soldier wasn't worried. You understand that, don't you, señor Faulques?" Mother and child were safe. As he lived through the miseries and alarms of war, rifle in hand, he consoled himself with the knowledge that they were in a secure place. You who have been a witness with a return ticket in so many disasters, you understand what I'm saying. Isn't that right? The relief of knowing that when everything is in flames, you have no loved ones burning in the ruins of the world.

Faulques was sitting in one of the canvas chairs, with the glass of cognac in one hand, as motionless as the figures painted on the wall. He slowly nodded.

"I can understand that."

"I know you can. At least *now* I know." Markovic, who hadn't moved from his place before the painting, waved vaguely toward a point on it, as if what he was going to say was illustrated there. "When I saw you on your knees beside the body of the woman in the ditch, a few days after you took my photograph, I thought that was the situation with her. One more corpse, one more image. A shame, of course. Our closest colleagues always die. But better, I thought you'd be thinking, better her than me. How many journalists fell in that war in my country?"

"I don't know. Fifty or so. A lot."

"That's what I mean. One among so many. One woman in your case. That's what I believed for a while. Now I know I was mistaken. She wasn't just one more."

Faulques shifted uncomfortably in his chair.

"You were telling me about yourself. Your family."

Markovic, who seemed about to add something, stopped, lips parted, gazing at Faulques intently. Then yet again he turned in a circle, eyes taking in the painting and the sketches on the white primer: ships sailing beneath the rain, men fleeing, soldiers, and the city in flames, the volcano erupting in the distance, the clash of cavalry, the medieval horsemen awaiting the moment to ride into combat, the men in anachronistic garments and weapons from thirty centuries ago slashing at one another in the foreground.

"The family of the soldier was safe," Markovic continued. "Meanwhile he was fighting for his country, although that was less important to him than his other, his true, concern: his wife and child. The fact is that the official fatherland was turned into a slaughterhouse called Vukovar. Into a fearsome trap." Markovic paused a moment, absorbed. "Can you imagine Serbian tanks bearing down on you, and you with no weapons to stop them? One morning, the soldier ran like a rabbit, along with his comrades, to save his life.

Then, when the survivors regrouped, still panting for breath, you took his photo."

Silence followed. Faulques drank a sip of his cognac. He sat still as stone in his chair, soaking up every word. The visitor had again turned toward the painting. Now he was studying the forest where men were hanging from the trees like clusters of fruit.

"In recent years I've read a lot," he continued. "Magazines, newspapers, sometimes a book. I know how to browse the Internet. I didn't use to be much of a reader, but my life has changed a lot. And then one day, I read something about you that interested me, an interview you gave on the occasion of the publication of your last book of photos. From what you said, there's a scientific formula: if a butterfly flutters its wings in Brazil, or somewhere, a hurricane will be unleashed on the other side of the world. Is that how it goes?"

"More or less. The theory is known as the Butterfly Effect."

Markovic smiled a little, pointing one finger at Faulques. A disturbing smile, however. As rigid as if it weren't his. It stayed on his face for a time, frozen, revealing the black hole between his ruined teeth.

"It's curious that you should mention it in that interview, because what happened was like the fluttering wings of the butterfly. The soldier didn't know that until the photo reached the hospital in Osijek. Everyone congratulated him. He was famous. A Croatian hero. Vukovar had just fallen, finally, and all his comrades had died fighting, or been killed by the Chetniks: Nikola, Zoran, Tomislav, Vinko, Grüber. That Grüber was his officer. They were walking together the day you took the photo. When the city fell, Grüber was in the basement of the hospital with his foot amputated. The Serbs pulled him out into the courtyard with the others; they beat them senseless before they shot them in the head and dragged them to a common grave."

Faulques could see that the smile, or whatever it was, had disappeared. Now Markovic's eyes were on him, though it seemed as if their true focus was on something far away, somewhere behind Faulques' back.

"The soldier in the photo," Markovic continued, "was luckier than his comrades. Or maybe he wasn't . . . Demobilized because of his wound, he'd been sent to Zagreb to recover. In a place called Okucani, his luck ran out. The bus ran into an ambush."

The passengers on the bus were civilians, he added after a pause. There were old men, women, and children. So instead of killing them all right there, the Serbs took them to an interrogation center under the command of the regular army, where the soldier was subjected to routine rough treatment. Later, between beatings, a guard recognized him. He was the man in the famous photo. The hero of Vukovar. The face of Croatian separatists.

"He was tortured for six months. Like an animal. Then, for some strange reason, or by chance, they let him live. He was transferred to a prison camp near Banja Luka; he spent two and a half years there. One day they loaded him onto a truck, and just when he thought they were going to shoot him, he found himself on a bridge over the Danube, and heard them say: 'Prisoner exchange, get out and walk, you're free . . .' "

Markovic's lips kept moving, but without words. Only silence. Faulques saw that he had stopped, as if surprised, and was looking around as if he had just found himself in bizarre surroundings. I hope it doesn't bother you if I smoke, he said suddenly. The painter shook his head, and Markovic went to his knapsack and took out a pack of cigarettes.

"Do you smoke?"

"No."

Markovic lit a cigarette, and when he blew out the match looked for an ashtray to put it in. Faulques pointed to an empty French mustard jar. His visitor picked it up, and with the cigarette in his mouth and the jar in his hand, he went and sat down in the other chair, facing his host.

"What do you think of that story?" he asked in an ordinary voice.

"It's terrible."

"Not especially," the Croatian said, grimacing. "It is terrible, of course. But there are others. Some are even worse. Stories that complement one another."

For a moment he said nothing, his eyes lost in the depths of the vast mural around them. One another, he repeated after a bit, pensive. And I'm talking, he said, about entire families being exterminated, of children killed before the eyes of their parents, of brothers forced to torture each other so that one might live. You can't imagine the things that prisoner saw. The pain, the indignity, the desperation. We men, señor Faulques, are bloodthirsty animals. Our ingenuity in creating horror has no limits. You must be aware of that. You learn something, I suppose, during a lifetime of photographing cruelty and wickedness.

"Is that why you want to kill me? To avenge all those things?"

That cold, somehow alien smile again crossed Markovic's face.

"The Butterfly Effect, you said. What an irony. Such a delicate word."

4.

THE VISITOR WAS SMOKING, concentrating exclusively on his cigarette, as if each puff of smoke were priceless. Faulques recognized the familiar habit of the soldier, or the prisoner. He had watched many men smoke in many wars, where often tobacco was the only companion. The only consolation.

"When that man was set free," Markovic said, resuming his tale, "he tried to find his wife and his son. Three years with no news of them, imagine . . . Well . . . Before long he had news. The famous photo had made its way to their town. Someone had come across a copy of the magazine. There are always neighbors willing to cooperate in that sort of thing: the girlfriend they couldn't have, the job someone's grandparents had taken from someone else's grandparents, the house or piece of land they'd wanted . . . The same old story: jealousy, maliciousness. All too predictable among human beings."

The setting sun shining horizontally through one of the narrow tower windows crowned the Croatian with an aureole red as the fires painted on the wall: the city burning on the hill and the distant volcano that illuminated rocks and bare branches, the fire reflecting off the metal of weapons and armor that now seemed to bounce off the wall and flood the room, its content, the figure of the man sitting in the chair, the curls of smoke from the cigarette he held between his fingers or left dangling from his lips, reddish spirals that in that light lent a singular animation to the scenes on the wall. Maybe, Faulques thought suddenly, this painting isn't as bad as I think it is.

"One night," Markovic continued, "a group of Chetniks came to the house where the Serbian woman and the son of the Croatian were living. They raped her, one after the other, as many times as they wished. Since the boy, all of five years old, cried and fought to defend his mother, they ran him through with a bayonet at the door. Just the way you pin butterflies—imagine, the butterflies of the effect you told me about. Then, when they were tired of the woman, they cut off her breasts and slit her throat. Before they left, they painted a Serbian cross on the wall and the words 'Ustacha pigs!' "

Silence. In the fiery splendor streaming through the window, Faulques tried to see his visitor's eyes, but couldn't. The voice that had recounted the story was as objective and tranquil as if the teller had been reading a pharmaceutical prospectus. Then Markovic slowly raised the hand that held the cigarette.

"Forgive me," he added, "if I tell you that although the woman was screaming all night, not a single neighbor turned on a light or came outside to see what was happening."

This time the silence lasted much longer. Faulques didn't know what to say. Slowly, the lower corners of the area were filling with shadows. The bloodred light slipped away from Markovic and spread across the wall to the charcoal sketch, black on white, of a man, hands tied behind his back, kneeling before another man raising a sword above his head.

"Tell me one thing, señor Faulques. Does a person ever get really hardened? By that I mean, after a time, is what passes before the lens of the camera something the witness is indifferent to, or not?"

The painter raised the glass to his lips. It was empty.

"War," he said, after thinking a moment, "can be photographed well only when, as you raise the camera, what you see doesn't affect you. The rest you have to leave for later."

"You've taken photographs of scenes like the one I just told you about, haven't you?"

"Of the aftermath, yes. A few."

"And what were you thinking about as you focused, read your light meter, and so on?"

Faulques got up to look for the bottle. He found it on the table beside the jars of paints and the empty glass of the visitor.

"The focus, the light, and all that."

"And that was why they gave you the prize for my photograph? Because I didn't affect you either?"

Faulques had poured himself two fingers of cognac. With the glass he pointed to the mural where shadows were beginning to gather.

"Maybe the answer is there."

"Yes." Markovic had half turned and was looking around him. "I think I understand what you mean."

The painter of battles poured more cognac into his questioner's glass and took it to him. Between drags on his cigarette, the Croatian took a swallow while Faulques went back to his chair.

"To accept the truth of things is not to approve that they are as they are," Faulques said. "Explication is not synonymous with anesthesia. Pain . . ."

He stopped himself. Pain. Spoken before his visitor, the word sounded out of place. Stolen from its legitimate owners, as if Faulques had no right to use it. But Markovic didn't seem bothered.

"Pain, of course," he said, understanding. "Pain . . . Forgive me if I pry into matters that are too personal, but your photographs do not show much pain. I mean, they reflect the pain of others but I don't perceive any sign of your own. When did the things you saw stop giving you pain?"

Faulques ticked the lip of his glass with his teeth.

"It's complicated. At first it was an amusing adventure. The pain came later. In bursts. And finally, the impotence. I suppose that nothing hurts any longer."

"Is that the hardening I was referring to?"

"No. I'm talking about resignation. Even if you don't decipher the code, you understand that there are rules. Then you resign yourself."

"Oh, but you don't," Markovic rejoined smoothly.

Suddenly, Faulques felt cruelly relieved.

"You're still alive," he said roughly. "That in itself is a kind of resignation. Your kind. You say you were a prisoner for three years, isn't that right? And when you learned what had happened to your family, you didn't die of the pain, you didn't hang yourself in a tree. You're here, now. You're a survivor."

"I am," Markovic conceded.

"Well, look. Every time I come across a survivor, I

ask myself what he was capable of doing in order to stay alive."

Silence again. Now, almost with jubilation, Faulques regretted that the growing darkness prevented him from making out the features of his interlocutor.

"That's not fair," the visitor said finally.

"Maybe. But fair or not, that's what I ask myself."

The shadow sitting in the chair, enveloped in the last splashes of light on the mural, reflected on Faulques' words.

"You may not be too far off," he concluded. "Maybe surviving when others can't implies a certain class of depravity."

The painter of battles raised the glass to his lips. Again it was empty.

"You should know." He leaned down to set the glass on the floor. "According to what you tell me, you have experience."

Markovic emitted a kind of grunt. Maybe a hint of a cough, or a surprised laugh. You're a survivor, too, señor Faulques, he said. You kept breathing when others were dying. That day I observed you kneeling beside the woman's body. I think you were showing pain.

"I don't know what I was showing. No one took my photograph."

"But you took hers. I watched you take up your camera and photograph her. And this is interesting: I know your photographs as well as if I had taken them myself, but I never found that photo. Did you keep it for yourself? Did you destroy it?"

Faulques didn't answer. He sat quietly in the darkness that was painting, just as he'd first seen it take form in the tray of developer, the image of Olvido lying facedown on the ground, the strap of her camera around her neck, one motionless hand almost touching her face, and the small red stain, the tiny dark thread beginning to trickle from her ear down her cheek until it met the other, larger, and more brilliant stain spreading beneath her. Antipersonnel mine, slivers of shrapnel, Leica 50-mm lens, 1/125 exposure, 5.6 aperture setting, black-and-white film—the Ektachrome of the other camera was at that moment rewinding—for a neither good nor bad photograph, perhaps a little underexposed. One photograph that Faulques never sold, and he had burned that one print some time later.

"Yes," Markovic continued without waiting for an answer. "Somehow that's how it is, isn't it? However intense it might be, there is a moment when pain ceases to register. Maybe that was your remedy. That photo of the dead woman. In a certain way, the depravity that helped you survive."

Faulques slowly came back to the tower and the conversation.

"Don't be melodramatic," he said. "You know nothing about it."

Then, in fact, he hadn't known, the other man conceded as he crushed out his cigarette. I was very slow to learn. But I came to understand things that had escaped me before. This place is an example. If I had come here ten years ago, before I knew you as I know you now, I wouldn't even have glanced at these walls. I would just have given you time to remember who I was before settling accounts. Now it's different. This confirms everything. It really explains my presence here.

Once he had said all that, Markovic leaned forward, as if to see Faulques better in the waning light.

"And is it?" he added suddenly. "Is it enough for you to assume responsibility?"

The painter shrugged his shoulders. I will know when I've finished my work, he said, and his answer sounded strange even to him, with that absurd threat of death floating between them. The visitor sat for a while, thinking, and then said that he, too, was making his own painting. That was what he said: his landscape of battles. When he saw that wall, he added, he realized what had brought him there. Everything has to fit together, didn't Faulques agree? Fit with uncommon precision. But it was strange. Markovic thought the author of the mural didn't seem to be a very classic painter. He himself had already confessed that he didn't understand painting, but he did know a few famous paintings, like anyone else. This one, in his opinion, had too many angles. Too many sharp edges and straight lines in the faces and hands of those people depicted on the wall. Cubism, is that what they called it?

"Not exactly. There's some of that, but the mural isn't Cubist."

"I thought it was, you know. Those books you have piled around everywhere. Do you get your ideas from them?"

" 'Enough that you could say that I've used old words . . .' "

"Is that your answer, or did someone else say that?"

Now Faulques laughed aloud, a dry laugh. His visitor and he were two shapes in the shadows. It was a quote, he answered, but it didn't matter. What he was trying to say was that those books helped him put his own ideas in order; they were tools like the brushes and paints and the rest. In truth, a painting, a painting like this one, posed a technical problem that had to be resolved efficiently. That efficiency was provided by tools in combination with each individual's talent. He didn't have much talent, he repeated. But that wasn't an obstacle to what he intended to do.

"I'm not able to judge your talent," Markovic replied. "But in spite of the angles, I think what you're doing is interesting. Original. And some of those scenes are . . . Well. They're real. More real than your photos, I suppose. And I guess that is what you're aiming for."

His features were suddenly illuminated. He was lighting another cigarette. With the match still burning in his fingers, he got up and went to the mural, holding the faint light to the images painted there. Faulques could see the face of the woman at the very forefront, broken down into violent strokes of ochre, sienna, and cadmium red, her mouth opened in a scream of coarse, dense, silent brush lines, as old as life itself. A fleeting glimpse before the light of the match burned out.

"Is it really like that?" Markovic asked, again in the dark.

"That is how I remember it."

Neither of the men spoke. Markovic moved, maybe looking for his chair. Faulques did not want to help him by lighting a lantern or the gas lamp he kept nearby. The darkness gave him a feeling of having a slight advantage. He remembered the palette knife on the table, the shotgun he had upstairs. But the visitor was speaking again, and his tone sounded relaxed, alien to the painter of battles' suspicions.

"The technical aspect must be complicated, no matter how good the tools you have at your disposal. Had you painted before, señor Faulques?"

"Some. When I was young."

"So you were an artist?"

"I tried to be."

"I read somewhere that you studied architecture."

"For a brief time. I preferred painting."

The tip of the cigarette glowed red for an instant.

"And why did you leave it? Painting, I mean."

"I quit very soon. When I realized that every painting I began had already been painted by someone before me."

"And that's why you became a photographer?"

"Maybe." Faulques was smiling in the darkness. "A French poet thought that photography was the refuge of failed painters. I think that in his moment he was right. . . . But it's also true that photography allows us to see in fractions of a second things normal people don't see no matter how hard they look. Painters included."

"You believed that for thirty years?"

"Not that long. I stopped believing it quite a while before that."

"And that's why you went back to your brushes?"

"It wasn't that quick. Or that simple."

Once again the tip of the cigarette glowed in the shadows. What did war have to do with it, Markovic asked. There were easier ways to practice photography, or painting. Faulques responded with a simple answer. It had to do with a trip, he clarified. When I was a boy I spent a lot of time looking at a print of an old painting. And finally I decided to go see it—well, actually, see the landscape in the background. The painting was *The Triumph of Death,* by Bruegel the Elder.

"I know it. It's in your book *Morituri.* A little pretentious, that title, if you don't mind my saying so."

"I don't mind."

Even so, Markovic commented, Faulques' book of photographs was original and interesting. It made you think. All those battle scenes hanging in museums, with people looking at them as if the paintings had nothing to do with them. Their error captured by your camera.

This Croatian former mechanic was intelligent, Faulques decided. Damned intelligent.

"As long as there's death," he murmured, "there's hope."

"Is that another quote?"

"It's a bad joke."

It was bad. It was hers, Olvido's. She'd made the comment in Bucharest, one Christmas day, after the slaughter by Ceausescu's Securitate and the revolution in the streets. She and Faulques were in the city after they'd crossed the border from Hungary in a rented car and made a mad dash through the Carpathian Mountains, twenty-eight hours taking turns at the wheel, slipping and sliding on icy roads past farmers who, armed with hunting rifles and blockading bridges with their tractors, watched them go by from high above on the cliffs, like you see in cowboy-and-Indian movies. And a couple of days later, as the families of the dead were digging graves in the frozen soil of the cemetery with pneumatic drills, Faulques had watched Olvido move with a hunter's cautious steps among crosses and headstones sprinkled with snow, photographing the miserable coffins nailed together from packing crates, feet aligned in open graves, the spades of the grave diggers piled atop icy clumps of black dirt. And when one poor woman in black knelt beside a newly closed grave, eyes closed and intoning something like a prayer, Olvido turned to the Romanian who was acting as their interpreter. *The house where you are living is dark,* he translated. She is praying to her dead son. Then Faulques saw Olvido nod slowly, with one hand wipe snow from her hair and her face, then photograph the back of the mourning-clad woman on her knees, a black silhouette beside a pile of black earth spattered with snow. Afterward, Olvido let her camera drop onto her chest; she looked at Faulques and murmured, "As long as there's death, there's hope." And as she said it she smiled absently, almost cruelly. As he had never seen her smile.

"You may be right," Markovic conceded. "When you think about it, the world has stopped thinking about death. Thinking that we're not going to die makes us weak, or worse."

For the first time with this curious visitor, Faulques felt a spark of real interest. That disturbed him. It wasn't interest in facts, in the story of the man sitting with him—as conventional as that of many he had photographed through his lifetime—but in the man himself. For a while now, a certain affinity had been floating in the air.

"It's odd," Markovic continued. "*The Triumph of Death* is the one painting in your book that isn't about a battle. As I see it, the subject is the Final Judgment."

"It is. But you're wrong about one thing. What Bruegel did was paint the last battle."

"Ah, of course. I hadn't thought of that. All those skeletons like armies, and the fires in the distance. Executions included."

A corner of a yellow moon could now be seen at a window. The rectangle, with an arch at the top, was lighter than the interior, a dark blue that defined the outlines of the objects inside the tower. The white stain of the visitor's shirt became more visible.

"So you decided that the best way to travel to a painting of war was to spend a long time in a war . . ."

"That could be one way to sum it up."

But speaking of places, Markovic commented, I don't know if what happens to me happens to you. In war you survive thanks to features of the terrain. That gives you a special sense of the countryside. Don't you agree? The memory of the places where you walked is never erased, even if you forget other details. I'm talking about the meadow you see while you await the approaching enemy, the shape of the hill you climb under fire, the design of the trench that protects you from a bombardment. Do you understand what I'm saying, señor Faulques?

"Perfectly."

The Croatian let a moment go by. The tip of his cigarette glowed for the last time before he crushed it out.

"There are places," he added, "you never come back from."

Another long pause. Through the windows, the painter of battles could hear the sound of the sea slapping the foot of the cliff.

"The other day," Markovic continued in the same tone, "something occurred to me as I was watching television in a hotel. In ancient times, men looked at the same landscape all their lives, or at least for a long time. Even the traveler did, because every road was a long road. That forced them to think about the road itself. Now it's different, everything is fast. Highways, trains . . . Even television shows us different scenes every few seconds. There's no time to reflect on anything."

"There are those who call that insecure terrain, something that shifts beneath your feet."

"I don't know what they call it. But I know what it is."

He didn't add to that, but finally he moved in his chair as if he were going to get up, although he didn't. He may have been looking for a more comfortable position.

"I had a lot of that kind of time," he said suddenly. "I can't say that it was a good thing, but I had it. For two and a half years, my only view was of a fence and a mountain of white rock. There was no uncertainty there, not even close. It was a concrete mountain, bare, no vegetation, and a cold wind blew off it during the winter. You understand? A wind that shook the fence with a sound I have in my head and can't blot out. The sound of a frozen, unyielding landscape, you know, señor Faulques? Like your photographs."

That was when he stood, felt around for his knapsack, and left the tower.

5.

THE PAINTER OF BATTLES EMPTIED his glass—too much cognac and too much conversation that night—and took one last look at the flashes from the distant lighthouse. The luminous streak traveled horizontally, like the trail of a tracer bullet on the horizon. Often when he was looking at that light Faulques remembered one of his old photos: an urban, night panorama of Beirut during the battle of the hotels, at the beginning of the civil war. Black and white, dark silhouettes of buildings highlighted by bursts of explosives and lines of tracer bullets. One of those photos in which the geometry of war was indisputable. Faulques had taken it during the early stage of his career, already aware that modern photography, given its technical perfection, was so objective and exact that at times it looked false—Robert Capa's famous photos on Omaha Beach owed their dramatic intensity to an error in the laboratory during the developing process. For that reason, exactly as television reporters and cameramen for action movies did, photographers now used little tricks to blur the camera's fidelity, going back to reproduce a few imperfections that helped the eye of the observer perceive the image in a slightly different way: in pictorial language, the same focal distortion that Matisse's broad brushstrokes imposed on Giotto's meticulous blades of grass. In reality, it was nothing new. Velázquez and Goya knew about distortion; and later, by now free of complexes, so did modern painters—all twentieth-century art proceeded from there—after figurative painting had reached the absolute extreme and photography had claimed the field of faithful reproduction of the precise instant, which was useful for scientific observation but not always satisfying in artistic terms.

As for his photo of Beirut, it was a good photo. It reflected the chaos of combat in the city, with its slight oscillation at the edges of silhouetted buildings standing amid the explosions and the luminous, parallel straight lines scoring the night sky. An image that gave you an idea, better than any other, of the disaster that could be unleashed upon a conventional urban space. Not even the photographs Faulques had taken twenty-five years later in Sarajevo, during the long siege, had matched that extreme of perfect geometric imperfection achieved because of the inferiority of the camera he had been using then—he hadn't as yet acquired good professional equipment—and his inexperience. The photo of the vast night combat, with fires in every direction and the city converted into a polyhedral labyrinth pounded by the ire of men and their gods, had been achieved by resting a Pentax with 400 ASA film on the sill of the window on the eleventh floor of a tall building in ruins—the Sheraton—and holding the shutter open for thirty seconds, with the lens at 1.8 aperture. In that way, each shot and explosion that occurred during that half minute had been recorded on a single 35-mm negative, with the result that when the image was printed, everything seemed to have happened at the same instant. Even the slight movement caused by Faulques' hands during the exposure, when he was shaken by nearby explosions, gave the outlines of the buildings that slight shiver that made everything seem so real; much more so than pictures taken by a perfect, modern camera capable of faithfully capturing the brief, authentic—and maybe commonplace—instant of one photographic second. Olvido had always liked that photo, maybe because there were no people in it, only straight lines of light and contours of buildings. The triumph of weapons of destruction over weapons of obstruction, she once commented. The ten years of Troy reduced to thirty seconds of pyrotechnics and ballistics.

Urban architecture, geometry, chaos. For Faulques, that photograph was a satisfactory graphic representation: insecure terrain. The memory of his conversation with Markovic drew a surprised grimace from Faulques. The Croatian might lack theoretical instruction, but no one could deny his intuition and perception. To survive any difficulty, whatever it might be, especially war, was a good education. It forced you to turn to your own resources and gave you a way of looking at things. A point of view. The Greek philosophers were right when they said that war was the mother of all things. Faulques himself, who when he was young and along with his photographic equipment carrying concepts still fresh from the architectural studies he had cut short, found himself stunned by the transformation war had imposed on the urban landscape, by its functionalist logic, by the problems of locating and concealing, of firing range, of dead angles. A house could be a refuge or a deadly trap; a river, an obstacle or defense; a trench, protection or tomb. And modern warfare made such dualities more frequent and more likely: the more advanced the technology, the more mobility and uncertainty. Only then did he come to truly comprehend the concepts of fortification, of the wall, the glacis, the ancient city and its relation, or opposition, to modern urbanism: the wall of China, Byzantium, Stalingrad, Sarajevo, Manhattan. The History of Mankind. To note to what point man's technical advances had made the cityscape mutable, modifying it, shrinking it, constructing and destroying it according to the circumstances of the moment. That was how, in the sequence of weapons of obstruction and destruction, you arrived at the third system: weapons of communication, something Olvido had seen with extreme lucidity in the photo of Beirut. The end of the aseptic and innocent image, or of that universally accepted fiction. In a time of information networks, of satellites and globalization, what modified territory and the lives that moved across it was specifying. To kill, you pointed a finger: a bridge framed in the monitor of a smart bomb, news of the ups and downs of the market broadcast simultaneously around the world. The photograph of a soldier who until that moment had been just another anonymous face.

The painter of battles went inside the tower. He lit the small gas lamp and stood a moment, hands in his pockets, looking at the dark panorama around him.

The light could not illuminate the entire fresco, but the parts in black and white stood out in the darkness, some faces, weapons, and armor, leaving in the shadows the background of ruins and fires, the masses of men with bristling lances battling on the plain beneath the dark red cone of lava—thick blood, it looked like—from the erupting volcano.

The volcano. Geological layers, geometry of the earth. Ballistics and pyrotechnics of a different nature perhaps, but not at all alien to the photo of the night battle. Cézanne had seen that clearly, thought Faulques. It was not simply a question of green accentuating a smile or of ochre shading a shadow. It was, above all, a way of looking into the very heart of the matter. The structure. He picked up the lamp and moved closer, observing the deliberate similarities between the city burning on the hill and the red volcano painted on a more distant plane and to the right, at the far end of despoiled fields ripped open as if the earth had been slashed by an enormous and powerful hand. He had met Olvido Ferrara near a similar volcano, or, to be more precise, near the volcano from which this one had taken inspiration, or tried to: the 168 x 168 centimeter painting hanging in a gallery in the Museo Nacional de Arte in Mexico. Faulques had discovered it, to his surprise, when he looked to the left, toward a corner of the wall: an easy place to be overlooked by other visitors as they came into the hall and moved forward toward other paintings that caught their eye at the back of the room and to the right. *Eruption of Paricutín.* Not until that moment had Faulques heard of Dr. Atl. He knew nothing about him, or his obsession with volcanoes, or his landscapes of ice and fire, or his true name—Gerardo Murillo—or about Carmen Mondragón, a.k.a. Nahui Ollin, the most beautiful woman in Mexico, who had been his lover until she more or less left him for a captain in the merchant marine with the name and look of an Italian tenor, a man called Eugenio Agacino. The day Faulques discovered Dr. Atl, he knew nothing of all that, but he stood very still before the painting, almost unable to breathe, contemplating the truncate pyramid of the volcano, the glowing trajectory of the lava flowing down its side, the land devastated by the reflections of fire and silver lending depth to the scene, the extraordinary effect of light on the naked trees, the flares of flames and the plume of black ash spilling to the right under the cold gaze of the stars in the clear night, indifferent and far above the disaster. A photograph, he thought in that instant, could never achieve that. And yet, everything—absolutely everything—was explained there: the blind and impassive rule translated into volumes, straight lines, curves, and angles by which, as if on inescapable rails, lava were flowing from the volcano to cover the world.

Later, after coming back to himself, Faulques glanced to one side and saw a pair of large, moist green eyes studying the same painting. Then came the exchange of two courteous, and to a degree, complicitous smiles, a certain brief discussion about the painting both were admiring—even nature, she pointed out, has its passions—a silent, impersonal good-bye, during which Faulques' trained eye noticed the small camera bag the woman had over her shoulder, and then a singular interweaving of footsteps and chance through the galleries of the museum, with another accidental encounter, this time without words or smiles, before a pool where the undulating reflections of a painting by Diego Rivera wove destinies that neither of the two was aware of. And later, when Faulques left the museum, and after walking past the bronze equestrian statue located at the door had wandered in the direction of the Zócalo, he saw the girl sitting at a table on the terrace of a cantina, the photography case on a chair, the grape-colored eyes greener still in the outdoor light, jeans emphasizing long, slender legs. Her amiable smile of recognition had made Faulques stop to say something about the museum and the painting they had both admired, not knowing that at that moment he was changing the meaning of his entire life. We are a product, he would think later, of the hidden rules that determine coincidences: from the symmetry of the universe to the moment you walk into a museum gallery.

Faulques held the lamp closer to the wall, in the area where he was painting the volcano. He studied it awhile and then went outdoors to connect the generator and halogen lights, chose brushes and paint, and set to work. The echo of his conversation with Ivo Markovic gave new shadings to the circular landscape that surrounded the painter of battles. Slowly, with extreme care, he applied Payne's gray, unmixed, for the column of smoke and ash, and then, intensifying the lower edge of the sky with cobalt blue mixed with white, forgot all precautions and built up the fire and the horror with vigorous, nearly brutal, brushstrokes of scarlet and white lacquer, cadmium orange and vermilion. The volcano that spilled its lava toward the edge of the field of battle, like an Olympus indifferent to the needs and wishes of the tiny ants bristling with lances and engaged in battle at its feet, was now furrowed with lines that opened into a fan; hills and valleys that seemed to channel the chaos of the red lava—more orange and vermilion—erupting interminably, semen ready to impregnate the entire earth with horror. And when finally Faulques put down the brushes and moved back a few steps to contemplate the result of his work, his lips curved in a smile of satisfaction before he moistened them with a new glass of cognac. Good or bad, the volcano was in a certain way different from those Dr. Atl had painted—and he had put his efforts into quite a few during his lifetime. His were marvels of a grandiose and heroic nature, an extraordinary vision of the transformation of the world and the telluric forces that create and destroy it. Something nearly congenial. What Faulques had created on the wall of the tower was more somber and more sinister: impotence in the face of the geometric caprices of the universe, Jupiter's contemptuous thunderbolt that, precise as a scalpel guided by invisible hands, strikes at the very heart of man and his life.

We don't have much time, she'd said shortly after that. Faulques would remember those words in years to come, just as he was remembering them this night, with the smell of Ivo Markovic's cigarettes on the air, and Faulques himself motionless before the mural of which Olvido was the direct cause. We don't have much time. She had said it quite casually, with a slight smile on her lips, the night of the day they met. A long, pleasant day of walking and conversation, of professional affinities discovered in an expression, in a phrase, in the blinking of an eye. She was young, and so beautiful that she didn't seem real. Faulques had noticed that in the museum with an unprejudiced eye, but it wasn't until they were walking below Rivera's frescoes in the Palacio Nacional and he observed her leaning along the railing, photographing the effects of light and shadow in the gallery among schoolchildren marching along hand in hand, that he realized hers was an exceptional beauty: she was slim, lithe, with the subtle movements of a doe, but one with a gaze that belied innocence. She had a characteristic way of looking at you, lowering her head a little and looking up, half irony and half insolence. The look of a dangerous hunter, Faulques suddenly thought. Diana with a photographer's quiver and a pair of cameras.

They'd had lunch together in a restaurant near Santo Domingo after strolling past the bustle of the art printing shops beneath the arches of the plaza. And by midafternoon, contemplating the large murals by Siqueiros, Rivera, and Orozco covering the walls of the Palacio de Bellas Artes, each of them knew the basic facts about the other. In Faulques' case it was simple, or at least as he told it: Mediterranean childhood in a mining city near the sea, abandoned brushes, a camera, the world through a lens. A certain professional reputation translated into income and status. As for her, she had no idea of what war was, she had only seen images on television. She'd studied art history and then worked as a fashion model for a brief time, until she decided to move to the other side of the camera. She worked for art, architecture, and interior-decorating magazines. Ridiculously expensive magazines, she added, with a smile that removed any pretentiousness from what she'd said. Twenty-seven years old, an Italian father—a well-known businessman with important galleries in Florence and Rome—a Spanish mother. Good family on both sides, with connections to the world of painting that went back three generations, including an octogenarian maternal grandmother, whom Faulques would meet: the painter Lola Zegrí, a disciple of the late Bauhaus, a friend of Duchamp, of Jean Renoir—she had a bit part in *The Rules of the Game,* dressed as a seminar student next to Cartier-Bresson—of Bonnard and Picasso. Olvido truly loved that old woman, who spent her last years in the south of France, where she lived awaiting news of Kikí de Montparnasse's latest lover or whether the Germans had entered Paris. Shortly before she died, Olvido had visited her there: a little white house with straight lines and austere décor, where in her garden, also perfectly linear, she grew vegetables instead of flowers after she'd sold the last of her paintings, and those she owned by other artists, and with no regret spent her last centime—including proceeds from the auction of an old and widely famous Citroën now in the Cortanza Museum in Nice; on one of its doors Braque had painted a gray bird and on another, Picasso a white dove. Olvido introduced Faulques—my lover, she said expressionlessly—to her grandmother, in whom he could still note the elegance displayed in the photo albums she showed them during their visit: Paris, Monte Carlo, Nice, breakfast on Cap Martin with Peggy Guggenheim and Max Ernst; one photo of Olvido at five, in Mougins, sitting on Picasso's knees, seemed taken from a Penagos drawing. I was one of the last women able to make men suffer, the old woman commented with a placid smile. My granddaughter, however, came too late to a world too old.

From the beginning, aside from her beauty, what fascinated Faulques were Olvido's mannerisms: her way of conversing; of tilting her head after a phrase or of listening with a sympathetic air, as if she never believed anything completely but was willing to listen; the manners of a well brought up and slightly haughty girl; her gentle cruelty—she was too young and too beautiful to know compassion devoid of calculation—all tempered by a scintillating sense of humor and puckish courtesy. Also, Faulques came to know, she was a woman who never passed unnoticed, though she tried: men held doors for her and helped her into cars, waiters came if she merely glanced their way, maître d's reserved the best table for her, and hotel managers gave her the best room with the most splendid view. Olvido reacted to all these attentions with her peculiar smile, at once ironic and affectionate, with clever banter and sophisticated observations, with her inexhaustible faculty of placing herself, without giving up anything, at the level of the person she was talking to. Even tips in restaurants and hotels were slipped to the person helping her quietly, confidentially, as if she were sharing a joke. And when she laughed, really laughed—like a mischievous and guilty little boy—any man would lay down his life for her, or for that laugh. She was very good at all these things. We people who have been well brought up, she would say, seduce others with a very simple trick: we always talk about what interests *them*. She could seduce with words and silences in five languages; she imitated voices and gestures with awesome ease, and she had an extraordinary memory for details. Faulques heard her call a myriad of concierges, waiters, and taxi drivers by name. She adopted every slang and every accent, and when she was furious, filthy words poured from her lips with amazing fluency—her Italian blood. She also had an unstudied skill for neutralizing the swinish side of the people who waited on her: the resentment hidden beneath the servility of those who grudgingly wait on others while dreaming of head-lopping revolutions, or of those who assume their role with dignified resignation. Women envied Olvido in a sisterly way, and men adopted her at first sight, immediately taking her side. Had Olvido been a male in the early years of the century, Faulques could easily imagine the transformation: still in his dinner jacket having breakfast in a *chocolatería* alongside the servants from the home where the night before he had attended a dinner or a ball.

That night of the first day, in Mexico City, he, too, succumbed to her charm. Despite his own reservations, his biography, his ideas about the world, he found himself with his wrists resting on the edge of a well-located table in a restaurant in San Ángel Inn—he in a dark blue blazer and jeans, she in a mauve dress so plain it might have been painted onto her hips and long legs; the maître d' had said, Good evening, What a long time, How is your father, señorita Ferrara?—gazing into the grape-green eyes identical to those of that Nahui Ollin she had told him about that afternoon. He stared, unconsciously, for such a long time that Olvido had lowered her head slightly and, looking at him through the wheat-colored hair falling over her face, had become serious for an instant, just long enough to say, We don't have much time, Faulques, not specifying whether she meant that night or the rest of their lives. She had called him that, Faulques, for the first time using his family, not his given, name. And she would always call him that, up to the end. Three years. Or nearly three. One thousand and fifty days confirming how directly proportional it all was to the product of two bodies' desire—it was she who had paraphrased Newton on a certain occasion when Faulques had his arms around her in the shower of an Athens hotel—and inversely proportional to the square of the distance that separated them. Three intense and peripatetic years begun that night that ended very late, alone in a cantina on the Plaza Garibaldi after closing hours, talking about painting and photography while the waiters turned chairs up on the tables and began to sweep the floor. And when Faulques looked at the clock, she had said she found it surprising that a war photographer could not sit and drink without being affected by the fire in the glances of the impatient waiters. She was unique in injecting non sequiturs here and there in the form of her own maxims, or of spontaneous reflections, ingenious in getting around obstacles by incorporating them into the original plan, skillful in lying, making you believe that she was lying openly and deliberately. Everything faux enchanted her; she collected little trinkets everywhere only to abandon them later in hotel wastebaskets and airports, or give them to maids, telephone operators, and airline stewardesses: faux Murano glass, faux Brussels lace, faux antique bronzes, faux eighteenth-century miniatures she bought in flea markets. She moved with complete ease among all that kitsch, with a word or a gesture making it something to be cherished. It was Olvido who conferred importance on things and people she had contact with, maybe because she had the unassailable self-confidence some few women have when the world is their exciting field of battle, and men a useful but disposable complement.

At any rate she had been right. Three years was not very long, although neither of them could have calculated how long. That first night in Mexico City, Faulques, who by then already considered the world in the light of its paradoxes and convergences, thought about the meaning of her name. Olvido. Forgetfulness. And suddenly he knew, with the fleeting precision of a photograph perceived in an instant, that she was the only thing he would never forget.

Now, through the open windows of the tower, the painter of battles heard the sound of the rising tide at the foot of the cliff accompanying his inspection of the volcano he'd painted. At that moment, the cognac he'd drunk, shadows, or some effect of the gas lamp caused a shadow to cross before his eyes. Shaken, he looked at the part of the vast mural where that shadow had gone to hide. After an instant, he shook his head. *The house where you are living,* he murmured, remembering, *is dark.*

6.

THE NEXT MORNING THE COLD WATER of the cove cleared his head. After swimming the usual one hundred and fifty strokes out to sea, and the same number back, he worked with only a quarter of an hour break to make coffee and drain a cup as he appraised the painting before going back to work on the caballeros who, located in a group on the near left of the tower door, were awaiting the moment to join in the battle taking place on the slopes of the volcano. Although the horses had not been dealt with—Faulques had technical problems to resolve—of the three horsemen, one in the foreground and the other two farther back, two were nearly finished: armor in cold colors, blue-gray and a violet blue, the angles and edges of their weapons gleaming with fine strokes of a white base, then Prussian blue, and a little red and yellow. The painter of battles had devoted special attention to the eyes of the horseman in the foreground, who because the visor of his helmet was raised was the only one of the three whose face—or part of it—could be seen; those of the other two were hidden behind sallet and bevor. Absorbed eyes, empty, fixed on some indeterminate spot, contemplating something the viewer couldn't see but could intuit. Eyes that looked without seeing, familiar in a man about to enter combat, stirred several of Faulques' professional memories; their pictorial execution, however, owed a great deal to the master hand of the classic painter who—among many others but above them all—from the fifteenth century guided the man working in the tower: the Paolo Uccello of the three paintings of *The Battle of San Romano* exhibited in the Uffizi, the National Gallery, and the Louvre. The choice was not fortuitous. Along with Piero della Francesca, Uccello had been the best artist/geometer of his time, with an engineer's intellect for resolving problems that still today impress specialists. The shadow of the Florentine fell across the entire circular fresco in the tower, among other reasons because the first thought of leaving cameras behind to paint the battle of battles had occurred to Faulques there in the Uffizi before Uccello's painting, the day that Olvido Ferrara and he had stood in the gallery, by good fortune empty for five minutes, admiring the extraordinary composition, the perspective, the magnificent foreshortening in that painting on wood, one of three representing the encounter between the armies of Florence and Sienna on July 1, 1432, in San Romano, a valley near the course of the Arno. It had been Olvido who called Faulques' attention to the horizontal line that ended on the horseman unseated by a lance, and who pointed out the broken lances on the ground beside the bodies of the fallen horses, crisscrossing in the simulation of a net, a pictorial underpinning—the perspective stretching back toward the background and the trees on the horizon—on which was arranged the mass of men fighting in the principal scene. Olvido had had a good eye from the time she was a little girl: the instinct to read a painting the way someone reads a map, a book, or a man's thoughts. It reminds me of one of your photos, she said suddenly. A tragedy resolved with almost abstract geometry. Look at the arches of the crossbows, Faulques. Look at the lances that seem to continue beyond the painting, the curved lines of armor that disrupt the planes, the volumes interrupted by helmets and breastplates. It wasn't by chance, was it, that the most revolutionary artists of the twentieth century had reclaimed this painter as a master? Not even he could have imagined how modern he was, or was going to be. Or you either, with your photographs. The problem is that Paolo Uccello had brushes and perspective, and all you have is a camera. That imposes limits, of course. From so much abuse, so much manipulation, it's been a long time since a picture was worth a thousand words. But that isn't your fault. It isn't the way that you see things that's been devalued, it's the tools you use. There are just too many photos, don't you agree? The world is saturated with photographs. When he heard that, Faulques had turned to look at her; she was profiled against the light beaming through the window on the right side of the gallery. Maybe one day I will compose a painting based on that idea, he thought of saying, but didn't. And Olvido died a little later, never knowing that he was going to do it; that, among other things, for her. At that moment she was studying the Uccello, fascinated: long neck, hair caught back at the nape, a statue sculpted with exquisite delicacy absorbed in the men killing and dying, in the dog by the head of the central horse, poised to give chase to some hares. And you? he had asked. Tell me how you resolve the problem. Olvido was slow to answer, but finally she tore her eyes from the painting and looked toward him out of the corner of her eye. I don't have a problem, she said finally. I'm a comfortable girl with no responsibilities and no complexes. I don't pose for couturiers or magazine covers anymore, or photograph luxurious interiors for magazines intended for society ladies married to millionaires. I am a simple tourist of disaster, happy to be that, with a camera that serves as a pretext for feeling I'm alive, as it was in those long-ago days when every human had a shadow glued to his heels. I would have liked to write a novel, or make a movie about the dead friends of a Knight Templar, about a lovesick samurai, about a Russian count who drank like a Cossack and gambled like a criminal in Monte Carlo before he became the doorman at Le Gran Véfour in Paris, but I don't have the talent to do that. So I look. I take pictures. And you are my passport, for the moment. The hand that leads me across landscapes like the one in that painting. As for the definitive image, the one that everyone is looking for in our profession—including you, though you never say it—that isn't important, I don't care whether I find it or not. You know that I would shoot—*clic, clic, clic*—with or without film in the camera. You know damn well I would. But it's different with you, Faulques. Your eyes, so charged with defensiveness, want to ask an accounting of God using their own rules. Or weapons. They want to peer into Paradise, not at the beginning of Creation but at the end, just at the brink of the abyss. Although you will never capture that with one miserable photo.

This place is known as Cala del Arráez. *It was once the refuge of Berber pirates . . .* The woman's voice, the sound of the tourist boat's motors, and music rose from the sea at the exact hour. Faulques stopped working. It was one o'clock. And Ivo Markovic still wasn't there. Faulques reflected on that, then went outside and took a cautious look around. He went to the shed and washed his arms, torso, and face. Back in the tower, he thought about fixing something to eat, but he couldn't make up his mind and he couldn't get the strange visitor out of his head. He had thought about him all night, and through the morning while he was working he couldn't help seeing places where the Croatian could be included in the mural. Markovic, independent of his intentions, was by rights part of it. But the painter of battles didn't have enough information. I want you to understand, the Croatian had said. There are answers you need as much as I do.

After wandering around for a while, Faulques went to the upper floor of the tower, where he pulled the Remington 870, wrapped in oily rags, from the bottom of the trunk, along with two boxes of shells. It was a weapon he had never fired, a shotgun that reloaded by means of a sliding mechanism parallel to the barrel. After testing that it worked, he put in five shells and injected one into the chamber with a quick movement that produced a metallic *crack!* accompanied by a flood of memories: Olvido, blindfolded with a handkerchief, blindly assembling and disassembling an AK-47 amid a group of militiamen in

Bulo Burti, Somalia. Like the soldier's war, the photographer's war was always one part action and the rest boredom and waiting. That was the case. They were waiting for the right time to attack a rival militia's position, when a training session for some young recruits caught Olvido's eye. They blindfold them, Faulques explained, in case their weapons jam during night combat and they have to put them right in the dark. Olvido had gone over to the recruits and their instructors, and asked to learn how to do it herself. Fifteen minutes later, she was sitting on the ground, legs crossed, in the center of a circle of armed to the teeth men smoking and watching. A skinny and very black militiaman was keeping time, Faulques' watch in hand, as Olvido, eyes covered, with precise movements, without error or hesitation, took apart and put back together an assault rifle several times, then lined up the pieces on a poncho before putting them back, one by one, by touch and pumped the bolt, *clac, clac,* with a triumphant, happy smile. She kept practicing the rest of the afternoon, while Faulques watched in silence close by, engraving in his memory the handkerchief around her head, the hair combed into two braids, the shirt wet with sweat, and the drops on her forehead furrowed with concentration. After a while, with the weapon again disassembled and as she was feeling the contours of each piece, Olvido divined his presence, and without slipping off the handkerchief offered an observation. Until today, she said, I never imagined that these things could be beautiful. So polished. So metallic and so perfect. Touching them reveals virtues that can't be seen. Listen. They fit together with such wonderful *click*s.

They're beautiful and sinister at the same time, aren't they? Through the last thirty or forty years, these strangely shaped pieces have tried to change the world, without success. A cheap weapon of the pariahs of the earth, millions of manufactured units, and here they are, innards exposed, on the knees of my very expensive jeans. The Surrealists would have been mad about this readymade. Don't you agree, Faulques? I wonder what they would have called it. *Opportunity Lost*? *Marx's Funeral*? *This Weapon Is Not a Weapon*? *When War Goes, Poetry Returns*? It just occurred to me that Kalashnikov's signature must be worth as much as R. Mutt's. Or much more. Maybe the representative work of art of the twentieth century isn't Duchamp's urinal after all but this collection of disassembled pieces. *Broken Dream of Blued Metal*. I think that's the name I like best. I don't know if the AK-47 is exhibited in any museum of contemporary art, but it should be, like this, in pieces. Like this one. So uselessly beautiful once it is taken apart and exposed, mechanism by mechanism, on an oil-stained military poncho. Yes. Please tie my blindfold again. It's coming loose, and I don't want to cheat. I do that often enough with a camera around my neck and a civilized passport and return ticket in my pocket. I am an indulgent technician; you know that, don't you? *Woman Who Assembles and Disassembles a Useless Rifle Over and Over.* Yes. Now I've got it. That, it seems to me, is the right title. And don't you even think of taking my picture, Faulques. I hear you digging into your camera bag. The true modern work of art is ephemeral, or it isn't art.

The painter of battles set the safety on the shotgun

and put it back in the trunk. Then he looked for a clean shirt—wrinkled and stiff since it had hung in the sun to dry and he had no iron—rolled his motorcycle from the shed, put on dark glasses, and drove down to the town backfiring along the dirt road that snaked among the pines. The day was luminous and warm. The soft breeze from the south was not enough to relieve the temperature on the dock when he stopped, kicked down the stand, and parked the bike. He stood for a moment admiring the cobalt blue of the sea on the other side of the breakwater where the port beacon was located, the brown and green nets piled beside the bollards for the fishing boats that at this hour were out at sea, the clinking of the halyards on the masts of a dozen boats moored at the dock below the sixteenth-century wall and the small fort that in another time had protected the cove and the original town of Puerto Umbría: some twenty whitewashed houses perched along a hill on either side of the ochre bell tower of a dark, narrow church—a Gothic fortress, with windows like embrasures—that had served as a refuge for the townspeople when renegades and pirates came ashore. The abrupt orography of the place had saved it from the surrounding urban development: boxed in among the mountains, the town stayed within reasonable boundaries. The zone of the tourist expansion began a couple of kilometers to the southeast, toward Cabo Malo, where hotels lined the beaches and where the mountains, spattered with little houses, glowed at night with the lights of the housing developments gnawing into their slopes.

The tourist tender was docked at the pier, with no

one aboard. Faulques took a look around, trying to pick out the guide from among the few people strolling back from the beach that stretched beyond the port, or eating beneath the awning of one of the bars on the fishing dock, but none of the women he saw resembled the one he imagined, and the office where tickets for the boat tour and sales of summer homes and rental cars were posted was closed. He devoted only a moment to that. There was another person he was interested in, although there was no trace of him, either. Ivo Markovic was not on the terraces, not in the narrow white streets behind them—a hardware shop where Faulques bought brushes and paints, a grocery and souvenir shops—where he walked for a while, looking relaxed and casual but keeping a sharp eye out. One of the pensioners who planted themselves in front of the local men's club greeted him as he passed, and he responded without stopping. Although he had no more to do with people than was necessary, or inevitable, he was known in Puerto Umbría and awarded a certain courteous status. He had the reputation of being an unsociable and somewhat eccentric artist, but one who paid punctually for what he bought, respected local customs, would buy you a beer or a cup of coffee, and left the women of the town alone.

Faulques went into the hardware shop and asked for four tins of green chromium oxide and several of natural sienna; he was getting low on those and needed them to finish the ground painted on the mural with superimposed layers: a heavy brush, wet over wet, taking advantage of the irregularities of the sand and cement layer on the wall around a scene of two men, arms locked around each other, one fallen on the other as he stabbed at him with rage, cooling the vivid colors of the violent foreshadowing with layers of ultramarine blue with a little carmine in the shadows, an effect owed to the intermingling splendors from the city in flames and the distant volcano. The painter of battles had worked for a long time on that detail, devoting special attention to it. He had vague recollections of Goya's *Duel with Cudgels:* two men struggling in water up to their calves, in the most brutal symbol of civil war ever painted. Compared to it, Picasso's *Guernica* was an exercise in style—although in truth the figures weren't that great, Olvido had said, the real painting is on the right of the canvas, don't you think? Our don Francisco was so modern that it hurts. At any rate, as Faulques himself knew all too well, the most direct antecedents of the scene he had painted in that part of the mural, Goya aside, could be found in Vicente Carducho's *Victory at Fleurus;* it too was exhibited in the Prado museum—the Spanish soldier run through by the sword of the Frenchman he was stabbing—and especially in an Orozco fresco painted on the ceiling of the Hospicio Cabañas in Guadalajara, Mexico: the conquistador sheathed in steel—those futuristic, angular planes of armor—crushing the slashed Aztec warrior, a bloody fusion of iron and flesh as a prelude to a new race. Years before, when he had not even thought about painting, or believed that he had given up attempting it forever, Faulques, lying on his back on one of the benches beside Olvido, admired that enormous fresco for almost half an hour, until he had imprinted all the details in his memory. I've seen this before, he said suddenly, and his voice echoed in the painted dome. I've photographed it many times but never been able to capture an image that expresses it with such precision. Look at those faces. The man who kills and dies, confused, blind, locked together with his enemy. The history of the labyrinth, or the world. Our history. Olvido looked at him and put her hand on his but didn't speak for a while, until finally she said: When I stab you, Faulques, I want to have my arms around you like that, looking for the chink in the steel as you bury yourself in me, or rape me, scarcely adjusting your armor. And now, reserving a space on the interior wall of the watchtower for all that, mixing it on his own palette of memories and images, the painter of battles was trying to reproduce not Orozco's terrifying fresco but the sensation of viewing it at Olvido's side, her words, and the touch of that hand, recorded so long ago in his heart and his memory. How subtle and how strange, he thought, the ties that can be established among things that appear not to be connected: paintings, words, memories, horror. It seemed that all the chaos of the world, scattered across the earth by the caprice of drunken or imbecilic gods—an explanation as good as any other—or by coincidences devoid of mercy, could find itself quickly rearranged, converted into a whole of precise proportions by the key to an unsuspected image, a word spoken by chance, an emotion, a painting contemplated with a woman who had been dead for ten years, remembered now and painted again in the light of a biography different from that of the one who conceived it. Of a gaze that perhaps enriched and explained it.

When Faulques walked past the hotel in Puerto Umbría—there was also a hostel a little farther away, on the same street—he stopped for a moment, quiet, reflecting, hands in his pockets and head to one side. Turning over in his mind a more immediate and urgent recollection: Ivo Markovic. Finally he decided to go in. The concierge greeted him amiably. And he was very sorry, but no. That gentleman was not registered in his establishment. At least not with that name, nor did he have anyone fitting the description. The same response ten minutes later from the clerk at the hostel. Faulques went outside, squinting from the reverberating glare off the white walls. He put on his dark glasses and went back to the port. He discarded the idea of going to the police. The local station was staffed with five officers and a chief: sometimes, as they made their rounds, they would drive in a black-and-white ATV almost up to the tower, and the painter of battles would invite them to have a beer. In addition, the wife of the police chief painted in her free time; Faulques had seen one of her oils in her husband's office—an atrocious sunset with stags and a vermilion sky—the day he went in to fill out some forms and the chief had showed it to him with pride. That put him in line for a certain warmth, and it would have been easy to have them look into Markovic. But maybe that was going too far. Aside from the strange declaration of what he intended to do, the Croatian had done nothing to justify strong measures.

The walk under the hot sun had made Faulques sweat, and his shirt was wet. He went and sat under the awning of one of the restaurant bars on the fishing dock. He stretched his legs beneath the table, leaned back in the chair, and ordered a beer. He liked this terrace because it offered the best view: the sea beyond the inlet, between the beacon on the breakwater and the rocks. When he came down to the town to buy painting supplies or provisions, he liked to sit there at dusk, as the water became tinged with red along the coast and silhouetted the fishing boats coming back one after the other to unload boxes for the market, followed by bands of noisy seagulls. Some evenings Faulques ordered a pot of rice soup and with a bottle of wine stayed to eat, watching the sea grow dark as the green beacon on the breakwater was turned on and he could see the intermittent flashes from the Cabo Malo lighthouse.

A waiter brought the beer and Faulques lifted it to his lips and quaffed half in one breath. When he put the glass down he noticed that he had paint, cadmium red, under the fingernails of his right hand. So like blood. And the mural, the circular wall of the tower, was again in his thoughts. A long time back, in a bombarded city—it was Sarajevo, although it could have been Beirut, Phnom Penh, Saigon, anywhere—Faulques had had blood under his nails and on his shirt for three days. The blood was that of a child blown up by a mortar grenade; he had died in his arms, bleeding to death as Faulques carried him to the hospital. There was no water to wash in, no clean clothes, so for three days Faulques had the child's blood on his shirt, on his cameras, and under his fingernails. The boy, or what was left of him in the memory of the painter of battles—often the image blended into other places, other children—was now represented with cold strokes, a leaden chiaroscuro in the tower fresco: a small silhouette lying faceup, his head resting on a stone, which also owed a great deal in its technical inspiration to Paolo Uccello. This time not his battle paintings, but a fresco recently discovered in San Martino Maggiore in Bologna: *The Adoration of the Child.* In the lower fragment, among a mule, an ox, and several figures decapitated by the assaults of time, a child Jesus lay with his eyes closed, in an almost cadaver-like stillness that announced, to the shudder of the attentive spectator, the tortured and dead Christ of any pietà.

Faulques was cleaning his fingernails when a shadow fell across the table. He looked up and saw Ivo Markovic.

7.

WHEN THE WAITER BROUGHT HIS BEER, Markovic stared at his glass without touching it. After a while he drew a line down the sweating glass and watched drops trickle down, leaving a wet circle on the table. Finally, still without taking a sip, he took a pack of cigarettes from the knapsack he'd set on the ground beside his chair, and lit one. The breeze off the sea sent smoke through his fingers, and he was still bent over the flame he was protecting in the hollow of his hands when he looked up and saw Faulques.

"I thought you'd be thirsty," Faulques said.

"And I am."

Markovic tossed the burnt match aside, again examined the glass of beer, and then moving as if the world had slowed, picked it up to drink. Halfway to his lips, he paused as if to say something, but seemed to change his mind. Only after he'd taken a sip and set the glass back on the table did he suck twice on his cigarette and smile at Faulques. Or maybe it was his lips that smiled, while his gray eyes, fixed on the painter of battles, remained uninvolved.

"There's something," the Croatian began impassively, "you learn in a prison camp, and that's to wait.

At first you get impatient, of course. Fear, uncertainty, well, you can imagine . . . Yes. The first weeks are bad. And that's also the time the weakest disappear. They can't take it, they die. Some take their own lives. I always thought it was a bad idea to commit suicide out of desperation, and even more when there's a possibility of getting back at your tormentors someday. It's a different matter, I suppose, to end everything with serenity when you know you have no further to go. Wouldn't you agree?"

Faulques looked at him but said nothing. Markovic adjusted his glasses with a finger and shook his head. What's bad, he continued, is that the desire for revenge, or the mere hope of surviving, can become a trap.

"Yes," he added after reflecting a minute. "I think the worst is hope. You hinted at that yesterday, although you may not have been speaking of the same thing . . . You have faith that there's been some kind of mistake, that it will soon be over. You tell yourself it can't last. But time goes by, and it does last. And there's a moment when everything comes to a stop. You don't count the days anymore, your hope evaporates. That's when you become a true prisoner. A professional, to be more precise. A patient prisoner."

The painter of battles was contemplating the blue line of the sea in the inlet. He shrugged his shoulders.

"You're no longer a prisoner," he said. "And your beer's going to get warm."

Silence. When he looked toward Markovic again he saw that the Croatian was observing him, almost with caution, from behind the dirty lenses of his glasses.

"You seem like a patient man to me, señor Faulques."

The painter of battles didn't answer. Markovic once again pulled on his cigarette and let the breeze blow the smoke from his open mouth. He tilted his head.

"It's strange, that painting of yours. I assure you that it was a surprise to me . . . I'd like to ask you something, if you don't mind. You've photographed wars, revolutions . . . Is what you're working on now a summary or a conclusion? I mean by that, are you limiting yourself to reproducing what you saw or are you trying to explain it? Explain it to yourself?"

Faulques grimaced, consciously. A disagreeable expression.

"Come back to the tower anytime you want, and take a better look. You decide."

As if he were considering the pros and cons of that proposition, Markovic stroked his unshaven chin. The stubble and dirty glasses were not the only things that were slovenly about him: his skin was oily and he was wearing the same clothes he'd had on the day before. The shirt was wrinkled, and frayed around the neck. The painter of battles wondered where he might have spent the night.

"I will come, thank you very much. Tomorrow morning, if that's not inconvenient for you."

He tossed away the nearly consumed cigarette, index finger flicking it off his thumb, and sat watching the smoke rise from where it lay on the ground. Then he drank a little beer and wiped his lips with his fist. I'd like to ask another question if I may, he said.

"Do you have any idea by now why humans torture and kill others of their species? In those thirty years of photographs, did you find an answer to that?"

Faulques laughed at that. A brief, involuntary snort.

"It doesn't take thirty years. Anyone can find that out, as soon as he pays attention. Man tortures and kills because it's his thing. He likes it."

"To his fellow, man is a wolf, as the philosophers say?"

"Don't insult wolves. They're honorable killers: they kill in order to live."

Markovic bowed his head, as if he were carefully considering what Faulques had said. Then he looked up at the painter of battles.

"And what, in your judgment, is the reason that man tortures and kills for pleasure?"

"His intelligence, I suppose."

"That's interesting."

"Objective, elemental cruelty isn't cruelty. To be truly cruel, there must be conscious calculation. Intelligence, as I just said. Think of whales."

"What about the whales?'

So Faulques explained what whales do. How those marine predators with evolved brains, who operate within a complex social group, communicating with refined sounds, swim near the beaches and catch young seals; they toss them back and forth, playing with them as if they were balls, then let them escape almost to the shore before they catch them again and continue the game until, weary of the sport, they abandon their battered, broken prey or, should they be hungry, devour it. That, Faulques concluded, was not something he'd seen on television or heard somewhere. He had photographed it on a beach in the southern hemisphere during the war in the Falkland Islands. Those whales had seemed nearly human.

"I'm not sure I really understand. Do you mean that the more intelligent the animal is, the crueler it may be? That a chimpanzee is crueler than a snake?"

"I don't know anything about chimpanzees *or* snakes. Not even about whales, when it comes down to it. Seeing them made me think, that's all. They must have their reasons, I suppose. Play? Training? But their exquisite cruelty reminded me of man. Maybe they don't have any awareness that they're being cruel and are simply obeying the codes of their kind. And maybe man does the same: be faithful to the fearsome symmetry of his intelligent nature."

Markovic blinked, taken aback.

"Symmetry?"

"Yes. A scientist would define it as the stable properties of the whole, despite their transformations . . ." When Faulques saw Markovic's expression, he held out his hands, palms up. "Put a different way, appearances are deceptive. There is a hidden order in disorder, I would say. An order that includes disorder. Symmetries and answers to symmetries."

Markovic scratched his chin with a slight, negative shake of his head.

"I don't think I understand."

"Well, yesterday you said that you'd come to know me. My photographs and all that."

Markovic squeezed his eyes, trying to think. He removed his glasses and checked the lenses, as if he had just discovered that they weren't really transparent.

He took a tissue from his pocket and carefully began cleaning them.

"I see now," he concluded after a few moments. "You mean that an evil person can't help being evil."

"I mean that we are all evil, and we can't help it. That those are the rules of this game. That our superior intelligence refines our evil and makes it more tempting. Man was born a predator, like most animals. It is his irresistible impulse. Going back to science, his stable property. But unlike other animals, our complex intelligence incites us to claw our way to wealth, luxuries, women, men, pleasures, honors . . . That impulse leads to envy, to frustration and anger. It makes us even more what we are."

Faulques fell silent and the Croatian had nothing to say. He had put his glasses back on. He looked at Faulques before turning in the direction of the breakwater, and sat that way, contemplating the scene.

"I used to hunt before the war," he said suddenly. "I liked to go out in the country in the early morning, with a neighbor. Walk toward the dawn, you know, with a shotgun. *Pum! Pum!*"

He was still looking at the sea, squinting against the sunlight glinting off the water by the fishing dock.

"Who was there to tell me?" he added, his face suddenly contorted.

Again he lowered his head to light a cigarette. Faulques studied the scar on Markovic's right hand and then the one on his forehead, vertical and deeper. An eyebrow had been split open, no doubt. By some very authoritative object. That scar wasn't in the photograph, and Markovic hadn't mentioned it when he told about being wounded in Vukovar. Maybe it was a souvenir of the prison camp. He had talked about being tortured. Like an animal, were his words. They tortured me—"he was tortured," he'd said, in the third person—like an animal.

"I don't know what people find beautiful about the dawn," Markovic said suddenly. "Or a sunset. For someone who's lived a war, the dawn is a sign of possible clouds, of indecision, of fear of what's going to happen. And dusk is a threat of the coming shadows; darkness, a terrorized heart. The interminable wait, freezing to death in some hole, with the rifle stock pressed against your face . . ."

He was nodding. His memories seemed to back up his arguments. His cigarette was in his mouth and it bobbed with his movements.

"Have you been afraid countless times, señor Faulques?"

"Yes. As you say, countless times. Yes."

The painter's half smile seemed to make Markovic uncomfortable.

"Is there something wrong about the word 'countless'?"

"No, nothing. It's correct, don't worry. Countless: impossible to count."

The Croatian studied him intently, looking for a trace of irony. Finally, he relaxed a little. He smoked his cigarette.

"I was going to tell you," he said through a mouthful of smoke, "that once I vomited, toward dawn, before an attack. Pure fear. I wiped my mouth with a tissue, threw it away, and it blew into some brush, a sort of blot of light. I sat staring at that tissue as the dawn came. Now every time I think about being afraid, I remember that tissue caught in a shrub."

Again he pushed up his glasses with an index finger. He shifted to a more comfortable position in his chair and turned his head from side to side with a distracted air, as if looking for something interesting in the scene.

"Symmetry, you say," he commented finally. "Maybe. And that painting in the tower . . . That really surprised me. I think. Though maybe I wasn't as surprised as I say I think I was."

Now he was focused on the painter again, his face showing misgivings.

"Do you know what I do think? That every hunter is marked by the kind of hunting he does. And I've spent ten years following your tracks. Hunting you."

Faulques held his eyes but said nothing. He was fascinated by the accuracy of Markovic's comment. Hunters, kinds of hunting, being marked. Olvido had said it in almost the same words. One spring day after the first Gulf War, they had seen a group of children waiting outside the Louvre museum, lined up and sitting on the ground beneath a dark, rainy sky under the eyes of the teachers walking among them. They remind me, Faulques had said, of prisoners in the Iraqi war. And Olvido had looked at him with amusement, before she walked over to him and kissed him, a loud smack, and said that there are hunts that mark the hunter for a lifetime. Yes. There are meteorologists who look at the sky and see nothing but isobars.

"Whales, chimpanzees, snakes," Markovic murmured. "Is that really how you see it?"

That same day, Faulques was remembering, she

had written a poem. She wasn't unduly talented as a poet, just as she had no outstanding talent as a photographer; she was too eager to speed through life, burning the candle at both ends. She wasn't a creative person. If she hadn't let herself be led by her search for the intense experience, by the need to explore the outer limits of what was reasonable without renouncing her memory and her culture, or by her desire to live enough to catch up with the shadow of herself she pursued with such long strides, Olvido would have been brilliant as an art historian, a university professor, or a gallery director, in line with her family tradition. Her talent lay in an incomparably clear vision of art, an extraordinary eye for understanding it in any of its manifestations, a gift for analysis, and, when it came to selecting the good from the thicket of the mediocre and bad, superb taste, at once evenhanded and unadulterated. There had been a time, she said, when art was the only story in which justice triumphed, and in which at the end, however long it took to happen, the good guys always won . . . but now she wasn't so sure. For some time Faulques had kept the lines of the poem Olvido had scribbled on a café napkin, until finally he lost it, he didn't remember where, just as he didn't remember the words written on it: something about children sitting beneath the same rain that fell on other places, distant cemeteries where other children lay who would never reach old age . . . reach anything. All he could remember were the two first lines:

Children sitting in front of a museum
(remarkably) intact . . .

He brushed aside that memory and gave his attention to Markovic, who had repeated his question. Is that really how you see it? he persisted. Whales and all that. Faulques waved his hand in an ambiguous gesture.

"It's here, under our skin," he said finally. "In our genes. Only the artificial rules, culture, the varnish of successive civilizations keep man within bounds. Social conventions, laws. Fear of punishment."

Markovic was listening intently, his smoking cigarette dangling from his lips. Again his eyes were squinted.

"And God? Are you a believer, señor Faulques?"

"God? Don't be a bore."

Faulques half turned. He gestured toward the people sitting on the terraces or walking beside the dock, with their tans and their shorts and their children and their dogs.

"Look at them. So civilized within their parameters, as long as it doesn't cost them too much effort. Asking for things with a 'please'; some still do. Put them in a locked room, take away their basic necessities and you'll see them destroy each other."

Markovic was also looking at them. Convinced.

"I've seen it," he nodded. "For a piece of bread, or a cigarette. Say nothing of staying alive."

"That's why you know, as well as I, that when disaster throws man back into the chaos from which he came, all the civilized varnish chips off in little pieces and he is once again what he was, or what he always has been: a dyed-in-the-wool sonofabitch."

The Croatian was staring at the butt between his

thumb and index finger. He flicked it away, as he had the one before it. It fell at the same spot.

"You are not a compassionate man, señor Faulques."

"No, I'm not. But it's a little strange that you should say that."

"And in your opinion, what protects us? Culture, as you hinted before? Art?"

"I don't know. I don't think so."

Markovic seemed disillusioned, so Faulques thought about it some more.

"I suspect," he added, "that nothing can change human nature. Or always keep it in line."

He thought still a little longer. An attractive young girl was walking toward the ticket office of the tourist boat. Maybe that's the girl, he thought. The guide on the tender who talked about the famous painter in the tower. She walked on by.

"Memory, maybe. In a certain way it's a form of stoic dignity. Lucidity at the moment of contemplating the guiding lines of an issue. Accepting the rules of the game."

He saw Markovic smile, as if this time he had been able to understand the speaker's allusions.

"The symmetries," the Croatian said, with satisfaction.

"Yes. An English poet wrote the words 'terrible symmetry,' referring to a tiger's stripes."

"Really. A poet, you say?"

"Yes. He meant that all symmetry encases cruelty."

Markovic frowned. "So how is it possible to accept symmetries?"

"Through the geometry that allows us to see them. And the painting that expresses the geometry."

I'm lost again, Markovic's wrinkled brow communicated.

"Where did you learn all that?"

Faulques' hands mimed turning the pages of a book. Reading, he said. Taking pictures. Looking, I suppose. Asking. It's all out there, he added. The difference is that some people notice and some don't. The Croatian was listening to every word.

"I've lost track again," he protested. "You have very idiosyncratic points of view." He stopped, suspicious. "Why are you smiling, señor Faulques?"

"It's that word 'idiosyncratic.' It's fine. It's interesting the way you use some words."

"Unlike you, I am not an educated man. In recent years I've read a few books here and there. But I'm far from being cultured."

"I'm not referring to that. Just the opposite. You use interesting words. Words you don't often hear. Cultured words."

I didn't have much schooling, the Croatian said then. Only a good technical training as a mechanic. But in the prison camp I came to know a man who had read a lot. A musician. We talked often, fancy, during that time. I learned things. You know. Things. After he repeated "things," Markovic sat engrossed for a few moments, his air evocative. I also knew a man, he said, who had been buried for eleven hours under his bombed-out house, trapped in the debris, and all he could see was an object before him: a broken straight razor. Imagine, eleven hours without moving, with that blade before your eyes. Thinking.

Something like me with the tissue caught in the brush. Or the photograph you took of me. So that man came to know everything there was to know about broken razors, and any idea that can be associated with them. After listening to him, I did too.

"After the prison camp, when I found out that I didn't have a family any longer, I traveled a little. I read a few things . . . I had a good motive: you. To know the man who had destroyed my life with a photograph required a bit of knowledge. The mechanic from before the war could never have achieved it. Without knowing it, the musician and the man with the broken razor opened doors for me. I didn't understand how useful those doors were going to be later, when I did know."

He stopped and looked around, leaning forward, palms of his hands on his thighs, as if he were going to get to his feet. But he remained sitting. Not moving at all.

"I read, I looked in old newspapers, browsed the Internet. I spoke with people who had known you . . . You became my broken razor."

His eyes on Faulques were as cutting as if they were new razors.

8.

FAULQUES NEVER USED PURE BLACK. That color created holes, like a bullet or burst of shrapnel on the wall. He preferred to get to it indirectly, mixing burnt sienna with Payne's gray or Prussian blue, maybe even a touch of red, not mixing them on the palette but on the wall itself . . . sometimes, on large areas, rubbing it on directly with a finger until he achieved the tone he desired, a very dark ash streaked with light shadings that enriched it and gave it volume. In a certain way, thought the painter of battles, it was equivalent to opening the aperture of a camera one more stop when photographing people with black skin. If you trusted the meter when you shot, people looked flat, black with no shadow detail. A hole in the photograph.

He recalled, as he applied paint with a finger—black of shadows, black of smoke from the fires, black of night with no hint of dawn—a black skin he had photographed twenty-five years before on the banks of the Chari. That photo was also in the book Ivo Markovic had left on the chair, and it was truly a good black and white, so good that in its moment it had won a double-page spread in several international magazines. Following a battle on the outskirts of N'Djamena, a dozen Chadian rebels, wounded and bound, had been dragged to the river and left to be devoured by crocodiles, not far from the hotel where Faulques was staying—shattered windows and walls pocked with holes that looked as if they had been painted on with cold black. For half an hour he photographed those men, one by one, calculating aperture and composition, preoccupied with the contrast between the sand and those black skins shiny with sweat and dotted with flies, the whites of horrified eyes leaping out at the camera. The humidity made the heat unbearable, and Faulques moved with caution, one step at a time, scrutinizing the men laid out on the ground, shirt soaked with sweat, conserving energy with every move, pausing with open mouth to breathe in the heavy, hot air that smelled of the river's foul water and the prostrate bodies along its shore. Raw meat. Never before that day had Faulques thought that African bodies smelled like raw meat. And as he bent over one of them—meat on the butcher's block, ready to be devoured—and held the lens of the camera close to a face, the wounded man lifted his bound hands to shield himself, beyond terror, the white of his eyes even more exaggerated. It was then that Faulques had opened the aperture one stop, focused on the wide, staring eyes right before him, and pressed the shutter release, capturing that image composed with terrible technical perfection: graduated volumes of blacks and grays; bound, filthy hands in the near foreground with lighter shadings of palms and fingernails; the shadow the hands projected on the lower part of the face; the upper part illuminated by the sun: brilliant black, sweaty skin, flies, light grains of sand adhered to one cheek. And in the exact center, those inordinately wide-open eyes, staring into fear: two white almonds with blackest black pupils fixated on the lens of the camera, on Faulques, on the thousands of viewers who were going to see that photograph. And behind, in the background, at the end point of the viewer's perusal of the photo, the sum of all those blacks and grays: the shadow of the head of the man on the sand, and, in the slightly out-of-focus background—master touches of chance and implacable nature—the track of feet and the dragging tail of a crocodile. Faulques had taken nineteen exposures when a guard, with rifle and sunglasses bearing the Ray-Ban quality-control sticker on the left lens, approached and indicated with gestures that that was enough, the picture-taking was over. Faulques, more as an automatic response than with any hope, signed his protest, a vague plea for indulgence that the man in the sunglasses received with a white, insolent smile that bared his gums before he shifted his gun to the other shoulder and returned to the shelter of the shade. Then, without a backward glance, the photographer went back to the hotel, rewound the rolls of film, labeled them with a felt-tip pen, and put them into a padded envelope to send the next day on an Air France flight. And at sunset, as he was eating on the deserted terrace of the hotel beside an empty swimming pool, along with the throbbing beat of the combo—a guitar, an electric organ, and a black chanteuse he'd paid in advance to take to bed—Faulques heard the screams of the prisoners being dragged into the river by crocodiles, and left the rare meat on his plate untouched, after an abandoned attempt to cut it with his knife.

Later, in a restaurant in Madrid, he told the story to a friend. I need to know if that's part of the game, he asked. If there is some scientific basis for all that rational meat lying in the sun, waiting to be dispatched. Some hidden law of life or the world. I need to know whether my photographs really are the shortest line between two points. The friend was a man of science, young, and with a good head on his shoulders, a member of two academies, and author of revelatory books. Aristotle, his friend began, and Faulques interrupted, saying, Don't start off on Aristotle, for Christ's sake. I'm talking about real life and real death. The smell of a corpse beneath the rubble, the smell of death slipping like fog along the bank of a river. His friend looked at him three seconds before speaking. Aristotle, he continued imperturbably, never limited himself to expounding on how things were, but searched for the reason why. To understand ourselves, he said, we must understand the universe; and to understand the universe, we must understand ourselves. What happens is that since then a lot of water has passed under the bridge. When we divorced ourselves from nature, we humans lost the ability to find consolation in the face of the horror awaiting us out there. The more we observe, the less meaning it all has and the more forsaken we feel. Think how—thanks to Gödel, who certainly rained on that parade—we can't find refuge any longer in the one place we thought was secure: mathematics. But look. If there's no consolation as a result of observation, we can find it in the act of observation itself. I'm talking about the analytical, scientific, even aesthetic act of that observation. Gödel aside, it's like a mathematical procedure: it has such certainty, clarity, and inevitability that it offers intellectual relief to those who know how to utilize it. I would say it's analgesic. And so we turn back to a somewhat battered but still useful Aristotle: understanding, including the effort to understand, is our salvation. Or at least it consoles us, because it converts absurd horror into serene laws.

They ate and talked about all those things, with Faulques asking the pertinent questions and listening to the answers in silence, like a student intrigued by his professor's exposition. He didn't know it then, but their conversation altered—"completed" was, in a way, the more precise word—a vision of the world to which until then, at least that's what he'd thought, the lenses of his cameras had been the only mode of access, of knowing. In sum, it arranged intuitions and unconnected images on the rigorously aligned squares of an enormous chessboard that encompassed the world, reason, life. And it is difficult, his friend was saying, to accept the universe's lack of emotion: its pitiless nature. The scientists of old contemplated it as an enigma that could be read if you possessed the right code: something like a hieroglyph provided by God. That means that in a certain way you may be right, since if you exchange the word "God" for the concept of a system of hidden laws, the idea is still valid, although it's difficult to establish. Do you really hear what I'm saying? It's like Goldbach's conjecture: we know things we can't demonstrate. Classical science knew of the existence of problems associated with nonlineal systems—I'm referring to those systems with irregular, arbitrary, or chaotic behaviors—but it couldn't understand them because of the mathematical difficulty of analyzing them. Now, as our capacity for observation progresses, we find more and more apparent chaos in nature. We have known for more than half a century that true laws cannot be lineal. In those comfortable systems with which science tranquilized us for centuries, minuscule changes in initial conditions did not alter the solution; but in chaotic systems, when the initial conditions vary slightly, the object follows a different path. That would be applicable to your wars, of course. And also to nature, to life itself: earthquakes, bacteria, stimuli, thoughts. We live in interaction with the confusion surrounding us. But it is also true that a chaotic system is subject to laws and rules. And further: there are rules made of exceptions, or of seeming chance, that can be described with laws formulated in classic mathematical expressions. To sum up this lecture, my friend, and before you pay the bill: although it doesn't seem so, there is order in chaos.

And that crack on the wall—one among many—was also part of the chaos. Despite the thick coat of plaster Faulques had applied to the circular wall of the watchtower, one of the largest lines had progressed a few centimeters in the last few weeks. It was already affecting one of the painted areas of the mural, between the black of the smoke and the city burning on the hill, dark geometry against a background of flames the painter of battles had rendered with reasonable success—a lifetime of photographing fires helped in that—with the application of English red at the edges of the zone and, in the center, cadmium red with a little yellow. The zigzag evolution of that crack—of that nonlineal system, Faulques' scientific friend would have said—was also responding to hidden laws, to a perceptible dynamic whose advance was impossible to foresee. He had attempted to repair the crack by filling it with an acrylic resin mixed with marble dust, applied with a palette knife and then painted over, but that had not greatly changed things: the crack slowly continued its implacable progression. While Faulques cleaned the gray and blue from his fingers with a rag and a little water, he studied the crazed surface of the wall with resignation. After all, he consoled himself, that was part of the cryptogram. The zigzag of chaos and its hidden meanings. Nature, too, he remembered, had its passions. From that perspective, he studied the course of the crack for a long time: its point of departure on the upper edge of the mural and the pattern of a fan or a shell it made as it descended, dividing into other, smaller cracks as the principal line followed its course toward the lower edge, cutting between the rainy dawn sky that spread toward the beach from which the ships were sailing, toward the open space between the two cities, the modern, distant, nearly Bruegelian tower of Babel still asleep and tranquil, unaware that the coming dawn was the beginning of its last day, and the ancient, wide awake, burning city from which a throng of refugees poured toward the lower edge of the painting, on the foreground plane: the terrified women and children walking between fenced-off areas and the futuristic metallic reflections of soldiers in whose eyes they attempted to read their destinies as if putting questions to the Sphinx. The crack, Faulques observed, had adopted the form of an irresolute lightning flash between the two cities, but the painter of battles knew that the indecision was only illusory, that there was a hidden norm beneath the paint and the acrylic primer and the layer of plaster, a rigorous and unavoidable law that would end by converting the distant towers of steel and glass dozing in the dawn fog into a landscape very like the hill in flames, and that somewhere in that crack, wooden horses were lurking and airplanes flying very low toward the twin towers of all the sleeping Troys.

Olvido had made fun of him when he began showing signs of questions and uncertainties. By that time, Faulques still hadn't dug into the fissures and convolutions of the problem but he was already living amid intuitions, as if a swarm of annoying mosquitoes were buzzing around him. As you photograph people, you've looked for the straight lines and the curves that will kill them, she said, suddenly bursting out laughing after silently scrutinizing him. You photograph objects while at the same time you look for the dark angles where they will begin to disintegrate. You go hunting for divined corpses and anticipated ruins. Sometimes I think you make love to me with that desolate and violent desperation because when you put your arms around me you feel the cadaver I will one day be, or that we both will be. For you, Faulques, it's all over and you're only halfway there. You're changing, leaving the slim, silent soldier behind. You don't know it, but you've contracted the virus that one day will keep you from doing your work. One day you'll hold your camera up to your face and when you look through the viewfinder see nothing but lines, volumes, and cosmic laws. I hope I won't be with you at that moment, because you will be unbearable: autistic, a Zen archer making movements in the air with empty hands. And if I am still with you, I'll leave you. Ciao. So long. I swear. I detest soldiers who ask themselves questions, but I hate even more the ones who have all the answers. And if there's something about you I like, it's the silence your silences protect, so like your cold, perfect photographs. I can't bear murmuring silences, you know what I mean? I heard once, or read, that if you overanalyze events you end up destroying the concept. Or is it the other way around? That concepts destroy events?

As she'd said those things, she was laughing from behind a crystal wineglass, in Venice, the last New Year's Eve they would have together. She had insisted on going back to where she'd celebrated several end-of-the-year holidays in her childhood, among other reasons, to see the Surrealist exhibit in the Palazzo Grassi. I want you to take me to the best hotel in that ghostly city, she said, and walk with me at night through the deserted streets, because that's the only time of year you can find them like that. It's so cold that backpackers freeze to death on benches around the city, everyone stays inside their hotels and *pensiones,* and outside there's nothing but gondolas silently rocking in the canals; the Calle degli Assassini seems narrower and darker than ever, and the four carved stone figures on la Piazzetta squeeze closer together, as if they have a secret that people looking at them don't know. When I was a young girl, I would sneak out in my wool cap and muffler, hearing the echo of my footsteps as cats watched me from their dark porticos. I haven't been back to that city for a long time, but now I want to see it again. With you, Faulques. I want you to help me look for the shadow of that little girl, and later when we're back in the hotel, take needle and thread and sew it back to my heels, then quietly and patiently make love to me with the window thrown open, the cold air from the lagoon raising gooseflesh on your back, and my fingernails digging into it until you bleed and I forget you, and Venice, and everything I've been and everything that awaits me.

Now Faulques was remembering those words and remembering her walking through the narrow, snow-covered streets, the slippery ground, the gondolas covered with white splashing in the gray-green water, the intense cold and sleet, the Japanese tourists huddled in the cafés, the hotel lobby with brocades adorning the centuries-old staircase, the chandeliers in the main salon that was decorated with an enormous, absurd Christmas tree, the manager and the aged concierges who came out to welcome Olvido, calling her signorina Ferrara, as they had ten or fifteen years before, breakfasts in their room with the view of San Giorgio Island and, to the right, through the fog, the Aduana and the entrance to the Grand Canal. On St. Silvester's night they had dressed for dinner but the restaurant was crowded with Slavic mafiosi and their blond women and noisy North Americans celebrating New Year's Eve, so they got their coats and walked through the white, frozen streets to a small trattoria on the Zattere pier. There, he in a dinner jacket, she in a pearl necklace and a black dress so filmy it seemed to float around her body, they dined on spaghetti, pizza, and white wine before walking on to the point of the Aduana to kiss at exactly twelve o'clock, shivering with cold, as a colorful display of fireworks exploded over La Giudecca and they slowly walked back to the hotel, hand in hand through the deserted streets. From that night on, for Faulques, Venice would always be images of that unrepeatable night: the glow of lights through the fog and pale flakes falling on the canals, tongues of water lapping over white stone steps and washing in gentle waves across the marble paving, the gondola they watched pass beneath the bridge carrying two motionless passengers covered with snow, and the gondolier singing in a low voice. Also the drops of water on Olvido's face and her left hand sliding along the banister of the stairway up to their room, the creaking of the wood floor, the carpet that snagged the heel of her shoe, the enormous mirror on the right wall of the stairs, where he saw her glance sideways at herself as she went by, the engravings on the walls of the corridor, the pale yellow light falling through the window when, near the large bed, after peeling off their wet coats, he very slowly lifted her dress up to her hips as in the dark shadows she looked into his eyes with a fixed and impassive intensity, only half of her face lighted, as beautiful as a dream. In that moment Faulques rejoiced in his heart—a savage and at the same time tranquil elation—that he had not been killed any of the times it might have happened, because were that the case, he wouldn't be there that night, slipping off Olvido's panties, and he would never have seen her back up a little and fall onto the bed, onto the unturned spread, the loose, snow-wet hair falling across her face, her eyes never breaking from his, her skirt now up to her waist, her legs opening with a deliberate mixture of submission and wanton challenge, while he, still impeccably dressed, knelt before her and placed his lips, numb from the cold, to the dark convergence of those long, perfect legs between which throbbed, warm, soft, deliciously moist at the contact of his lips and tongue, the splendid flesh of the woman he loved.

The painter of battles stirred, running his fingers along the cold, rough edges of the crack in the wall. Raw meat, he remembered suddenly, beside amphibian tracks in the sand. Horror always lying in wait, demanding tithes and first fruits, poised to decapitate Euclid with the scythe of chaos. Butterflies fluttering through all wars and all peaces. Every moment was a blend of possible and impossible situations, of cracks predicted from that first instant at a temperature of three billion kelvins within the fourteen seconds and the three minutes following the Big Bang, the beginning of a series of precise coincidences that create man, and that kill him. Drunken gods playing chess, Olympian risk-taking, an errant meteorite only ten kilometers in diameter that, when it struck the Earth and annihilated all animals weighing more than twenty-five kilos, cleared the way for the then small and timid mammals that sixty-five million years later would become Homo sapiens, Homo ludens, Homo occisor.

A predictable Troy beneath every photograph and every Venice. Venerating wooden horses, their bellies bulging with bronze, cheering Florentine maestros through the streets, or, with identical enthusiasm, burning their works in Savonarola's bonfires. The balance sheet of a century, or of thirty centuries, was how Olvido summed it up that night on the point of the Aduana, watching the crowd congregated on the other side of the mouth of the canal, on San Marco, firecrackers and rockets exploding and the shouts of people celebrating the arrival of the new year, not knowing what it held in store for them. There are no barbarians now, she had murmured, shivering. They are all inside us. Or maybe it is we who have been left outside. Shall I tell you why you and I are together tonight? Because you know that the pearl necklace I'm wearing is made of real pearls. Not because you know pearls but because you know me. Do you understand what I'm saying? This world frightens me, Faulques. It frightens me because it bores me. I hate it when every idiot proclaims he is part of humankind and all the weak take up the shield of Justice, when artists smile, or spit, which is the same thing, on the dealers and critics who invent them. When my parents baptized me they missed my name by a hair. Today, to survive in the cave of the Cyclops you have to be named Nadie. No One. Yes. I think that soon I will need another strong jolt. Another of your beautiful and hygienic wars.

The painter of battles decided to leave the crack as it was. After all, it was part of the painting, like everything there. Like Venice, like Olvido's pearl necklace, like himself. Like Ivo Markovic, who at that moment, without Faulques' having heard him arrive, was silhouetted in the tower door.

9.

"SO AM I ON THERE YET?"

He was standing before the mural, and the smoke of the cigarette dangling from his lips made him squeeze his eyelids behind the lenses of his glasses. He had shaved recently, and was wearing a clean shirt with the sleeves rolled up to his elbows. Faulques followed the direction of his gaze. In an area he hadn't yet painted, the carbon sketch and a few strokes of color on the white primer described some forms stretched out on the ground that when the mural was finished would be corpses being stripped by crow-like pillagers. There was also a dog sniffing human remains, and trees with bodies hanging from their branches.

"Of course," the painter of battles replied. "You were there already. That's what it's about, I guess . . . *know*, actually. Since you showed up, I've been convinced of it."

"And what about your responsibility?"

"I don't understand."

"You, too, are responsible for what goes on in the painting."

Faulques put down the short brush he had in his

hand—the acrylic paint had dried and was hardening, he found to his annoyance—and then, with his arms crossed over his chest, he walked to where Markovic was standing. Looking where he was looking. The drawings were reasonably eloquent, he thought to himself. Even though he did not hold himself in any great esteem as a painter, he was consoled by the knowledge that he had a certain skill in drawing. And after all was said and done, these expressive, if disparate lines did speak of war. Of desolation and solitude: that of the dead. Every dead person he had ever photographed looked terribly alone. No solitude was more perfect, absolute, and irreparable than death. He knew that very well. Drawing and color aside, that might be his advantage, he decided. What gave consistency to the work he was carrying out in that tower. No one had told him what he was telling.

"I'm not sure about that word 'responsible.' I always tried to be the man who was looking. A third, objective man."

Markovic turned his head but did not take his eyes from the painting.

"I'd say you were mistaken. I don't think anyone is objective. You're in the painting, too . . . But not just a part of it, you're the agent as well. The cause."

"It's strange that you say that."

"What seems strange about it?"

Faulques didn't answer. He was remembering, a little disconcerted, what his scientist friend had added when they were talking about chaos and its rules: that a basic element of quantum mechanics was that man created reality by observing it. Before that observation, what truly existed was all possible situations.

Only through observation did nature become concrete, take a stance. There was, inevitably, inherent indetermination, of which man was more the witness than the protagonist. Or, to put a fine point on it, both things at once: victim as well as guilty party.

They both were staring at the mural, not speaking, not moving. Side by side. Then Markovic took the cigarette from his mouth. He leaned forward a little to better see the two men in the foreground of the lower edge of the painting, locked in a death embrace, slashing wildly at each other.

"Is it true that some photographers pay people to kill in front of their cameras?"

Slowly, Faulques shook his head. Twice.

"No. That was never something I did." His head moved from side to side a third time. "Never."

The Croatian had turned to look at him with interest. After a moment, he took another pull at his cigarette before crushing it in an empty mustard jar on the table among the paints and brushes. *The Eye of War* was still there. He leafed through a few pages, distracted, and stopped at one.

"Good photo," he said. "Is this the one that won the other prize?"

Faulques went to look. Lebanon, near Daraia. Four hundred ASA black-and-white film, 1/125 shutter speed, 50-mm lens. A snow-covered mountaintop, barely visible through the mist, served as background for the principal scene: three Druse militiamen at the moment of being executed by six Christian Phalangists, the latter kneeling three meters from their victims, rifles aimed and firing. The Druse were facing them, eyes blindfolded; the two in the background of the image had already been struck by bullets, the smoke of the shots was rippling their clothing—one was clutching his belly, knees buckling, the other was falling backward, hands over his head, as if the world had evaporated behind him—and the third, the one closest to the photographer, about forty, dark-skinned, short hair, two or three days' beard, erect and strong, was stoically awaiting the bullet that hadn't as yet been fired, head high, eyes covered with a black cloth, a wounded hand supported in a bandage slung around his neck and tight against his chest. So serene and dignified in his attitude that the men aiming at him, two young Maronites, fingers on the trigger of their Galil assault rifles, seemed to be undecided about killing him. The Druse with the wounded hand had been shot a second after Faulques took his photo—he pressed the shutter release when he heard the first burst of fire, convinced that they would all fire at the same time—struck in the chest when his companions were already on the ground. Faulques did not get a picture of him falling because he was shooting with the Leica; it didn't have a motor drive but was wound by hand, and as the men fell he was advancing film for the following exposure. By the time he shot again the man already lay sprawled on the ground, bandaged hand slightly raised and rigid amid the smoke of gunfire floating in the air and the dust his body had raised when he fell. Faulques took a third photo when the leader of the executioners was standing among the corpses, having delivered the coup de grâce to the first Druse and preparing to do the same for the second.

"This is interesting," Markovic commented, one

finger on the image. "Man's dignity, and so on and so on. But not every man dies that way, right? In fact, very few die that way. They weep, beg, crawl. That base behavior we were talking about the other day. Anything to survive."

The editors at the agency Faulques had sent the undeveloped roll to had selected the photo of the Druse waiting to be shot because of his dignity in the face of death, the apparent hesitation of the executioners, and the drama of the fallen men behind him. It got great exposure. *Pride in the Face of Death,* an Italian magazine grandiloquently titled it, and that same year it won the twenty-thousand-dollar International Press Photo prize. In the book Markovic was holding, that image was paired, on facing pages, with one Faulques had taken in Somalia fifteen years later: a member of the Aidid militia executing a looter in the Mogadishu market. The two scenes were different in motif and composition, and Faulques had been very doubtful before deciding to place them side by side in the book; what finally convinced him was that they made more sense together. The Lebanese photo was in black and white, serene, the lines balanced despite the subject, planes well defined, a perfect vanishing point—the peak of the snow-capped mountain barely visible through the concealing fog—and diagonals running from far in the distance to converge there, with the executioners and the fallen Druse soldiers as chorus or background to the principal scene: the exact coincidence of the rifles in the foreground, two deadly parallels aimed at the chest of the third, the erect, Druse, precisely at the heart over which his hand lay in the sling, an almost circular harmony of curved lines, straight radii, and shadows, the center of which were that hand and that heart whose beating was about to be interrupted. The Mogadishu photo was just the opposite: color film, an image with no volume, nearly flat, with the ochre background of an adobe wall onto which the shadows of a group of onlookers outside the picture were projected, and in the center of the scene, a Somali militiaman wearing short pants that gave him a strangely juvenile air, his arm holding an AK-47 extended so the mouth of the barrel touched the head of a man lying faceup on the ground. The muscles and tendons of that thin black arm were clenched from the kick of the weapon's recoil; its bullets had destroyed the face of the fallen man not yet dead, hands and knees jerking upward, jolted by the impact of the bullets, dust rising around his head, his face exploding in red fragments—an absolutely pure *action painting,* Olvido would say afterward, still pale from fright—and two empty shells, just ejected from the chamber of the weapon and caught by the photo, frozen as they somersaulted through the air, golden and gleaming in the sun. That image had no depth, no background, no distant lines, nothing except the wall with the shadows acting as anonymous witnesses and the closed, equilateral, geometrically perfect triangle—like the symbolic triangle that represented God in Faulques' schoolbooks—formed by the standing man, the victim lying on the ground, and the weapon as an extension of the arm and rational will that had executed him. They weep, they beg, they crawl, Markovic had said. Anything to survive. That wasn't the case, Faulques thought, of the three Druse in the first photo, who would be killed without a by-your-leave or loss of composure, but it was true of the Somali in the second, who had dragged himself to the feet of his executioner, begging for his life as the latter kept kicking him—to the delight of the children watching the scene; it was their shadows that were projected onto the wall—and so, on his knees and clinging to the militiaman's legs, he had first been clubbed with the butt of the weapon, a blow that flung him onto his back, and then, pleading and with his hands lifted to protect his face, he had screamed when he saw the barrel of the gun so close, before his body was shaken by the hammering of the bullets. That time Faulques was using a motor-driven camera that advanced between shots, *clic, clic, clic, clic, clic, clic, clic, clic,* eight times, a complete series at 1/500 shutter speed and f-stop of 8. The fifth exposure was the best: the one in which the dying man's face was barely visible among his own red explosions, his arms and legs lifted in a reflex defense. Later, when the militiaman noticed the photographer—Faulques had approached with impeccable tactical stealth as Olvido whispered, You'd better not, Please, Stay here, Don't even move—the Somali struck a swaggering pose, rifle held in both hands and one foot on the chest of the cadaver in the manner of the hunter posing with his trophy. *Maik mee uan photo.* Smiles and relaxing. And Faulques, raising the camera again, pretended to take that image, although he didn't. He had already shot an identical scene in Tesseney, Eritrea: two FLE guerrilla fighters posing guns in hand, one with his foot on the neck of a dead Ethiopian soldier. He had no wish to publish the same picture twice: it was ridiculous to plagiarize himself. As for that *Maik mee uan photo* and all the rest, the most insightful summary would come from Olvido the night of the Mogadishu incident as they were having a drink in the dark by a hotel window. Africa fascinates me, she said, it's like a trial run of the future. It surpasses the most extreme Dadaist absurdity. It's like those video games in which the characters, armed with machetes and guns and grenades, go absolutely crazy.

"Anything to survive," Markovic repeated.

Faulques, who was slowly returning from his memories, grimaced.

"It doesn't do a lot of people any good to beg," he murmured. "Not even baseness, crawling on your belly when you face your executioner, guarantees anything."

The Croatian leafed through more pages of the book. Finally he closed it.

"They try," he said. "Almost everyone, in fact. Some succeed."

He was staring pensively at the cover of the closed book. A black-and-white photograph, the asphalt of the Saigon airport: a dead woman on the ground with her dead baby in her arms. The husband a little farther away, clutching another child's hand. Also dead. All of them. In the middle, a conical straw hat sitting in a pool of blood. It wasn't Faulques' favorite photo, but at the time he and his editors had thought it would make a good cover.

"When they let me go," Markovic continued, "there were others with me, in a bus. We didn't have much to say. We didn't even look at each other.

Ashamed. We knew things about each other, you know? Things we wanted to forget."

He was still standing beside the table with the book of photographs, lost in his own thoughts. Faulques went to get the bottle of cognac and motioned to it, querying. Markovic said no, thank you, no, without turning his head. The painter poured himself a little, wet his lips, and set the glass on the book. Then Markovic looked up.

"There was a young kid. Handsome. About sixteen or seventeen. Bosnian. A Serbian guard took a fancy to him."

He smiled a little, evocatively. If it hadn't been for the expression in his eyes, you would have said it was a pleasant memory.

"When some nights the guard took him away with him," he continued, "that boy always came back with something. A little chocolate, a tin of condensed milk, tobacco . . . He gave it all to us. Sometimes he brought medicine for those who were sick . . . Even so, we scorned him. How about that? We did, however, take everything he brought us. Greedily, I assure you. Yes. Down to the last cigarette."

The sun shining through one of the tower windows illuminated the Croatian's face, and his pupils looked lighter than ever behind the lenses of his glasses. The trace of a smile evaporated from his lips as if the light had erased it: his eyes revealed their true dominion, giving the impression that the smile had never existed. Faulques was thinking how in a different time he would have moved cautiously, lifting the camera slowly in order not to disturb his prey, with the goal of capturing a look that not just anyone would ever see. You had to have a specific biography to have a look like that. Olvido called it the look of one hundred steps. There are human beings, she said, who walk one hundred steps farther than the rest of us, and never retrace those steps. They go into bars and restaurants, ride buses, and almost no one notices them. That's absurd, isn't it? We should all wear our biography on our face, like a military record. Some do, of course. Let me look at you. You do. But other people don't always know how to read that look. People walk past them and don't realize a thing. Maybe that's because no one really *looks* anymore. At eyes.

"One night," Markovic picked up his tale, "several of my companions sodomized the kid. If you let the Serbian do it, they said, then let us. They had stuffed a rag in his mouth so he wouldn't yell. We did nothing to defend him."

A long silence followed. Faulques was studying the mural, at the spot where the child half squatting in the sand was looking at the woman lying on her back, her thighs naked and bloody. The stream of people fleeing the city in flames, watched by armed militiamen, passed by without a glance. The woman was just one more story, and everyone had his own problems.

"The boy hanged himself the next day. We found him behind the barracks."

Now Markovic was looking at the painter of battles as if inviting him to offer some judgment on what he'd said. But Faulques had nothing to say. He merely nodded, still staring at the violated woman and boy painted on the wall. Markovic followed the direction of his gaze.

"Did you ever stop anything, señor Faulques? Even once? A beating? A death? Were you ever able to stop something, and did?" He left a deliberate pause. "Or try to?"

"A few times."

"Many?"

"I never kept count."

The Croatian smiled malevolently.

"Fine. At least I know that once you did try."

He seemed disappointed that there was no comment from Faulques, whose eyes were still on the mural. There were two half-painted figures behind the foreshortened soldier in the foreground guarding the refugees; another soldier, medieval in appearance but carrying modern weapons, a faceless specter behind the visor of his helmet, was aiming his gun at a man whose only finished features were his head and shoulders. Something in the victim's expression was not entirely convincing to the painter of battles. He was going to be killed an instant later, and Faulques knew it. The man who would shoot him knew it, too. The problem lay in the emotions of the man who was going to be killed. His face, touched with burnt sienna and Prussian blue to accentuate angles and foreshortening, was contorted with fear; he was not, however, turned toward the executioner but toward the viewer, or the painter, or anyone witnessing the scene. And that was why it didn't look right, Faulques realized. It wasn't terror that should be reflected on the face of that man who was about to die. He wasn't looking at his executioner but at the viewer, at the camera become the brushes and eye of the painter, the imaginary eye that was preparing so brazenly to witness his death; the condemned man's expression shouldn't reflect fear, but indignation. Indignant surprise was the exact nuance. Of course. The man was in pajamas, he had just been pulled out of his house, hair mussed, not really awake, before the passive, cowardly, rejoicing, or complicitous eyes of his neighbors. He was exactly like the man whom Faulques had photographed on the Corniche in Beirut as he was being pushed at rifle point, barefoot and dressed in a pair of ridiculous red-and-white diamond-patterned pajamas, to a place where another four neighbors from his apartment building already lay on the ground murdered. The man in the pajamas knew what awaited him, but his fearful expression—he arrived looking ill, his skin an ashen yellow—turned to surprise and irritation when behind his killers he saw the camera with which Faulques, who a week before had turned twenty-five, was photographing him. And he, the photographer, had pressed the shutter release at the precise moment to capture that irate expression of invaded privacy when the man in the pajamas registered the injustice of being photographed as he was about to die, and looking the way he did. The photo was taken just in time, for when Faulques again pressed the release, the bullets had already penetrated the victim's body and he was collapsing atop the other corpses. There was a possible third photo, but Faulques didn't take it. When he saw one of the executioners go to the body and bend over him, he changed the aperture from f 8 to f 5.6 and prepared to shoot. But when through the viewfinder he watched the man take a pair of pliers from his pocket to yank out the dead man's gold teeth, a wave of nausea prevented him from focusing. He let the camera drop onto his chest, calmly walked some distance to the rattletrap taxi with the *Press-Sahafi* sign stuck to the windshield and, before the amused smile of the Lebanese driver to whom he was paying two dollars' commission for every good photo he helped him get, vomited up everything he'd had for breakfast that morning in the Commodore Hotel.

"An objective, ideal witness," Markovic commented. "Is that what it's about? For no one would say that, seeing what you're painting here. And it didn't seem to me that you were being objective that day I saw you kneeling in the ditch along the Borovo Naselje road . . . At least not until you picked up the camera and photographed the woman."

No answer from Faulques. He'd gone right up to the wall and, leaning a little over the scene he'd painted, was studying it closely. It was so obvious that he cursed himself for not having noticed it before. He went to get a green kitchen scrub pad and softly and very carefully rubbed the face of the man who was going to die, lightly erasing his features, especially the part around his mouth, until some of the sandy irregularities of the white primer on the cement wall showed through. Then he used a pastry brush to clean the scratched surface before returning to the table, where he poked through the dried brushes clumped together in the tins that had held fruit preserves and coffee, until he found a round number 4. He could feel Markovic's eyes on the back of his neck. The painter of battles had never worked while anyone watched, but at that moment he didn't care.

"How strange," the Croatian murmured. "There

are people who identify art with something cultivated, and delicate. I thought that myself."

It was difficult to decide whether he was referring to the dramatic motifs of the mural or to the scrubbing pad, but Faulques was not interested in finding out. He unscrewed the tight lids on two glass jars in which he had mixed colors—he liked to prepare the ones he used most in large quantities so he didn't waste time looking for the shade he wanted—and with his brush daubed some paint on his large oven-tray palette. The mixtures had the right consistency. He wet the brush, dried it with a rag, sucked the tip, put a bit from each jar onto the tray, and went back to the wall. Markovic followed right behind. He had picked up a flat, inch-and-a-half-wide English brush he was studying with curiosity.

"Is this real hair? From a squirrel, or a marten, or some animal like that?"

Synthetic, Faulques answered. Painting on the rough wall wore brushes down. Nylon was stronger and cheaper. Then he stood for a minute studying the figure, the eyes painted a week ago, the oval of the face, the violent and well-executed mat of disheveled hair—up close it was a simple muddle of superimposed colors—and finally he applied flesh color, Naples yellow with blue, red, and a pinch of ochre, with strong vertical strokes around the scrubbed mouth of the man dead nearly thirty years before.

"That conversation we had yesterday, about torture," Markovic said suddenly. "There's something I didn't tell you. I once tortured a man."

He was close at Faulques' side, watching him work. He kept turning the brush over in his fingers, drawing its softness across the back of his hand. The painter had squatted down to rinse his brush, and after he dried it on a rag he applied the other mixture, burnt sienna with Prussian blue, with the idea of shading the sunken cheeks beneath the strong cheekbones and giving the effect of light on the face turned toward the viewer. He took risks as he worked, wet over wet, letting the two mixtures fuse before the rapidly drying acrylic set. Then he stood back from the wall to view what he'd done. Now the expression of the man who was going to die was right: astonishment, indignation. What the hell are you looking at, observing, photographing, painting? Faulques knew that everything would depend on his skill, or lack of it, as he painted the still scratched and smudged mouth: but he would take care of that later, when the rest was dry. He stooped down to leave the brush in the spiral of the water-filled tin, took a good look from that angle at what he had done, and when he stood up continued working on getting the contours right, this time rubbing directly with his thumb and middle finger. Then once again he was listening to what Markovic was saying. It was at the beginning of the war, the Croatian recounted. I'm referring to my war, of course. My war. Before Vukovar. We had been mobilized for a week when they ordered us to rout out the Serbian civilians from the outskirts of Vinkovci. The system was the same they used: you went to a house, brought everyone outside, opened the gas tap in the kitchen, tossed in a grenade, and went on to the next house. We separated the combat-age men, fourteen to sixty more or less. Nothing you don't know. But we didn't rape the women as others did. At least, not in any organized way. Not as part of a deliberate program of terror and ethnic cleansing. They took the men away in trucks. I don't know what they did with them. It didn't matter to me, I didn't care. The thing is that when we got to one house, in Vinkovci, one of my comrades said that he knew the family, that they were wealthy farmers, and that they had money hidden. Older father and mother. One son. Young. Twenty-something. Mentally retarded.

"I don't think I'm interested in that episode," Faulques interrupted, still rubbing on paint with his fingertips. "It's too predictable, and not very original."

Markovic paused, thinking about that.

"He laughed, you know?" he suddenly continued. "That bastard laughed as we were beating him in front of his parents. He looked at us with his eyes wide open, and he was drooling on himself, but he never stopped laughing. As if he wanted us to like him."

"And of course there was no hidden money."

Markovic looked at the painter with respectful attention. Then he gave a slight nod.

"Nothing. Not a centime. But the thing is that it took us a long time to find that out."

He put the brush back in its place and stood with his thumbs hooked in his pants pockets, watching what Faulques was doing.

"When we left there, it also took us a long time to look each other in the eye."

The painter stopped rubbing, stepped back and assessed the result. The face was greatly improved—he needed only to finish the condemned man's mouth.

Indignation in place of fear. And those vertical, dirty shadows that brought out the expression of the face. Volume and life, one step from death. As real as his memories, or nearly so. Satisfied, he went to the basin and washed his paint-stained hands.

"Why did you participate in it? You could just have watched. Maybe you could even have stopped it."

Markovic shrugged his shoulders.

"We were comrades, don't you get it? There are group rituals. Codes."

"Of course." Faulques' mouth twisted with sarcasm. "And what would you have done had there been a rape? Which codes would you have followed?"

"I never raped anyone." The Croatian shifted his feet, uncomfortable. "And I didn't see anyone do it."

"Maybe you didn't have the opportunity."

Markovic's expression was strangely malicious.

"You did some pretty foul things yourself, señor photographer. Be careful. Your camera was a passive accomplice many times . . . Or active. Don't forget your damned butterfly. Don't forget why I'm here."

"The difference is that everything vile I did, I did alone. My cameras and me. Period."

"It's presumptuous to say that."

"Really?"

"You were lucky."

"No." Faulques lifted a finger. "It was deliberate. I chose to do it that way from the beginning."

"Maybe you're wrong. It may be that you have always been the way you are, and the word 'chose' has nothing to do with it. That would explain everything, even your survival."

As he said that, Markovic pointed to his head, indicating what kind of survival he was referring to. Then he pointed to the painting. That also explains your work here in the tower, he continued. It confirms what I always suspected from your photographs. Nothing of what you're painting is remorse or expiation. It's more like a . . . Well. I don't know how to express it. A formula? No? A theorem.

"A kind of scientific conclusion?"

The Croatian's face lighted up. That's it, he replied. I've finally understood that nothing has ever hurt you. Not even now. Seeing what you saw didn't make you any better or more committed to your fellow man. What happened was that your photos weren't enough any longer. What happened to them is what happens to certain words: from being overused they lose their meaning. Maybe that's why you're painting now. But painting, photos, words . . . with you it's all the same. I think you feel the same compassion the researcher feels as he observes the battle in the infection of a wound through his microscope. Microbes against amoebas.

"Leukocytes," Faulques corrected. "The things that fight microbes are leukocytes. White corpuscles."

"Right. Leukocytes against microbes. You look and you take note."

Faulques walked right up to Markovic and stood beside him, drying his hands on the rag. Neither spoke for a moment as they stared at the painting.

"You may be right," said the painter.

"That would make you worse than I am."

A beam of light was falling through the window

onto the lines of refugees in the mural. In it were little golden specks, motes of dust suspended in the air, that made it appear almost solid. It resembled the guard tower searchlight in a concentration camp.

"Once I photographed a fight in an insane asylum," Faulques said.

10.

WHEN HE WAS ALONE, FAULQUES worked all evening and far into the night on one area of the lower part of the mural: the warriors who, located to the left of the tower door, were mounted on their horses awaiting the opportunity to ride into battle, though one had moved ahead of the group, lance in socket, advancing alone toward a cluster of lances painted a little farther to the left, where the plaster showed only the charcoal sketch, black on white, of a confusion of silhouettes that when the painting was completed would be the vanguard of an army. The form for representing that solitary horseman—at first he was going to be in a serene stance, in the style of Dürer's *Knight, Death, and Devil*—had been suggested to Faulques by a scene from *Micheletto da Cotignola Engages in Battle,* one of the three panels of the triptych based on the battle of San Romano: the one in the Louvre. The devastations of time had faded contours and imposed a strange modernity upon the original scene, converting what initially had been five mounted caballeros, five lances upraised, into a sequence given extraordinary movement, as if it were a single person whose forward motion had been visually broken into segments: an amazing augury of the temporal distortions of Duchamp and the Futurists, or of Marey's chromographs. In the Uccello painting, the group that at first view seems to represent a single horse is composed of five almost superimposed horses, and of their riders the viewer can make out four heads and three plumed helmets, one of them suspended in air. A single warrior at the left seems to be holding two of the five lances, forming a fan-like pattern, as if they were one lance in different phases of movement. All of it fused into an extraordinary, dynamic, interrupted-action composition reminiscent of a film sequence shown frame by frame; not even a modern, deliberately planned photograph taken with slow shutter speed and long exposure would ever obtain the same effect. Time and chance had also painted, in their own way.

Faulques, a graphic predator free of complexes, had executed the horseman in his mural with all this in mind; hence the appearance of a moving photograph of an individual and the various outlines he seemed to leave behind like ghostly traces in space. As Faulques worked, he had sprayed water to keep the first layers fresh, moist over moist, diluted colors and quick brushwork on the bottom and thicker and stronger strokes on top. Now the painter of battles got up from the paint-stained mattress he had been kneeling on as he worked; he put the paintbrush in the spiral of the water can, rubbed his kidneys, and stepped back. It was right. Not a self-conscious Uccello, of course, but a humble Faulques, who would not even sign his name when he was finished. But it looked good. The group of horsemen was now complete, lacking only a few touch-ups that would be done later. Above their heads, at the planned vanishing point between them and the lone rider who was approaching the forest of enemy lances, rose—or would rise when they were something more than schematic lines in charcoal—the towers of Manhattan, Hong Kong, London, or Madrid: any city of the many that lived trusting in the power of their arrogant colossi; a forest of modern, intelligently engineered buildings inhabited by people convinced of their youth, beauty, and immortality, certain that sorrow and death could be kept at bay with the *Enter* key of a computer. Ignorant, all of them, of the fact that to invent a technical object was also to invent its specific undoing, in the same way that the creation of the universe brought with it, implicit from the moment of primordial nucleosynthesis, the word "catastrophe." That was why the history of humankind was so well supplied with towers built to be evacuated in four or five hours but able to withstand the fury of a fire for only two, and of intrepid, unsinkable *Titanic*s waiting for the iceberg placed by Chaos at an exact point on its nautical chart.

As sure of it as if he were seeing it—in truth he had seen, and was seeing it—Faulques shook his head, pleased with those lines on the wall that already had form and color in his imagination or in his memory. He had no need to invent anything. All that glass and steel was a direct continuation of the beplumed and ironclad horsemen whose armor had chinks through which any humble peon could, with a little desperation combined with a little boldness, insert the sharp blade of a dagger.

Olvido had expressed it with great precision in Venice. There are no barbarians now, Faulques. They are all inside us. And there aren't even ruins like those of the past, she would add later, in Osijek, as he was photographing a house whose façade had disappeared during a bombing; behind the rubble piled in the street one could still see the intimate grid of rooms, complete with furniture, domestic utensils, and family photographs on the walls. In a different time, she'd said—moving with care among chunks of cement and twisted iron, camera to her eye, searching for the right framing—ruins were indestructible. Isn't that true? They stayed there for centuries and centuries, though people used the stones for their houses and the marble for their palaces. And then a Hubert Robert or a Magnasco came along with his easel and painted them. It isn't like that now. Just look at this. Our world creates rubble instead of ruins, and as soon as possible a bulldozer comes and everything disappears, ready to be forgotten. Ruins are disturbing, they make you uncomfortable. And of course, without stone books for reading the future, suddenly we find ourselves on the shore with one foot in the boat and no coins in our pockets to give to Charon.

Faulques smiled inside, his eyes absorbed by the mural. The boatman on the river of death had been a private joke between Olvido and him ever since the time when in company of Sahrawi guerrilla fighters they'd had to cross the sandy bed of a *uad* near Guelta Zemmur under Moroccan fire. While they were waiting for the moment to leave the shelter of some rocks and run fifty meters in the open—Who goes first? the guerrilla who was going to cover them with fire from his Kalashnikov asked uneasily—Olvido made a playful face and patted Faulques' pocket, staring hard at him, green eyes glittering in the glare of the sun on the sand, tiny drops of sweat beading her forehead and upper lip. I hope you have a coin for Charon, she said, her breathing ragged from her eagerness to confront the moment. Then she'd touched the lobes of her ears, where two small ball-shaped gold earrings gleamed through her hair—she almost never wore jewelry; she liked to tell about the ladies of Venice who to circumvent the laws against ostentation went out for strolls followed by servants decked out in their mistresses' jewels. These will do for me, she added. And then she got up, stretched long legs sheathed in sand-covered jeans—she was laughing quietly, and that's what Faulques would hear as she left—adjusted her camera pack, and started running after the Sahrawi preceding her, while another guerrilla emptied half a clip on the Moroccan position. Faulques photographed her—motor at four frames per second—slim and swift, running forward over the sand like the gazelle with which he associated her at every instant. And when finally it was his turn to cross, she was waiting for him on the other side, under cover, still throbbing with excitement, her mouth open as she caught her breath. With a smile of savage happiness. Go to hell, Charon, she said, touching Faulques' face with her fingertips. And smiling.

He felt the warning pain again, so the painter of battles washed down two tablets and squatted on his haunches, back against the wall. He waited, not moving, gritting his teeth, for them to take effect. When he got up, his clothing was soaked with sweat. He went to the switch and turned off the two strong lights illuminating the wall. Then he took off his shirt and went outside to wash his face and hands; still dripping with water he plunged into the night landscape with long, slow strides, wet hands in his pockets, as the breeze off the sea cooled his face and naked torso and the deafening crickets urged him on from the brush and the black woods. He could hear the sea below, breaking among the rocks of the unseen cove. He walked to the edge of the cliff—he stopped a little short, cautious, still blinded by the brilliance of the halogen bulbs—and stood there until his retinas adjusted to the dark, watching the moon and stars, and the distant flash from the lighthouse. He was thinking about Ivo Markovic. It seems—the Croatian had said that morning, when they were both looking at the mural—that what we have here is a place where a lot of broken straight razors come together, señor Faulques. The painter of battles had just recounted an experience, in the usual way he told things: long pauses, as if he were reviewing some memory inside rather than telling it to a stranger who was not really a stranger any longer. An asylum, he was saying. Once he had photographed a battle in an insane asylum. With real lunatics. The line of combat passed through the courtyard of the building, a huge run-down house near San Miguel, in El Salvador. By the time he got there, guards and attendants had fled. The guerrillas were inside and the soldiers outside, on the other side of the wall and in the house across the street, some twenty meters away. They were attacking with everything they had, guns, grenades, while the inmates wandered around as they pleased, from position to position, walking across the courtyard between bursts of shots or standing near the combatants, staring at them, jabbering at them, laughing uproariously, shrieking with terror when a bomb burst near them. Eight or ten died, but that day the best photographs Faulques took were of the living: a calm old man in a pajama top, naked from the waist down, who, steadfast amid the fire, hands clasped behind his back, was watching two guerrillas firing from a prone position. He also photographed a middle-aged woman in a blood-stained bathrobe, fat, hair flying, rocking a young combatant who'd been wounded in the neck as if he were a baby or a doll. Faulques had left there when one of the inmates picked up the gun of a wounded man and started shooting in every direction.

"I went back two days later, to take a look . . . There were holes in the walls and the ground was covered with spent shells. The soldiers and the guerrillas weren't there any longer, but some of the patients had stayed on in the asylum. There was excrement and dried blood everywhere. One man came up to me, acting very mysteriously, to show me a jar of something that looked like peaches in syrup. When I looked more closely I saw they were cut-off ears."

Markovic half turned toward Faulques. He seemed sincerely interested.

"You took the photo?"

"It would never have been published. So I didn't take it."

"But oh yes, you have, and those were published,

the ones of men with burning tires around their necks . . . Wasn't that in South Africa?"

"Don't believe that. They threw out the rawest ones. Companies that advertise automobiles, perfume, and expensive watches don't like to see their advertisements run alongside those kinds of scenes."

The Croatian kept looking at the painter of battles. His smile was placid. That was when he'd said, *It seems that what we have here is a place where a lot of broken straight razors come together, señor Faulques.*

With those words Markovic had turned back to the mural. He stood a long time before he lightly shrugged his shoulders, as if in answer to internal reflections.

"Who was it who said that words had been exhausted by wars?"

"I don't know. It sounds like something from a long time ago."

"And a lie, besides. Whoever said that had never been in a war."

"That's what I think, too." Faulques smiled. "Maybe war exhausts stupid words, but not the rest. The ones you and I know."

Facing Faulques, Markovic half closed his eyes in a look of shared complicity.

"Do you mean the words that are seldom spoken, or that come out only before someone who knows them?"

"Yes, those words."

Markovic had not taken his eyes from the mural.

"You know what, señor Faulques? After I left that prison camp, I was taken to a hospital in Zagreb, and the first thing I did when I got out was go and sit in a café in Jelacic Square. To watch people, hear their words. And I couldn't believe what I heard: the conversations, the preoccupations, the priorities . . . Listening to them, I wondered. Don't they realize? What does a dented car matter, a run in your stocking, the payment on the TV? Do you know what I mean?"

"Perfectly."

"That still happens to me . . . doesn't it to you? I get on a train, go into a bar, walk along a street, and I see them all around me. Where do they come from? I ask myself. Am I an extraterrestrial? Can it be that they're not aware that theirs is not a normal state?"

"No. They aren't aware."

Markovic had taken off his glasses and was checking to see if the lenses were clean.

"You know what I think after having looked at so much of your work? That in war, instead of your camera catching normal people doing abnormal things, it does just the opposite. Doesn't it? You photograph abnormal people doing normal things."

"The truth is that it's something more complex than that. Or simpler. Normal people doing normal things."

That stopped Markovic. After a while he slowly nodded a couple of times and put his glasses back on.

"All right. I don't really blame them. I didn't know that myself until . . ." Suddenly he turned. "And you? Has it always been what your photos say it is?"

The painter of battles held Markovic's eyes but his lips didn't move. After a moment, the Croatian shrugged again.

"You were never an ordinary photographer, señor Faulques."

"I don't know what I was . . . I know what I wasn't. I began the way everyone does, it seems to me: as a privileged witness of history, danger, and adventure. Youth. The difference is that most of the war photographers I knew discovered an ideology after the fact. With time they were humanized, or pretended to be."

Markovic pointed to the book on the table.

" 'Humanitarian' is not a word I would use to label your photos."

"It's just that when you apply the word 'humanitarian' you spoil the photograph. It makes it self-conscious, and that means no longer seeing the external world through the viewfinder. The photo ends up photographing itself."

"But that isn't what made you retire . . ."

"In a way it did, yes. At the end, I, too, was photographing myself."

"And were you always suspicious of the landscape? Of life?"

Faulques, who was distractedly rearranging some brushes, reflected on that a moment.

"I don't know. I suppose that the day I left home with a pack on my back, I still wasn't. Or maybe I was. Maybe I became a photographer in order to confirm some suspicion I had in advance."

"I know what you mean. An educational journey. Scientific. The leukocytes and all the rest."

"Yes. The leukocytes."

Markovic took a few steps into the room, examining everything as if he had just taken a new interest in it: the table covered with jars of paint, rags, and brushes—the photography book was still lying there—books stacked on the floor and on the steps of the spiral staircase that led to the upper floor of the tower.

"Do you always sleep up there?"

The painter of battles looked at him with mistrust, and didn't answer, and the Croatian made a mocking face. It's an innocent question, he said. Curiosity about your way of life.

"In fact," Markovic added, "I was just going to pose a more impertinent question and ask whether you always sleep alone."

This place is known as the Cala del Arráez. It was once a refuge for Berber pirates . . . The woman's voice and the amplified music echoed off the cliff, above the noise of the engines of the tourist tender passing by, as it did every day. Faulques turned toward the window the sound was coming through. *A well-known painter lives in that tower* . . . and there he was, standing stock-still until the boat moved on and the sound faded away.

"How about that," said the Croatian. "You're a local celebrity."

He had walked to the foot of the stair and was studying the titles of the books stacked there. He picked up a copy—underlined on nearly every page—of Pascal's *Pensées* and put it back where it had been atop an *Iliad,* Franco and Stefano Borsi's *Paolo Uccello,* Vasari's *Lives,* and Sánchez Ron's *Diccionario de la ciencia.*

"You are a refined man, señor Faulques. You read a lot."

The painter of battles pointed to the wall. Only things that relate to this, he replied. And Markovic again turned to the mural. Finally his face lighted up.

I understand now, he said. You mean that the only things that interest you are those that can be useful to this enormous painting. Things that give you good ideas.

"That's it."

"Well, the same's true of me. I've already told you that I was never a person to read much. Although because of you I tried several times. I read books, I assure you. But only when they had some connection to you. Or when I thought they would help me understand. Many of them were difficult books. Some I couldn't finish, no matter how hard I tried . . . But I read a few. And it's true: I learned things."

As he was talking, his eyes went from the windows to the door to the upper floor. Faulques felt a flash of apprehension. The Croatian reminded him of a photographer studying how to slip into hostile territory and how to get out. Also a murderer studying the future scene of a crime.

"There's no woman?"

Faulques had no intention of answering. However, he did, some five seconds later. You just heard her, he said, passing by down there. Markovic, surprised, seemed to consider the possibility that Faulques was pulling his leg. And he must have come to that conclusion, for he smiled a little and shook his head.

"I'm being serious," Faulques insisted. "Or almost."

Now the Croatian was studying him. His smile was a little broader.

"Come on," he said. "What does she look like?"

"I don't have the least idea . . . All I know is her voice. Every day, at the same hour."

"You haven't seen her in the port?"

"Never."

"And you're not curious?"

"Only relatively so."

A pause. Markovic wasn't smiling anymore. His gaze had become suspicious. Intelligent.

"Why are you telling me that?"

"Because you asked me."

The Croatian pushed his glasses with a finger and for a moment looked at Faulques without speaking. Then he sat down on a step of the stairway, beside the books, and without taking his eyes from the painter of battles made a gesture that encompassed the entire tower.

"How did you get the idea for all this? To do something like this? Here?"

Faulques told him. Old story. He'd been in an ancient, ruined mill near Valencia, where an anonymous seventeenth-century author, no doubt a soldier passing by, had painted chiaroscuro scenes of the siege of the Salses Castle in France. That had left certain ideas in his head that later hatched somewhere between visiting a hall of battle paintings in the Escorial and a certain painting he'd seen in a museum in Florence. That was it.

"I don't believe that was all there was to it," Markovic protested. "There are those photos of yours . . . And isn't it extraordinary. I never thought of you as a man who was dissatisfied with his work. Horrified, maybe, I told myself. But not dissatisfied. Although in this painting the last thing you seem to be is horrified. Maybe that's because paintings aren't painted with emotion. Right? Or are they? Maybe what can't be painted with emotion is a painting like this."

"Photographing a fire doesn't mean you think you're a fireman."

And yet, thought the painter of battles, though he didn't say it, Markovic was right. Or at least partly right. A painting like the one he was working on could not be painted with emotion, but neither could it be done by ignoring your feelings. First you had to have them, and then know you had rid yourself of them. Or be liberated from them. It was Olvido who had truly changed him, two times, and in two directions. She had also taught him to look. And, in a certain way, to paint. It was luck. When she died and the lens of the camera clouded over, painting became his salvation. Painting with the eye that she had trained.

"Tell me one thing, señor Faulques. . . . Does feeling horror blur the focus of the camera?"

Now the painter of battles couldn't help but laugh. This individual had done a good job of tracking, or interpreting, although not a hundred percent. He often lightly touched the truth without penetrating the heart of it, but some of his elementary guesses were on the mark. He had to admit that the man had good intuition. A certain style.

"That," he admitted, "is very perceptive."

"But answer the question, please. I'm talking about mercy, not technique."

Faulques fell silent. His discomfort was growing. This was all going too far. But there was a certain sinister pleasure in it, he decided. Like the husband who is suspicious of his wife and searches until, triumphant, he comes up with the proof. Passing a finger gently down the sharp edge of a broken razor.

Markovic was still sitting on the stair. He nodded slowly, agreeing, as if he had just heard an answer no one had given. I thought it was something like that, he said.

"Honestly, there's no real woman?" he asked suddenly.

Faulques didn't answer. He had collected a few brushes and was washing them with soap under the spigot of the water tank. He shook them with care, sucked the tip of the finest ones, and put them back in place. Then he set about cleaning the oven-tray palette.

"I apologize for my persistence," the Croatian continued, "but it's important. It's part of what brought me here. As for the woman on the Borovo Naselje road . . ."

He stopped himself at that point, never taking his eyes from the painter. Faulques was dispassionately cleaning the tray.

"Earlier," Markovic continued, "we were talking about horror and losing the clean focus of the camera. And you know what I think? That you were a good photographer because to take a photograph you have to frame, and to frame is to select and exclude. Save some things and eliminate others . . . Not everyone can do that: set himself up as a judge of all that's happening around him. You understand what I'm talking about? No one who is truly in love can make that kind of judgment. Put in the position of choosing between saving my wife or saving my son, I wouldn't have been able to . . . No. I don't think so."

"And which *would* you have chosen among saving your wife, your son, and yourself?"

"I know what you're getting at. There are people who . . ."

Again he interrupted himself, staring at the floor between his feet. You're right, Faulques said then. Photography is a process of visual selection. You frame a part of your line of vision. It's a matter of being in the right place at the right time. Of seeing what move to make, the way you do in chess.

Markovic's eyes were still on the floor.

"Chess, you say."

"I don't know if that's a good example. It would also work with soccer."

The Croatian looked up, smiled a strange, almost challenging smile, and waved a hand toward the mural.

"And where is she? Have you reserved a special place in your mural for her, or is she just one among that mass of people?"

Faulques set down the tray. He didn't like that sudden insolent smile. And, to his own surprise, for an instant he found himself calculating the possibilities of attacking Markovic. The Croatian was strong, he decided. Shorter than he was, but also younger and more robust. He would have to hit him before he had time to react. Catch him off guard. He looked around. He needed a forceful weapon. The shotgun was upstairs. Too far away.

"That's not your problem," he said.

Markovic's lip curled in an unpleasant way.

"I don't agree with you there. Everything that has any bearing on you is my business. Including that chess you talk about so cold-bloodedly . . . And the woman you photographed when she was dead."

There was a section of scaffolding on the floor beside the door, some three meters from where Markovic was sitting. Heavy aluminum pipe about the length of his forearm. With a practiced sense of space and motion, as if he were taking a photograph, Faulques calculated how many steps it would take to get to the pipe and then to the Croatian. Five to the door, four to the objective. Markovic would not get up until he saw Faulques pick up the pipe. In two quick steps he could be near him before he was on his feet. One more to strike him. On the head, naturally. He couldn't allow him the chance to gather himself. Maybe two blows would do it. Or just one if he was lucky. He had no intention of killing him, or of calling the police. In fact, he didn't have any intention of doing anything. He was simply irritated and wanted to hurt him.

"They say she was a photographer of fashion and art," Markovic said. "That you cut her out of her world and took her with you. That you became companions and . . . which is it? Husband and wife? Lovers?"

Faulques dried his hands on a rag. Who told you that? he asked. Then slowly he walked toward the door, his air casual. First only a step. Out of the corner of his eye he glanced at the tube on the floor. He picked up the can of dirty water he'd washed the brushes in and started outdoors to empty it, to justify his movements. People told me, Markovic was saying, who knew her and knew you. I assure you that I talked with a lot of people before I came here. And I worked a lot of nasty jobs in several countries, señor Faulques. Traveling costs money. But I had a powerful motive. Now I know it was all worth it.

"I think a lot about mine, you know?" he added after remaining silent for a moment. "About my wife. She was blond, and sweet. She had hazel eyes, like my son . . . You know . . . I can't stand to think about the boy. This black despair settles over me, I want to scream until my throat is raw. Once I did; I screamed till my throat was almost bleeding. That happened in a *pension,* and the owner thought I was crazy. I couldn't talk for two days, imagine. I can think about her. It's different. I've been with other women since. I'm a man, after all. But there are nights that I toss and turn in my bed, remembering. Her skin was very white, and her flesh . . . She had . . ."

Faulques was at the door. He threw out the dirty water and bent down to set the can on the floor beside the piece of scaffolding. His fingers had almost touched it when he realized that his anger had dissipated. Slowly, he stood up, his hands empty. Markovic was studying him with curiosity. For a moment the Croatian's eyes focused on the aluminum pipe.

"That tourist boat goes by at the same hour, with the same woman, and you never think about going down to the port to see what she looks like?"

"Maybe I'll do it some day."

Markovic smiled slightly with a distracted air.

"One day."

"Yes."

You may be disappointed, Markovic warned him. The voice sounds young and pretty, but maybe she isn't either of those things. He spoke those words as he moved over to leave room for Faulques to go up to the second level, open the turned-off refrigerator, and take out two beers.

"Have you been with women since what happened on the Borovo Naselje road, señor Faulques? I suppose you have. But it's curious, isn't it? At first, when you're young, you think it's impossible to get along without women. Then when circumstances or age force you to, you get accustomed to it. Maybe you resign yourself. But I'm not sure that 'accustomed' is the right word."

He took the can Faulques offered him and stood looking at it without opening it. The painter pulled the tab to open his. The beer was warm, and a gush of foam spilled over his fingers.

"So you live alone, then," Markovic murmured, pensive.

Faulques drank with quick sips, observing him. Without a word he swiped his mouth with the back of his hand. Markovic nodded. He seemed to have confirmed something. Finally he opened his beer, drank a little, set it on the floor, and lighted a cigarette.

"Do you want us to talk about the woman who died on that road?"

"No."

"I've told you about mine."

The two men stared at each other a long time. Three pulls on Markovic's cigarette, two swallows of Faulques' beer. It was the Croatian who spoke first.

"Do you think my wife tried to ingratiate herself with the men who raped her, to save her life? Or save our son? Do you think she yielded out of fear, or out of resignation, before they killed the boy and mutilated her and slit her throat?"

He put the cigarette between his lips. The tip glowed, and for an instant a mouthful of smoke veiled the pale eyes behind the lenses of his glasses. Faulques said nothing. He was watching a fly that after dancing between them had lighted on the Croatian's arm. Who looked at it. Impassive. Without moving or waving it away.

11.

THE BREEZE WAS BLOWING OFFSHORE toward the sea and the night was very warm. Despite the bright moonlight, Faulques could see nearly all the constellation Pegasus. He was still outdoors, hands in his pockets, surrounded by the shrilling of the cicadas and the fireflies flickering beneath the black mass of the pines that stood out with each flash from the distant lighthouse. He was thinking about Ivo Markovic, his words, his silences, and the woman the Croatian had mentioned as he left. What was there between you two, señor Faulques? he'd asked, already on his feet and on his way to the door with the empty beer can in his hand, looking for a place to put it down. I mean, what was really in that last photograph? He had said it in an offhand way, making some vague gesture, sure that he would not have an answer. Then he'd crushed the can in his hand and deposited it in a cardboard box filled with trash, and shrugged. The photo in the ditch, he repeated as he walked away. That strange photograph that was never published.

Faulques slowly returned to the tower, its dark mass rising from the cliff. It served no purpose to remember, he thought. But it was inevitable. Between the two points determined by chance and time, the Mexican museum and the ditch on the Borovo Naselje road, Olvido Ferrara had loved him, he had no doubt. She had done so in her deliberate, vital, and self-centered manner, with a sediment of intelligent sadness in the pauses. Faulques had always moved with supreme caution around the subtle melancholy latent in the depths of her gaze and her words, like a prudent plunderer trying not to provide a reason to make the latent explicit. Flowers just keep growing, detached and sure of themselves, she had once said. We're the fragile ones. Faulques was worried about the eventuality of confronting aloud the reasons for the hopeless resignation that coursed through her veins, as precise as the healthy and regular beating of her heart that could be perceived, as if it were an incurable illness, in the pulse at her wrists, at her throat, in her embraces. In her impulses and in that peculiar jubilation of hers—she was capable of laughing boisterously, like a happy child—that she shielded herself behind the way other humans tend to do with a book, a glass of wine, or a word. Olvido was similarly cautious in her relationship with Faulques. During the time they were together, she always observed him from afar, or rather, from the outside, perhaps fearing to penetrate the surface and discover that he was like other men she had known. She never asked about women, about years past, about anything. Nor about the nomadic rootlessness he used as defense in a territory that from the time he was young he had decided to consider hostile. And sometimes, when in moments of intimacy and tenderness he was on the verge of confiding a memory or an emotion, she would put her fingers to his lips. No, my love. Don't talk, look at me. Don't talk, kiss me. Don't talk, come here, right here. Olvido wanted to believe that he was different, and that that was why she had chosen him, less as a companion for an improbable future—Faulques noted, impotently, the signs of that improbability—than as a path to the inevitable destiny her own hopelessness was guiding her toward. And maybe he was, in a certain way, different. Once she had told him that. They were climbing the stairway of a hotel in Athens, near dawn, Faulques with his sport coat over his shoulders. Olvido in a white, form-fitting dress that closed with a zipper from waist to neck. He, one step behind her, was suddenly struck by a thought: One day we won't be here. And he slowly unzipped the dress as they went up the stairs. Olvido continued without any reaction, one hand on the brass railing, her dress open to her hips, revealing her splendid back, her naked shoulders, as elegant as an imperturbable gazelle—she would have done the same even had they met a guest or hotel employee. When she reached the landing, she stopped and turned to look at him. I love you, she said serenely, because your eyes don't betray you. You never allow that. And that adds silent weight to your baggage.

He went into the tower, felt around for a box of matches, and lighted the gas lamp. As an effect of the darkness, the images painted on the wall seemed to encircle him like ghosts. Or maybe it wasn't the darkness, he told himself as he took a slow look around the entire perimeter of the painting, which on that night, as on many others, spirited him toward the river of the dead, to its dark and tranquil waters where bloody shadows were gathered on the opposite bank, eyes on him, answering him with sad words. Faulques searched for the bottle and poured three fingers of cognac into a glass. Night flies by, he murmured after the first sip. And we lose ourselves in weeping.

No one who truly loves, Markovic had said that evening. And have you always been the person your photos say you are? And nevertheless, the painter of battles knew that only in that way was it possible to get through it all and keep the camera's lens focused. Unlike Markovic himself, even Olvido, both of whom were caught up in war, voluntarily or involuntarily, changing their lives or destroying them, in thirty years of traveling around the world shielded behind a camera, focusing, observing, Faulques had learned a lot about humankind, but nothing had changed in him. At least, nothing that altered his premonitory vision of the problem. The Croatian was right in a certain way. That mural surrounding him with its shadows and its ghosts was a scientific exposition of what he had observed, not remorse or expiation. But there was a crack in the wall, in the circular painting, that in essence was confirmation of what in a different time Faulques had intuited and now knew. Despite his technical arrogance, the scientist who studied man from the icy solitude of his observation did not find that he himself was outside that world, although he liked to think he was. No one was completely indifferent, however much he pretended to be. If only that were possible, he thought, draining the glass and pouring himself more cognac. In their relationship, Olvido had forced him to come out of himself. But her death had ended that truce. Those steps executed with geometric precision on the Borovo Naselje road—almost the elegant moves of a knight on the chessboard of chaos—had sent Faulques back to his solitude, had in some way had a calming effect, put things in place. The painter of battles took another swallow after lifting his glass in a silent toast to the wall, nearly all its circular length, the way a torero salutes the crowd from the center of the ring. Now Olvido was on the dark shore where shadows spoke with the barking of dogs and the howling of wolves. *Gemitusque luporum.* As for Faulques, Olvido's last steps had consigned him for all time to the company of the shadows that populated the tower: a man standing beside the black river, watched from the other side by the melancholy specters he had known with life.

Olvido and he, he remembered, had looked from that same shore at a river in a painting in the Uffizi: Gherardo Starnina's *Thebaid,* which some attributed to Paolo Uccello or to the young Fra Angelico. Despite its pleasant, folkloric quality—scenes of the eremitic life with colorful, allegorical, and mythic touches—a more careful observation of that wood panel revealed a second level beyond first appearances, where beneath the Gothic synthesis could be noted strange geometric lines and disquieting content. Olvido and Faulques had stood rooted before the painting, enthralled by the attitudes of the monks and the other human characters in the painting, by the allegorical intensity of the numerous separate scenes. It reminds me of those nativities they set up with miniature figures at Christmastime, Faulques commented, ready to go on to the next painting. But Olvido had caught him by the arm, eyes still glued to the painting. Look, she said. There's something dark and disturbing here. Look at the ass crossing the bridge, the confused scenes in the background, and on the right, the woman who seems to be fleeing furtively, and the monk behind her, peering from a cave in the rock. When you look closer, some of these figures become sinister, you know? It makes you worry that you don't know what they're up to. What they're plotting. What they're thinking. And look at the river, Faulques. I've seldom seen one so strange. So deceptively peaceful and so dark. It's a fabulous painting, no? There's nothing naïve about it. Whether it's by Starnina, or Uccello, or whoever—I suppose it would please the museum if it were Uccello, that would raise the value—you begin by being entertained, but little by little your smile freezes.

They had talked about the painting all afternoon: first by the river and the old bridge, beneath the statue of Giovanni dalle Bande Nere in the Vasari façade, and then during an early dinner on the terrace of a restaurant on the other side of the river, from which they could see the bridge and the Uffizi galleries illuminated by the late afternoon light. Olvido was still fascinated by the painting, which she had seen before but never, until she was with Faulques, viewed in that way. It is abstract order become reality, she said. And it's as dense as Bellini's *Sacred Allegory,* don't you think? So surreal. Its enigmas talk among themselves, and leave us out of their conversation. And we're back in the fifteenth century, no less.

Those old masters, more than anyone, knew how to make the invisible visible. Did you really look at the mountains and rocks in the background? They make you think of the geometrical landscapes of the end of the nineteenth century, of Friedrich, Schiele, Klee. And I wonder how we would title that painting today. Maybe *The Ambiguous Shore.* Or better, *Pictorial Theology of a Strictly Geological Topography.* Something like that. My God, Faulques. We are so wrongheaded. Seeing a painting like that makes it clear that photography isn't good for anything. Only painting can do what that painting does. Every good painting has always aspired to be a landscape of another landscape not yet painted, but when the truth of a society coincided with that of the artist, there was no duplicity. True magnificence came when they separated, and the painter had to choose between submission and deception, and call upon his talent to make one look like the other. That's why the *Thebaid* has what all masterpieces have: allegories of certainties that become a certainty only after a lot of time has gone by. And now, please, pour me a little more of that wine. She had said all that as she rolled pasta around her fork with enviable ease, wiped her lips with her napkin, or looked into Faulques' eyes with all the light of the Renaissance reflected in them. In five minutes, she added, suddenly lowering her voice—she had leaned a little toward him, elbows on the table and fingers laced together, gazing at him seductively—I want us to go back to the hotel and for you to make love to me and call me a whore. *Capisci?* Here I am eating spaghetti with you exactly eighty-five kilometers from the place where I was born. And thanks to

Starnina, or Uccello, or whoever really painted that work, I urgently need you to make love to me with reasonable but conclusive violence and to blank out the odometer in my brain. Or break it. I have the pleasure of informing you that you are very handsome, Faulques. And I find myself at that exact point when a French woman would shift to a more intimate word for "you," a Swiss would try to find out how many credit cards you have in your wallet, and a North American would ask if you carry a condom. And so—she glanced at the clock—let's be off to the hotel, if you have no objection.

That evening they went back to the hotel with the last light, walking slowly along the banks of the Arno, enveloped in a melancholy Tuscan autumn sunset that seemed to have been copied from a painting by Claude Gellée. And then, once in the room, with the windows open over the city and the river below, where they could hear the murmuring sound of the current flowing over the dikes, they made long, methodical love, unhurried, pausing only to rest a few minutes and then pick up again, attacking each other in the semi-dark, with no light other than that from outside, enough, though, that Olvido, head turned toward the wall, could contemplate both their shadows on the wall. Once she got up and went to the window, and as she looked at the dark, unornamented wall of San Frediano in Cestello, spoke the only ten words in a row that Faulques heard that night: They're all gone, the women I wanted to be like. Then she wandered aimlessly around the room, so beautiful, so provocative. She had a natural tendency to walk around naked, to move in her indolent fashion, with the elegance of her fine lineage and of the model she had been for a short time. And that night, as from their bed he watched the movements of a delicate and perfect animal, Faulques thought that Olvido didn't need any illumination. Day or night, naked or clothed, light followed her as if a portable spotlight were tracking her everywhere she went. He was still thinking of that the next morning as he watched her sleep, mouth slightly open, forehead creased with the line of sorrow you see in some Sevillian images of virgins. In Florence, no doubt influenced by the place, and because she was so close to where she'd been born, Faulques discovered with calm consternation that his love for Olvido Ferrara was not merely intensely physical, *or* intellectual. It was also an aesthetic emotion, a fascination with all the possible soft lines, angles, and fields of vision of her body, the serene movement so much a part of her nature. That morning, contemplating the sleeping woman between the wrinkled hotel sheets, Faulques felt the claw of future jealousy superimposed on retrospective jealousy: from the men who one day would watch her move through museums and city streets and hotel rooms above ancient rivers to those who had known her that way in the past. He knew, because she had told him, that a fashion photographer and a bisexual designer had been her first lovers. He learned that unsought, when Olvido mentioned it even though the issue hadn't come up and he hadn't asked. Casually, or deliberately, she had told him and then observed him, studied him, lying in wait, until he, after a brief, silent pause, had changed the subject. Nonetheless, the idea had awakened in Faulques—it still happened—an icy internal anger, irrational and inexplicable. He never mentioned what she had confided, or alluded to his own experiences, unless as a jest or casual comment, or as when he'd become aware of how well known she was in some of the best European and New York hotels and restaurants he had joked, laughingly, that *he* was recognized in some of the best whorehouses in Asia, Africa, and Latin America. In that case—was Olvido's reply—try and see that I get the benefit of it. She was perceptive in the extreme; she knew how to read paintings and how to read men. And above all, she was capable of listening to a silence with deep concentration, as if she were a zealous student absorbed in a problem the professor had just written on the blackboard. She dismantled silence, piece by piece, the way a watchmaker dismantles a watch. And so she easily perceived Faulques' irritation in the sudden tightening of his muscles, the expression in his eyes, the way he kissed her. Or didn't. You men are all amazingly stupid, she would say, interpreting things he had never voiced. Even the cleverest of you. I can't bear that. I detest men who take me to bed thinking about the woman they bedded before me, or the one who will be next.

Faulques went up the spiral stairs carrying the glass of cognac in one hand and the gas lamp in the other. The liquor was making his fingers clumsy as he dug through the large box he used as a table beside the military cot where he slept. He went through papers, documents, notebooks, until he came upon the photo he was looking for: the only one he had kept of himself . . . and it had been a long time since he looked at it. Actually, it was a picture of both of them, for Olvido was there as well: a house later destroyed in a bombing raid, with Faulques—this time it was he—asleep on the floor, mouth dropped open, chin unshaven, head resting on his backpack, boots and pants stained with mud, the two Nikons and the Leica on his chest, and a wool cap covering his eyes. And Olvido, at the moment she pressed the shutter release, face half hidden by the camera and partially reflected in the broken mirror on the wall. She had taken the photo in Jarayeb, in the south of Lebanon, after an Israeli bombing raid, but Faulques hadn't realized that until much later, until everything had ended and he was packing her belongings to send them to her family. It was a black-and-white photo with a beautiful dawn light that lengthened shadows on one side of the image, framed Faulques, and on the other side illuminated the figure of Olvido, fragmenting her three times in the broken mirror. One of the reflections showed her face behind the camera, her braids, her torso clothed in a dark T-shirt, jeans molded to her waist; a second, the camera, the right side of her body, an arm, and a hip; the third, only the camera. And in each fragment of that incomplete image, Olvido seemed to fade into her own reflection, every instant of that flight disintegrating and fixed in time in the emulsion of the film, like Paolo Uccello's guerrilla and the one Faulques was painting in his mural.

12.

SHE HAD GONE WITH HIM, just like that. Very soon. I want to go with you, she said. I need a silent Virgil and you are good at that. I want a nice-looking guide, silent and strong like the ones in the safari films of the fifties. Olvido had said that one winter twilight as they stood at the edge of an abandoned Portman mine near Cartagena, beside the Mediterranean. She was wearing a wool tam, her nose was red from the cold and her fingers protruded from the overly long sleeves of a heavy red sweater. She spoke very seriously, and then came the smile. I'm tired of doing what I do, so I'm going to stick with you. Mind made up. Oh, death, let us set sail . . . and so on. My own work bores me. It's a lie that photography is the only art form in which your training is not decisive. Now they're all that way. Any amateur with a Polaroid can rub shoulders with Man Ray or Brassai, you know? But also with Picasso or Frank Lloyd Wright. Centuries of accumulated traps weigh heavily on the words "art" and "artist." I don't know very well what it is you do, but it attracts me. I watch you; you're all the time taking mental photos, as focused as if you were practicing some strange Bushido discipline, with a camera in place of a samurai sword. I suspect that the only contemporary, living art is what emerges from your merciless hunting trips. Don't laugh, silly. I'm being serious. I began to understand that last night, when you held me as if we were about to die. Or as if someone was going to kill us both at any moment.

She was intelligent. Very. He'd noticed that he never had to explain, resolve, or change anything. That all she wanted was to see the world in its true dimensions, without the varnish of false normality; she wanted to place her fingers on the terrible pulse of life even if she drew them away stained with blood. Olvido was aware that she had lived in a fictitious world since she was a girl, like the young Buddha from whom, it was told, his family had for thirty years hidden the existence of death. The camera, she said, you yourself, Faulques, are my passport to what's real: there where things can't be embellished by stupidity, rhetoric, or money. I want to shred my former naïveté. My badly battered and overvalued innocence. And that may be why when she made love she whispered steamy provocations and sometimes wanted him to be rough with her. I detest, she'd told him once—they were in the National Gallery in Washington, D.C., looking at van der Weyden's *Portrait of a Lady*—the hypocritical, chaste mien of women painted by those northern types. Do you know what I mean, Faulques? What a contrast with Italian madonnas and Spanish saints, all of whom, should an obscenity escape their lips, look as if they know precisely what they're saying. Like me.

From that moment on, Olvido never produced a

single work that evolved from the aesthetic and the glamour in which she'd been educated and had lived, but deliberately turned her back to them. Her new photos had to be a reaction to all that. Her work never had people in it, no beauty, only a jumble of things you'd find in a secondhand store, leftovers from lives now gone that time flung at her feet: ruins, rubble, skeletons of blackened buildings set against somber skies, ripped curtains, shattered china, empty armoires, broken furniture, spent shells, the tracks of shrapnel on the walls. That was the sum of her work for three years, always in black and white, the antithesis of the scenes of art or fashion that she had previously photographed or played a part in; none of the color, light, and perfect focus that made the world more beautiful than it was in real life. See how pretty I was in these pictures, she once said, showing Faulques a magazine cover—Olvido, impeccably made up, posed on the rain-slick Brooklyn Bridge. How incredibly pretty—and take note, if you will be so kind, of the adverb. So I want you please to give me what was missing in my old world. Give me the cruelty of a camera that is not an accessory to the crime. Photography as art is a perilous terrain; our era prefers the image over the object, the copy over the original, the representation over the reality, appearance over being; it prefers that I, dressed by the best designers, steal phrases from Sasha Stone or Feuerbach. That's why I love you . . . for the moment. You are my way of saying to hell with fashion magazines, to hell with the spring collection in Milan, to hell with Giorgio Morandi, who spent half a lifetime painting still lifes with bottles, to hell with Warhol and his cans of soup, to hell with the canned artist's shit they sell at millionaire auctions at Claymore's. Soon I won't need you, Faulques, but I will always be grateful for your wars. They free my eyes from that past. They give me perfect license to go wherever I want: action, adrenaline, ephemeral art. They liberate me from responsibilities and make me an elite tourist. I can look, finally. With *my* eyes. Ponder the world using the only two possible systems: logic and war. In that, too, there isn't much difference between you and me. Neither of us subscribes to ethical photojournalism. Who does?

Olvido made the decision to go with him as she was contemplating the devastated landscape of Portman. Or at least that was when she told him. I know a place, Faulques had suggested, that's exactly like a painting by Dr. Atl, except without the fire and lava. Now that I know those paintings, and I know you, I would like to go back there and photograph it. She looked at him, surprised, over her cup of coffee—they were having breakfast in Faulques' house in Barcelona when the idea came to him—and said, But that isn't a war, and I thought that all you photographed was wars. It is war in a way, he replied: now those paintings and that place are also part of a war. So they rented a car and traveled south until one winter day at dusk, in the silence of winding dirt roads bordering ravines and mountains of mineral slag, demolished towers and collapsed houses, walls without roofs, old strip mines open to the sky, revealing their brown, red, and black guts, ochre oxide lodes, exhausted veins, enormous buddles where cracked gray mud had escaped through crumbled walls and carpeted the bottom of the ravines, creeping among dead prickly pears and dry fig trees like tongues of old, solidified lava. It looks like a dormant volcano, Olvido murmured with awe when Faulques stopped the car; he picked up the pack with his cameras, and they walked through the landscape of somber beauty, hearing the crunch of stones beneath their feet in the absolute silence of the vast wasteland abandoned by the hand of man for nearly half a century; wind and rain, however, had continued to erode it into capricious forms, flumes, crisscrossing gullies, landslides, collapses. You might think that a gigantic and chaotic hand had wielded powerful implements to strip the earth until mineral and stone had been torn from its viscera and then left it to time to work on the scene like a demented artist in a chaotic workshop. Then the sun, which was about to set behind slag heaps that stretched to the nearby sea, peered out for an instant from beneath the layer of leaden clouds, and a brilliant red splendor burst over the water and spilled like an eruption of incandescent lava across the tormented land, over the eroded tops of the buddles, the deep gullies of slag, and the ruined mine towers silhouetted in the distance. And as Faulques lifted the camera to photograph it, Olvido stopped rubbing her hands together to keep warm; her eyes opened wide beneath the wool tam, she struck her forehead with her open palm, and said, Of course! My God! That's exactly what happens. It isn't the pyramid of Giza, or the Sphinx, it's what's left of them after time, wind, rain, and sand storms have done their work. It won't be the real Eiffel tower until the iron structure, finally rusted and crumbling, rises over a dead city like a specter in its watchtower. Nothing will truly be what it is until the unfeeling Universe wakes like a sleeping animal, stretches its legs, stirring the skeleton of the Earth, yawns, and takes a few random slashes. Do you realize that? Yes, of course you do. Now I understand. It's a question of geological amorality. Of photographing the useful certainty of our fragility. Of keeping a sharp eye on the roulette of the cosmos, the wheel spinning on the exact day that, yet again, the mouse of the computer fails to work, Archimedes triumphs over Shakespeare, and a disconcerted humanity pats its pockets, confirming its fear that it has no change for the boatman. Photographing not man, but the traces of man. The naked man descending a staircase. But I had never seen it that way before. It was only a painting in a museum. My god, Faulques. My god—the red light illuminated her face like the flames of a volcano hung on a wall. A museum is nothing but a question of perspective. Thank you for bringing me here.

From that day on, she went everywhere with him. She hunted in her own way, concentrating on her vision of the world, which was not identical to Faulques' but was nourished from the same desolation. The first place was Lebanon. He took her there because it was familiar territory, and he had spent a lot of time there during the civil strife. He knew its highways, towns, cities, and in all of them he had groups of friends and contacts that allowed them, up to a certain point, to keep the situation under control. The war had dropped back south of the Litani River, to incursions and bombings by Islamic guerrillas on the northern border of the Hebrew state, and to Israeli retaliations. The couple traveled by taxi along the coast, from Beirut to Sidon, and from there to Tyre, where they arrived one luminous, blue Mediterranean day, with a blinding sun gilding the stones of the ancient port. Faulques' septuagenarian friend Father Georges, still alive and immediately seduced by Olvido, showed her the crypt of his medieval church; there they'd seen the recumbent figures of knights of the Crusades—their stone features disfigured by hammers when the city fell into Turkish hands. The next day, Olvido had her baptism of fire on the Nabati highway: an attack by Israeli armored helicopters, a missile fired at a car carrying leaders of the Hezbollah, a man without legs dragging himself from the wreckage of smoking sheet metal as from a Rauschenberg anti-Futurist bricolage. Out of the corner of his eye, Faulques saw her working, pale, avid, between photos examining the scene around her with burning eyes, but never a word. Neither lament nor commentary; prepared and patient, like a dedicated student. Do what I do, he'd told her. Move the way I do. Make yourself invisible. Do not wear military or flashy clothing, do not step off the blacktopped roads, do not touch abandoned objects, do not stand motionless in doorways or windows, never lift a camera to the sun when airplanes or helicopters are flying over, and remember that if you can see a man with a rifle, he can see you. Don't ever hold your camera too near people who are weeping or suffering; they might kill you. The only thing about you they should be aware of, the first thing they should notice, is the sound of your shutter. Calculate your distance, focus, light, and frame before you get close, and do it discreetly; work in silence and disappear with caution. Before you go into a risky area, check out a way to leave, study the terrain, look for protected spots, go from one to the next in stages or dashes. Remember that every street, trench, hill, tree, has a good side and a bad side; make no mistake when identifying them. Don't complicate your life unnecessarily. And especially don't complicate mine.

Olvido liked to be with Faulques, and she told him that. I like to watch how you move, alert as a fox, focusing in advance, mentally preparing the photograph you're going to take before you attempt it. I like seeing you in jeans you've worn out at the knees and shirts with the sleeves rolled up, see your hard, thin body and watch you change lenses or film while you're pressed against a wall and they're shooting at us, working with the same intensity a soldier has when he's changing the clip in his rifle. I like to watch you in a hotel room, one eye glued to the loupe, marking the best images on negatives held to the light against the window glass, or to see you spend hours over prints with your pica-pole and felt-tip pen, selecting the frame and writing instructions as you calculate where the editor is going to place the fold. I like it that you are so good at your work, and that tears have never caused you to miss what your camera is focused on. Or that's how it seems.

She, too, was reasonably good when she was working; Faulques had discovered that on dangerous roads and at hostile checkpoints in the rain, in deserted towns threatening in their silence, where all they could hear was the crunch of their own footsteps over broken glass. Olvido was not a brilliant photographer, but she was conscientious and original in conceptualizing her image. Soon she began to reveal the right talents: instinct, and a technical coolness vital in extreme situations. She also had a knack for knowing how to be adopted by dangerous people, an essential quality when roaming about in wars with a camera. She was able to convince anyone without words, with just one of her elegant smiles, that it was to everyone's advantage to let her remain there as a kind of necessary witness. That she was more useful alive than dead, or raped. But almost immediately she stopped photographing people, or nearly so. They didn't interest her. She could, however, spend an entire day wandering around inside an abandoned house, or a village in ruins. Despite her fondness for buying trinkets she found behind the line of conflict—the faux or banal objects she collected with frivolous passion and then gave away or left behind everywhere—she never took anything, not a book, not a piece of china, not the spent shell of a bullet, taking only rolls and rolls of film, photographing everything. War, she said, is filled with found objects, her *trouvés*. It puts Surrealism in its place. It's like the meeting on the dissecting table between a human without an umbrella and a meat grinder.

Faulques, who until then had almost always worked alone, and never with women—it was his opinion that they created problems in a war: among them, that men would kill you to get a woman—found that Olvido's company had professional advantages: she closed some doors but she opened others with her special talent for awaking men's protective instinct, admiration, and vanity. And she took advantage of it. The way she had in Ras al Khafji during the first Gulf War, when a flirtatious Saudi colonel not only let them wander wherever they wanted—they'd arrived from Dhahran without a permit, in a vehicle camouflaged with allied military markings—he also offered them coffee in the midst of a battle, and then asked Olvido where she would like him to direct the artillery, so she could get the best photos. She thanked him with elegance and a radiant smile, pointed toward something at random—the tall water tower occupied by Iraqis—and readied her camera fitted with a 90-mm lens. The amiable colonel had a chair brought for her so she would be comfortable, and had time to direct four cannons and a TOW missile at the place she'd chosen before a detachment of North American marines came rushing up, chewed out the colonel, and made them all leave. I want a child, she told Faulques that night as they were drinking fruit juice in the alcohol-free bar of Le Meridien Hotel, laughing uproariously as they remembered the day. I want one just for me; I will carry him in my backpack and bring him up in airports, hotels, and trenches. If I don't, what will I do when our sweet camaraderie comes to an end? That night they made love till dawn, in silence, uninterrupted even during a raid of Iraqi Scud missiles, not opening their mouths except to kiss, bite, or suck. And then, exhausted, she licked Faulques' body until she fell asleep.

As for photographing things and not people, he had scarcely ever seen her focus on anything alive. Truth is in things, not in people, she said. But it needs us in order to be manifest. She was patient. She waited until the natural light was exactly as she wanted, and with time developed her own style. Later, in Barcelona—very soon she moved into the high-ceilinged flat he had near the Boquería—when she came out of the darkroom she would drop down on the rug, surrounded by all those black-and-white images, and spend hours marking details with a felt-tip, grouping images according to codes that only she knew and that Faulques never succeeded in penetrating completely. Then she would go back to the developing trays and the enlarger, and work on the parts of the photos she had marked earlier, blowing them up again and again in new frames, until she was satisfied. Things, Faulques heard her murmur once, bleed like people do. One of her obsessions was the photos she found in devastated houses. She photographed them just as they were, never touching or arranging them: stepped on, scorched by fires, hanging on the wall with curling edges, shattered glass, broken frames, open and torn family albums. Abandoned photos, she affirmed, are like pale spaces in a Tenebrist painting: they don't illuminate it, but they obscure the shadows. The first and only time Faulques saw her cry during a war was over an album in Petrinja, Croatia, twenty-two days before the ditch on the Borovo Naselje road. They found it on the floor, covered with plaster dust and wet from the rain leaking through the damaged roof, opened to two pages of photos of a family at Christmastime: parents, grandparents, four small children, and a dog, happy photos around a decorated fir tree and a table set with a festive meal: the same family, grandparents, and dog that she and Faulques had just seen outside lying in a puddle in the garden, a jumble of soaked clothing and raw flesh riddled with bullets and finished off by a fragmentation grenade. Olvido didn't take any shots there: she stood looking at the corpses, her cameras protected under her raincoat, and only when she went inside and saw the album on the floor had she begun to work. It was a very humid and stormy day, and her hair and face were covered with raindrops, so Faulques was slow to realize that she was crying, and noticed only when he saw her lower the camera and rub her eyes to dry away tears that prevented her from focusing. She had never spoken of that moment, nor had he. Later, when he was back in Barcelona, when everything was over and he was looking at the contact sheets Olvido hadn't had time to develop, Faulques found that by one of those singular symmetries with which chaos and its rules were so prodigal, she had taken exactly twenty-two frames of the photos pasted in the album: as many as the days she had left to live. He had checked that with a calendar in one hand and the contact sheets in the other, remembering. He hadn't been that dumbfounded since the time they'd returned from a trip to Africa—Somalia, the hunger and the killing were intense—and she'd spent a week in an industrial slaughterhouse, photographing sharp blades and great slabs of meat impaled on hooks, wrapped in plastic, and stamped with health department seals. All in black and white, as usual. Olvido had developed that strange body of work and kept it in a file on which she'd written: *Der müde Tod.* Weary Death. In those images, as in the war photos in which there was no human presence—at most, a dead foot with a worn-through shoe sole, a dead hand with a wedding ring—blood resembled the tongues of dark gray mud she had seen around the collapsed buddles at the Portman mine. Lava from a cold volcano.

The silence in the tower was absolute. He could not even hear the sea. Faulques put away the photo they both appeared in—he and her ghost in the broken mirror—and closed the lid of the box. Then he drained his glass and went down the spiral staircase in search of something more to drink, feeling as if the steps were yielding beneath his feet. I hope, he thought fleetingly, that Ivo Markovic doesn't get the urge to visit me right now. The bottle was still sitting among the jars and brushes, asking no questions and adding nothing more than what Faulques brought with him. That's good, he told himself. It's the right thing, no question. Perfect. He poured more cognac, emptied it in one gulp, and as he felt the alcohol burn his throat spoke Olvido's name aloud. An unusual name, he meditated. Deceptive word. Again he picked up the bottle, hazy, standing by the river of the dead, glimpsing on the other side slow-moving shadows surrounded by darkness and the black shadows of their shadows. The painter of battles studied the shadowy mural as he considered the paradox: some words committed semantic suicide, disavowing themselves. Olvido was such a word. From the dark shore of his memory, she watched him drink cognac.

13.

IVO MARKOVIC CAME BACK the next day at midmorning. When Faulques went outside to get water from the tank, he found him sitting beneath the pines on the cliff, gazing at the sea. Without a word, the painter returned to the tower and continued to work for a little more than an hour, putting the last touches to the warriors on horseback, until he considered that part of the mural finished. Then he went out again, squinting in the strong noon light flooding over everything, and washed his hands and arms; then, after thinking a moment, he walked to where the Croatian was sitting, still motionless in the shade of the pines. Between his boots were crushed-out cigarette butts and a plastic bag with ice and four cans of beer.

"Beautiful view," said Markovic.

Both men observed the sweep of blue that opened in a fan toward the horizon: the Bocas de Poniente to the north, with Los Ahorcados Island and the dark, hazy gray outline of Cabo Malo reaching out to sea toward the southwest. It looked, Faulques thought, and not for the first time, like a Venetian watercolor. The effect of lights and fog was more evident in the late afternoon, when the sun began to go down behind the successive irregularities of the coast as they receded into the distance, different planes and tones ranging from charcoal to light gray.

"How much do you think light weighs?" the Croatian asked suddenly.

Faulques thought it over for a moment. Then shrugged his shoulders.

"The same as darkness, more or less. About three kilos per square centimeter."

Markovic frowned an instant.

"You're talking about air."

"Of course."

Markovic seemed to reflect on the answer. Finally he made a gesture that encompassed the scene before them, as if there were a relationship between one thing and the other.

"I've been thinking over what we've been talking about all this time," he said. "My photo, your enormous painting, and all the rest. And it may make sense. You may not be too far off when you talk about rules and symmetries."

After he said that he fell silent, then softly tapped his temple with a finger. I'm not very swift up here, he added. I need time to turn things over in my head. You understand?

"I come from a family of peasants. People who never made decisions lightly. They studied the sky, the clouds, the color of the earth . . . All those things determined the abundance of a harvest, the damage from bad weather, hail, freezes."

Again he was silent, still looking at the sea and the rugged coastline. Finally he took off his glasses and began to clean them with the tail of his shirt, thoughtful.

"Chance is the name we put on our ignorance. Is that it?"

It wasn't a question. The painter of battles sat down beside him, studying the Croatian's hands: wide, with short fingers and blunt fingernails. A scar on the right hand. After holding his glasses to the light, Markovic put them back on and was again taking in the view.

"Really a beautiful sight," he insisted. "It reminds me of the coast of my country. You know it, of course."

Faulques nodded. He knew the 557 kilometers of the curving road between Rijeka and Dubrovnik very well, the shoreline of cliff-lined coves and countless islands green with cypresses and white with Dalmatian stone peppering an Adriatic of quiet blue waters, each inlet with its little village, its Venetian or Turkish wall, its tall, pointed bell tower. He had also seen a part of that landscape demolished by cannon during the week Olvido Ferrara and he spent in a hotel in Cavtat, witnessing the spectacle of Dubrovnik under Serbian bombing. Some people argued that a war photograph was the only thing that could not arouse nostalgia, but Faulques wasn't sure about that. Every night after dinner during that time, Olvido and he sat on the terrace of his room, glasses in hand, watching the city burn in the distance, the flames reflected in the black waters of the bay as flashes and explosions lent the scene a mute, unreal, and distant flavor reminiscent of the background, red among the silhouettes and shadows, of a silent nightmare by Bruegel or

Bosch. I know restaurants in Paris and New York, Olvido commented, where people would pay a fortune to have dinner overlooking a panorama like this. They sat there, the two of them, quiet, mesmerized by the spectacle, and at times the only sound was that of ice clinking in their glasses as they drank, distracted, with movements that the situation and the strange reddish light made exceptionally slow, almost artificial. From time to time a gentle land breeze blew from the northeast carrying the strong odor of burning, and also a muffled, syncopated thrumming like the beat of a kettledrum or rumbling of prolonged thunder. And at dawn, after they'd made love in silence and slept to the sound of the distant bombardment, Faulques and Olvido had coffee and toast as they watched the columns of black smoke rising straight up from the ancient city of Ragusa. He awoke one night to find her not at his side, and when he got out of bed saw her standing on the terrace, naked, her splendid body foreshortened in that light and stained with red from the far-off fires, as if Dr. Atl's brushes had slipped across her skin or as if the distant war were enveloping her, but with extreme delicacy. I'm taking a fire bath, she'd said when he put his arms around her from behind and asked her what she was doing there at three in the morning, and she had tilted her head to one side and rested it against his shoulder, never taking her eyes off Dubrovnik burning in the distance. Some people take sun baths or moon baths, like that Italian song about the girl on the tile roof. I'm taking a night bath, a fire-flames bath. And when he stroked her goose-pimply skin, tinted with a red tone that didn't warm because it was as distant and cold as light from a volcano hanging on a museum wall, or as the tortured land of Portman, Olvido stirred slightly in his arms, and he pondered for a moment the differences between the words "perdition" and "volition."

Ivo Markovic was gazing at the sea. I think that you're right, señor Faulques, he said. Truth corresponds to what you've said about the rules and the tiger's stripes and the hidden symmetries that suddenly are manifest and you discover that maybe they have always been there, ready to surprise us. And it's true that the least detail can change your life: a road you don't take, for example, or that you're slow to take because of a conversation, a cigarette, a memory.

"In war, of course, all those things are important. A mine you miss stepping on by centimeters . . . Or that you don't."

He looked up toward the sky, and Faulques imitated him. Very high, almost invisible at six or seven thousand meters, they saw the minuscule glint off a plane that left a long straight vapor trail from east to west. They followed it with their eyes until the line, white on blue, was hidden behind the branches of the pines. Some call it chance, Markovic continued. But you don't really think it is. After I heard what you have to say, I only had to remember your photographs. Or look at that painting. I've already told you that I've been sniffing along your trail like a hunting dog for a long time.

"And I think," he concluded, "that I agree with you. If we set aside the natural disasters in which man has no part . . . Or at least ones he didn't intervene in, because now, with the ozone layer and all that . . . If we set those aside, I mean, it turns out that war is the best expression of how things are . . . Do I have it right?"

He was staring at Faulques, very attentive, as if he had just posed a definitive question. Faulques shrugged. He still hadn't opened his mouth. Markovic waited a moment, and when he didn't get an answer he, too, shrugged, imitating Faulques. I guess so, he said. War as the sublimation of chaos. Order with laws disguised as a throw of the dice.

"Is that what you truly believe?" he persisted.

The painter of battles spoke at last. He smiled a crooked smile, evidencing no sympathy at all.

"Of course . . . It's nearly an exact science. Like meteorology."

The Croatian raised his eyebrows. "Meteorology?"

You could know a hurricane was coming, Faulques explained, but not the precise point it would hit. A tenth of a second, one additional drop of humidity here or there, and everything would take place a thousand kilometers away. Minimal causes, imperceptible to the naked eye, gave rise to dreadful disasters. It had even been proposed that the invention of a certain insecticide had modified the mortality rate in Africa, changed its demography, put pressure on colonial empires, and altered the situation in Europe and the world. Or think of the AIDS virus. Or a chip that could transform traditional forms of work, cause social upheaval, revolutions, and changes in world hegemony. Even the chauffeur of a principal stockholder in a major company, running a red light and killing his boss in the accident, could unleash a crisis that would create havoc in world markets.

"It's just more visible during wars. After all, wars are nothing more than life carried to dramatic extremes. Nothing that peace cannot contain, in small doses."

Markovic was regarding Faulques with renewed respect. When he paused, the Croatian nodded slowly, with an air of conviction. I understand, he said. I understand completely. And look, here's a coincidence. When I was a boy, my mother used to sing me a song. Something about those laws or links tied up with fate. Because someone was careless a nail was lost, for lack of the nail a horseshoe, for lack of the shoe a horse, and without the horse, a horseman. And in the end, because of all those things, a kingdom was lost.

Faulques got to his feet, brushing off his trousers.

"It's always been that way, but we forget. The world has never known as much about itself and about nature as it does now, but it doesn't do any good. We've had tidal waves forever, you know. What's different is that in the past we didn't try to build four- and five-star hotels along the beach. Man creates euphemisms and smoke screens to deny natural laws. And also to negate his own abominable state. And every time he wakes up it costs him two hundred dead in a plane crash, two hundred thousand in a tsunami, or a million in a civil war."

For a moment, Markovic said nothing.

"Abominable state, you say," he murmured at last.

"Exactly."

"You're good with words."

"You're not too bad yourself."

Markovic picked up the bag with the beers, stood up, and nodded again. He stared at the sea, reflecting.

"Dishonor, lost nails, carelessness, symmetries, chance. And all the time we're talking about the same thing, aren't we?"

"If not, then what?"

"And also about broken razors and photographs that kill."

That, too, the painter of battles replied, and looked at him closely. In that light, he saw things in the Croatian's face he'd never noticed before.

"Nothing is innocent, then, señor Faulques. And no one."

Without answering, the painter of battles turned and walked toward the tower, and Markovic followed right along. Their shadows, walking side by side, looked like two friends strolling beneath the noonday sun.

"You know, it's possible that this business of chance is deceptive, ambiguous." Markovic's tone was assured. "Is it chance that leaves an animal's tracks in the snow? Was that what put me in front of your camera, or did I walk toward it for subconscious reasons I can't explain? And the same could be said about you. What made you choose me, and not someone else? In any case, once the process is begun, when chance and inevitable circumstances come together, it all becomes too complex. Don't you agree? Remember, all this is new to me, and strange."

" 'Choose,' you said."

"Yes."

"I'll tell you what it is to choose."

Then Faulques talked for a while—his way; talk

punctuated by long pauses and silences—about choices and about chance. To illustrate, he told about the sniper he had spent four hours with, lying flat on the terrace of a six-story building that afforded a broad view of Sarajevo. The sharpshooter was a Bosnian Serb of about forty, thin, with calm eyes, who had charged Faulques two hundred marks in exchange for being allowed to stay while he was shooting at people running by on foot or speeding in a car along Radomira Putnika Avenue—on the condition that Faulques photograph him and not the street, so no one could identify his position. They had conversed in German as they waited, while Faulques played with his cameras to get the Serb accustomed to them and his subject smoked one cigarette after another, lowering his head from time to time to sight down the barrel of an SVD Dragunov rifle on which he'd mounted a powerful telescopic lens; it was aimed at the street, firmly secured between two bags of earth in a narrow opening in the wall. With no reticence, the Serb had admitted that he shot at women and children just as easily as at men, and Faulques asked no questions of a moral nature; among other reasons because that wasn't why he was there, and for another, because he knew full well—this wasn't the first sniper he'd talked to—the simple motives for which a man with the proper dose of fanaticism, rancor, or drive for monetary reward could kill indiscriminately. Instead, he asked technical questions, professional to professional, about distance, field of vision, the effect of wind and temperature on the trajectory of a bullet. Explosives, the Serb had detailed with detachment. Capable of bursting a head like a melon struck with a hammer, or rupturing guts with absolute efficacy. And how do you choose? Faulques asked. I mean, do you shoot at random or do you pick your targets? And then the Serb revealed something interesting. It's not random, he explained. Or at least not very often: maybe the reason why someone decides to cross there at just that time. The rest was up to him. Some he killed and others not. It was that easy. It depended on the way they walked, ran, or stopped. On the color of their hair, the way they moved, their attitude. On things that he associated with them when he saw them. The day before he had aimed at a young girl about fifteen or twenty meters away, and suddenly something she did very casually reminded him of his little niece—and at that point, the sharpshooter opened his billfold and showed Faulques a family photo. So I didn't shoot that one, and instead chose a woman nearby who was leaning out a window, and, who knows? maybe waiting to see how the girl who was walking so distractedly, so unprotected, was killed. That's why he said that randomness was relative. There was always something that decided things for this one or that one, operative difficulties aside, of course. It was more difficult, for example, to get a bead on children because they never stood still. The same was true of the drivers of cars passing by: sometimes they were moving too fast. Suddenly, in mid-explanation, the sniper had tensed, his features seemed to thin and his pupils contract as he leaned over the rifle, snugged the butt against his shoulder, put his right eye to the sight, and softly stroked the trigger. *Jägerei*, he had whispered in his bad German, muttering as if they could hear him below. Prey in view. A few seconds went by as the rifle described a slow circular movement toward the left. Then a single explosion; the butt kicked against his shoulder and Faulques was able to photograph a close-up of that tense, thin face covered with a few days' stubble, one eye shut and the other open, lips pressed together in an implacable line: just an ordinary man, with his selective criteria, his memories, antipathies and sympathies, photographed at the exact moment of killing. Faulques even took a second exposure when the sharpshooter took his cheek away from the rifle butt, looked into the lens of the Leica with icy eyes, and, after kissing the thumb and two fingers of the hand that had just pulled the trigger, gave the Serbian victory salute. You want me to tell you who I picked? he asked. Why I chose that target and not another? Faulques, who was measuring the light with his meter, did not want to know. My camera didn't photograph that, he said, so it doesn't exist. The Serb stared at him without a word, barely smiled, and then turned very serious. He asked if two days ago Faulques had driven by the Masarikov bridge at the wheel of a white Volkswagen with a shattered windshield and the words *Press-Novinar* taped with red adhesive over the hood. For an instant Faulques froze, then he put the light meter into his canvas bag and answered with another question whose answer he could guess. The Serb softly patted the Zeiss telescope on his rifle. Because I had you, he answered, in these sights for fifteen seconds. I had only two bullets left, and after thinking about it I told myself, I'm not going to kill that *glupan* today. That asshole.

14.

WHEN THE PAINTER OF BATTLES finished telling the story of the sharpshooter, Ivo Markovic sat thinking for a while, without commenting. They were inside the tower, drinking the Croatian's beer. Markovic on the lower steps of the spiral staircase and Faulques in a chair beside the table that held his paints.

"As you see," he said, "the uncertainty corresponds with the player, not the rules. Of the infinite possible trajectories of a bullet, only one happens in reality."

The Croatian nodded between sips. He was looking at the scar on his hand.

"Hidden and terrible laws?"

"Yes. Including the microscopic origin of irreversibility."

"I'm amazed that you claim to know about that."

Faulques again shrugged his shrug.

" 'Know' isn't the right word. Imagine a guy who doesn't know anything about chess but who goes every evening to the café to watch games . . ."

"Right. Sooner or later he will learn the rules."

"Or at least, learn they exist. What he will never be

able to know on his own, even if he watches all his life, is the number of possible games: one followed by one hundred and twenty zeros."

"I understand. You're talking about a game in which the rules are not the line of exit but the point of arrival . . . Isn't that so?"

"Damn. To be frank, that definition is very good."

Markovic set his beer can on the floor and took out a cigarette. He felt his pockets, looking for a match, and Faulques threw him a plastic lighter that was on the table. Keep it, he said. The Croatian caught it on the fly.

"So," he concluded through a mouthful of smoke. "I think I know now what you're doing here. In truth I suspected something like that but I wasn't capable of thinking it through that far. Although when I saw this"—he pocketed the lighter and gestured toward the mural—"I should have foreseen the ultimate consequences."

Faulques was hungry. If his strange visitor hadn't been there, he would have cooked a little pasta on the gas ring he had on the upper floor of the tower. He went upstairs, stepping between Markovic and the books, to look in the trunk where he kept clothing, tins of preserves, and the shotgun. There wasn't much left. Soon he would have to go to the village for supplies.

"And you think there isn't any way out?" the Croatian asked from below. "That we're governed by inevitable laws? The hidden rules of the universe?"

"It sounds extreme, put that way. But it's what I believe."

"Including the tracks that allow the hunter to follow the animal?"

"Absolutely."

Leaning over the railing, Faulques showed Markovic a tin of sardines and a loaf of cellophane-wrapped bread, and the Croatian nodded. After picking up another tin, two forks and two plates, the painter of battles came back down and set everything on paper napkins on a free corner of the table. The two men ate standing up, washing down the sardines with the remaining two, still cold, beers Markovic had brought.

"I respect tracks and hunters," Markovic emphasized between mouthfuls. "Maybe that sharpshooter, in his own way, is an artist, too."

Faulques laughed.

"Why not? In questions of art, the original work of the ego has greater social importance than philanthropy. Or that's what they say."

"Can you repeat that?"

The painter of battles said of course I can, and did. His guest mulled that over for a while and nodded with his mouth full, seeming almost to savor the idea. An artist, he repeated thoughtfully. Right for the times he lives in. The truth is that it would never have occurred to me to think of it in that way, señor Faulques.

"Well, or me," Faulques admitted. "It's taken me a few years to see it that way."

Halfway through his tin of sardines, the painter of battles felt the warning stabs of pain. Taking his time, he looked for tablets, swallowed two with a sip of beer, excused himself, and went outside, into the sun, where he leaned against the tower wall and waited for the pain to pass. When he went back in, the Croatian observed him with curiosity.

"Trouble?"

"At times."

They exchanged looks without commenting. Later, when they had finished eating, Faulques went to the upper level to brew coffee and returned with a steaming cup in each hand. The visitor had lighted another cigarette and was studying the mural at the place where the column of refugees was fleeing the burning city under the eye of the heavily armed guards, with their look of being halfway between medieval warriors and Futurist soldiers.

"There's a crack in the wall, up there," said Markovic.

"Yes, I know."

"What a shame," the Croatian shook his head, disturbed. "Damaged before it's finished. Although, at any rate . . ."

He fell silent, and Faulques could see his profile, all his attention absorbed by what he was contemplating, face upturned, chin unshaved, cigarette dangling from his lips, gray, attentive eyes running over the images on the wall, stopping on the beach where the ships were sailing away in the rain, and where, in the foreground, the boy contemplated his mother, who lay faceup, her thighs stained with blood. Aside from the painter of battles' professional memories, that woman owed a lot, in terms of composition, to a painting by Bonnard: *The Indolent Woman.* Although for the woman in Faulques' mural, "indolent" was not the right description.

Markovic was still studying the figure.

"Will you allow me a rude question?"

"Of course."

"Why is everything so geometrical, with so many diagonals?"

Faulques handed Markovic his cup of coffee, and drank a sip from his own.

"I believe that diagonals do a better job of establishing order. Every structure has its own code of movement. Its own traffic signals."

"Including war?"

"Yes. This painting is how I see it. It's a question of form, of law, or principle, or whatever we want to call it, set against disintegration into periods and commas, into blobs . . . Set against the disorder of color and of life. A fellow named Cézanne was the first one to see that."

"I don't know this Cézanne."

"Doesn't matter. I'm talking about painters. People I used to know nothing about, or scorned, and who with time I came to understand."

"Famous painters?"

"Old and modern masters. Some of their names are Piero della Francesca, Paolo Uccello, and Picasso, Braque, Gris, Boccioni, Chagall, Léger . . ."

"Oh, of course . . . Picasso."

Markovic stepped a little closer to the painting, leaning to get a better view of the details, cigarette in one hand and coffee cup in the other. I seem to remember, he said, that Picasso, too, had a big painting about war. *Guernica,* he called it. Although in fact it can't really be called a war painting. At least, not like this one. Isn't that right?"

"Picasso never saw a war in his life."

The Croatian looked at the painter of battles and nodded gravely. That he could understand. With intuition that surprised Faulques, he turned toward the hanged men in the trees, in the part drawn in charcoal on the white wall.

"And that other compatriot of yours, Goya?"

"That one did. He saw it and he suffered."

Again Markovic nodded, carefully studying the sketches. He paused for a long time at the dead child beside the column of refugees.

"Goya drew good illustrations of war, I think."

"His are the best engravings that have ever been made. No one saw war as he did, nor came as close to the darkness of the human condition . . . And finally he lost respect for all mankind and all academic conventions; not even the rawest photograph has gone that far."

"Then why is this painting so big?" Markovic's eyes were still on the dead child. "Why paint something that someone did better before you?"

"Each person has to paint his own thing. What he saw. What he sees."

"Before he dies?"

"Of course. Before he dies. No one should go without leaving a Troy blazing behind him."

"A Troy, you say?"

Markovic, who was now moving slowly along the wall, smiled pensively.

"You know something, señor Faulques? Thanks to you I no longer believe in the certainties held by people who have a house, a family, friends."

His smile revealed the gap in his teeth as he stopped

beside the group of warriors waiting to enter the combat, the area Faulques had been working on the day before. The afternoon light, as the sun began to descend, was pouring through the window, giving the scene an extraordinary clarity, making the armor shine as if it truly were metal, although that effect was owed to the fine lines of titanium white over a neutral gray, and to the repetition, in soft, slightly lighter touches, of the tones of burnished metal.

"They say that before you die," the Croatian commented, "you should plant a tree, write a book, and have a child. Once I had a child, but I don't have him now. And they burned the trees I had planted . . . Maybe I should paint that, señor Faulques. Do you think I would be capable of painting that?"

"I don't see why not. Everyone works things out the best way he can."

"And capable of collaborating on this one?"

"Yes, you can if you want."

The Croatian adjusted his glasses, and put his face close to the painting. He studied the weapons, the details of the helmets and gauntlets. Then he took one step back, looked around the entire wall, looked at the painter of battles, and gestured timidly toward the table with the brushes, tubes, and jars.

"May I?"

Faulques smiled a little, and nodded.

"Help yourself."

Markovic hesitated, set down his cup and cigarette, and finally pointed to the two men struggling on the ground, looking for chinks in the armor bristling with screws and nuts that made them look like robots. Faulques went to the table, opened one of the tightly sealed jars in which he kept small quantities of mixed paint, and put a little bluish-white paint on a number 6 brush.

"Let's make one of those knives gleam," he suggested. "All it takes is a fine line along the edge. You can brace yourself against the wall, the paint is dry."

He indicated the spot, handed the brush to Markovic, who, kneeling on the floor, and after studying the metal already painted with the white, traced a line along the edge of the knife one of the combatants held high above his head. He worked slowly and with great concentration, applying what was on the brush. After a while he stood up and handed the brush back to Faulques.

"What do you think?" he asked.

"Not bad. If you stand over here, you'll see that now the blade looks more dangerous."

"You're right."

"You want to paint something else?"

"No, thank you. That's enough."

Faulques washed the brush and set it to dry. The Croatian's attention was concentrated on the wall.

"Your soldiers look like machines, don't you think? With so many screws and all that metal." He turned toward the painter of battles as if he'd just been asked a question and was thinking about the right answer. "Killing machines?"

"You see it really isn't difficult. You just have to pay attention." Faulques gestured toward the mural. "My structure is compatible with common sense."

Markovic's face lighted up.

"So that's what it was."

"Of course."

"Your painting is filled with riddles, I think. With enigmas."

"All good ones are. Otherwise they'd be nothing but brushstrokes on a canvas or a wall."

"Do you think your painting is good?"

"No. It's mediocre. But I intend for it to look like the ones that are."

The Croatian picked up his coffee cup, drank a sip, and looked at Faulques with a frown of interest.

"So you're saying that every painting tells a story? Even the ones they call abstract; modern paintings and the rest?"

"The ones that interest me do tell a story. Look."

He went to the books stacked on the stairway, chose three, brought them to the table, and leafed through the pages until he found what he was looking for. One illustration was of a painting by Aniello Falcone, a classic seventeenth-century painter of battles: *Scene of Sacking Following a Battle.*

"What do you see in this painting?"

Markovic looked closely, scratching his head. He set the cup of coffee on the table and lighted another cigarette. I don't know, he said, exhaling smoke. There had been a hard fight, and now the victorious soldiers are taking clothing and jewels off the dead. The horseman with the armor is the leader, and he seems merciless. He also seems to be claiming for himself the women they're about to rape. At that point, the Croatian looked at Faulques. I see a story, he said. You're right.

"Now look at this painting," Faulques said.

"What is the painter's name?"

"Chagall. Tell me what you see."

"Well, I see . . . Uh . . . A painting that's a little abstract, right?"

"It isn't abstract. There are concrete human figures, objects. But all the same. Go on."

"All right. Well, it's . . . I don't know. Geometric like your mural there on the wall, although you don't exaggerate the angles as much or distort the look of persons or things. A man, a samovar, and a small couple dancing . . . Does that tell a story, too?"

"It does."

"What is the painting called?"

"Chagall put it at the bottom, in small letters: *The Soldier Drinks*. That soldier is Russian. He's come from the war, or is on his way to it, and he's so drunk that by now he can't tell vodka from tea. His cap has flown off his head; he's surprised to see a country girl he knows dancing on the table. And she's dancing, maybe, with the man who painted the painting."

Again Markovic scratched his brow, confused.

"A strange story, anyway."

"Everyone tells things in his own way. Besides, I've already told you that the soldier is soused. Now look at this painting . . . How do you like it?"

Markovic turned to it. He seems to be a capable fellow, Faulques thought. An interested and discreet pupil.

"Well, it's stranger yet. It's like some of those paintings you see on the walls in some neighborhoods. *In Italian,* it says at the bottom. Whose is it?"

"It was done by Jean-Michel Basquiat, a black Hispano-Haitian. He painted it in the eighties."

"It doesn't seem to be related to war."

"But it is. Not with cavalry charges, or drunken

soldiers, of course. It tells of another war different from the one you and I think of when we hear the word. Though they're not really that different. Do you see those inscriptions, and the circle on the left? Money, blood, *In God We Trust.* Liberty as a registered trademark. That painting, too, is talking about war, in its way. The slaves rebelling against Rome. Barbarians painting on the walls of the Capitolio with aerosol cans."

"That part I don't understand very well."

"It's all the same. Doesn't matter."

A memory flitted through his mind, painful and swift. Olvido's last job before she went off with him to war had been to photograph Basquiat for the magazine *One+Uno,* a few months before the graphic painter lost it completely, between an overdose of heroin and Charlie Parker tapes. Leaving the book open to the page with the Basquiat painting, the painter of battles drained his coffee. It was cold.

"Although in fact," Markovic suddenly commented, "it may be that I understand what he wants to say."

He had turned and was looking at Faulques, smoking, musing. And there's something, he added, that I would like for you to understand, too, señor Faulques. Using your own arguments. I'm talking about the story of a specific picture, the one of me. When it comes down to my life, you played a part in a process that you didn't initiate but that you influenced with your famous prize-winning photo. A photo that destroyed my life. Now I know enough to agree that it wasn't entirely the work of chance, since there are circumstances that brought you and me to that exact moment on that exact day. And as a consequence of the process begun by you, by me, by whoever, I'm here now. To kill you. Don't forget that.

Faulques held his gaze.

"I don't forget," he said. "Not for a minute."

The fact is, the Croatian continued in the same tone, that you can't hold any anger against me for that. You know? As I can't hold any against you. Just the opposite. I'm grateful to you for helping me understand things. From your point of view, the two of us are coincidences and determinations of those laws you mean to reflect in this tower after you tried, without success, to decipher them with your photographs. In fact, hatred and cruelty should have no place in this world. They're inadequate. Men destroy one another because the law of their nature, a serene and objective law, demands it. Isn't that true . . . ? In your opinion, intelligent people should kill one another when the time is right, like the executioner who carries out a sentence that means nothing to him . . . Is that it?

"More or less."

Markovic's eyes were like ice water.

"Well, I'm happy I've understood and that we're in agreement, because that is how I am going to kill you. There's nothing personal in it, really."

The painter of battles reflected on what he'd just heard. He was composed, as if he were considering the fate of a third person. To his surprise, he felt perfectly calm. The man before him was in the right: everything was as it should be. Right for the norms, or for the only norm. He looked at the painted wall and then again focused on his visitor. Markovic was serious, but nothing about him communicated threat or hostility. He seemed only to be waiting for an answer or a reaction. Expectant, tranquil. Courteous.

"Do you see it the way I do, señor Faulques?"

"Absolutely."

Of course, as the Croatian said then, it was more entertaining, thrilling, to kill out of good, solid hatred. More satisfactory, more common. With your blood boiling, howling with jubilation as you polished off your victim.

"It's like alcohol or sex," he added. "They're very calming. They bring relief. But for men like us who have spent a long time looking at the same scenery, that relief is a long way away. A broken razor in the rubble of a house, a bare mountain beyond barbed wire, the background of a painting you've been traveling toward your whole life . . . Places, remember, you can never go back to."

He looked around, as if to be sure he hadn't forgotten anything. Then he turned on his heel and went outside. Faulques followed him.

"One of these visits may be different," Markovic said.

"I suppose."

The Croatian tossed his cigarette on the ground and meticulously crushed it out with the toe of a boot. Then he looked the painter of battles squarely in the eye, without blinking, and for the first time held out his right hand. Faulques hesitated a moment and finally took it in his. It felt rough, strong. A countryman's hand. Hard and dangerous. Markovic turned to leave but paused. You should go down to the village, he said suddenly, his air thoughtful. And meet that woman from the boat. There's not much time left.

Faulques smiled. A gentle, sad smile.

"And what will happen to the painting . . . ? Who will finish it?"

Markovic revealed the gap in his teeth. His smile, almost timid, seemed an apology.

"I'm afraid it won't be finished. But the important thing is that you painted it. As for the rest of it, we'll finish it, you and I. In a different way."

15.

THE NEXT DAY FAULQUES WENT down to the village. He parked his motorcycle in a narrow street with no shade, squinting before the blinding perspective of white fronts of buildings stair-stepped down the hill toward the ochre mass of the ancient wall of the port. Then he went into the bank to take money from his account and on to pay his outstanding bill at the hardware shop where he ordered his paints. Then he slowly walked down to the fishing dock and lingered there awhile, looking at the boats tied up at the pier piled with nets. When behind him the clock in the town hall struck twelve, he went and sat beneath the awning of the nearest restaurant bar, the one that offered the best view of the inlet to the port and expanse of water, rippled by wind from the east, that reached to the gray line of Cabo Malo. He ordered a beer and sat there facing the sea and the empty pier where the tourist tender was usually docked, thinking about Ivo Markovic and about himself. About the last words the Croatian spoke before he left. *You should go down to the village. And meet that woman. There's not much time left.*

Meet that woman. Almost unconsciously, the corners of Faulques' mouth lifted in a smile. There were no women left to paint in the great circular fresco in the tower. They were all there; the raped woman with bloody thighs, the women grouped like a frightened flock under the rifles of the executioners, the one with African features staring in her death throes at the viewer, the woman in the very front opening her mouth to scream a silent howl of horror. And also Olvido Ferrara, in all the corners and in all the lines of the vast landscape that would have been impossible to have noticed, or composed, without her. As, for instance, in that red, black, and brown volcano that served as the vertex of the mural, the point at which all the lines converged, all the perspectives, all the complex and merciless plot lines of life and its chance and coincidences ruled by rigorous lines as straight as the trajectory of sinister arrows from the quiver of Apollo. He who in the Trojan War, as he drew back the arrow in his murderous bow—a lethal combination of perennial curves, angles, and straight lines—moved like the night. Obedient to the inescapable thread spun by the Fates.

Now I understand what you're looking for, Olvido had once commented. They were in Kuwait, an area only recently abandoned by Iraqi troops. They had gone in the day before with a mechanized North American unit, and were on the fifth floor of the Hilton; no electricity, no panes in the windows—they had plucked a key at random from behind the deserted counter of the concierge—with water from ruptured pipes running along the floor and down the stairs. They took off the spread covered with soot from burning petroleum and slept all night, exhausted, indifferent to the panorama of the burning oil wells and the booming of the last cannons. I understand at last, Olvido persisted—she was looking out the window, wearing one of Faulques' shirts and holding her camera in her hand as she gazed out over the city—and in the process I have invested time, kisses, and a lot of looking. Studying you as you move through catastrophes with the caution of a hunter, so reliable, so secure in what you are doing and not doing, as tight-lipped as an old soldier. Preparing each photo with your eyes before you make a move, evaluating in tenths of a second whether or not it's worth the trouble. Don't laugh, because that's what you do. I swear. And I also know what I know from feeling you explode in me as you hold me in your arms, how it is to have you there, deep inside me, finally relaxed in the only moment of your life in which you lower your guard. I see what you see. I observe you as you think before and after, but never while you're taking a photograph, because you know that otherwise you will never get it. My one doubt is whether I owe this horrible understanding of mine to contagion, as if it were some virus or secret and incurable illness. Whether I'm catching the war or if it was already in me and you have merely been the inciting agent, or witness. It's all something like what my grandmother—how well you two understood each other, the Bauhaus girl and the Zen archer—as she lined up her cauliflowers and lettuces in her garden, called gestalt: a complex structure that can be described only in its whole, as its parts are indescribable. Right? But you have a problem, Faulques. A serious problem. No photograph can capture what you're seeking. I am more practical, and I limit myself to collecting broken links: ruins with classic antecedents, a discovery of imbecilic, romantic literati revisited by still more imbecilic artists. But it isn't the aroma of the past that I'm looking for. I don't want to learn, or remember, only to cast off ties. Put in your psychopathic jargon, those deserted places, broken mechanisms and objects, are mathematical formulas that point the way. My way. A little flashing phosphorus in the meninges of the world. I don't pretend to solve the problem, understand it, or take it on. It's only a part of the journey toward where I am going: a place I will recognize when I reach it. Your case is different: you are in that place for your lifetime, and you were born suspecting it was there. But I doubt that you will see it this way. How many times have critics and the public judged photos of beauty? Remember the dead Che Guevara, as beautiful as a Christ in Freddy Alborta's photograph. The beauty of Salgado's outcasts, the beauty of Gerva Sánchez's mutilated children, the beauty of that African woman you photographed as she died, the beauty of the photos Roman Vishniac took in the ghettos of Poland, the beauty of the six thousand photographs taken by Ehem Ein, one of each prisoner, including children, who were going to be executed by the Khmer Rouge. The beauty of *all* those beautiful people we knew were going to die. No, my love. Do you remember that old Kodak ad? You press the button, we do the rest. In a world in which horror is sold as art, in which art is born with the hope of being photographed, in which coexisting with images of suffering has no relation to conscience or compassion, war photos have no meaning. The world does the rest: it appropriates them as soon as the camera shutter clicks. *Clic, oop hah, thanks, ciao.* At least a photo is more effective than a fleeting image on the television. It doesn't race by so indiscriminately. But not even there. It may be that for what you want to do, painting can offer that opportunity—but far away from the public and its interpretations. Painting has its own focus, frame, and perspective, qualities impossible to achieve through the lens of a camera. Although I doubt that any painter has ever achieved it all. Goya? Maybe. It isn't the same to make a transfer from reality to canvas as it is from retina to canvas. You know what I mean? It's one thing to reproduce an aspect of life, imitating it or interpreting it: pleasure, beauty, horror, pain, things like that. All that takes is a good eye, a matter of technique, and of talent. It would be something else to be guided by the fatalism of the retina. To paint horror with cold lines—she was still at the window, naked beneath the man's shirt, observing the umbrella of black smoke that covered the city, and from time to time half lifting her camera as if to take a photo, but immediately lowering it. A homicidal landscape where engendering executioners was no virtue. But let's see who the daring person is who sees that, and paints it.

Faulques shut off that memory with a sip of the beer the waiter had just brought. Then he looked to the east, where the pier blocked out the sea. He heard the distant sound of engines coming from the other side of the breakwater, and at that moment saw a red-and-black smokestack moving along behind it toward the beacon at the port entry. A few moments later, the tender was crossing the inlet and preparing to dock near the terrace. After a quick, precise maneuver, a sailor leaped ashore to secure the mooring lines around the bollards and lower the gangplank, and some twenty passengers left the boat. The painter of battles watched with curiosity, trying to identify the woman with the loudspeaker as the tourists scattered. Finally a smaller group was left, and in it one woman stood out, still young, blond, tall, strong, with a pleasant face. She was heading in the direction of the tourist office, wearing leather sandals and a white linen dress that emphasized her tan, with the strap of her large purse looped over her head and across her chest. She seemed tired. Faulques saw her open the office door and go in. He stayed where he was, watching the tourists as they moved along the dock shooting their last photographs or videos among the fishing nets beside the boats, with the background of the port and the open sea beyond the inlet.

Tourists. Public. And again came memories. We do the rest, said the Kodak ad Olvido had referred to. The association made Faulques smile. For some time he had kept trying the photography, or almost. As a final objective, it would have resulted in a mixed and unsatisfactory formula, but it was actually a preparation, a warm-up, training for the project developing in his head. A way to sharpen his eye, obliging him to see photography and painting in a different light. After the change of course the ditch on the Borovo Naselje highway had imposed on his life—he had held back the secondary effects with two years of intense work that included Bosnia, Rwanda, and Sierra Leone—Faulques had left war photojournalism behind. The decision was made after a long, cumulative process: the raw earth of Portman, the black cloud over Kuwait, Dubrovnik burning in the distance and Olvido's body stained with red light, and even later, cold, solitary nights in a room with blown-out windows in the Sarajevo Holiday Inn, with a panoramic view of urban geometry outlined in explosions and fires, had all set Faulques on the path—with the inevitability of his straight and converging lines—to the hall of a tribunal. There, one winter morning at the midpoint of that war, a Bosnian Serb named Borislav Herak, an old member of the Boica brigade of ethnic cleansing, had related with meticulous coolness, massive executions aside, the story of his thirty-two personal assassinations—he had trained earlier by beheading hogs in a slaughterhouse—including the deaths of sixteen women, students, and housewives whom he, as his comrades had done to hundreds more, had raped and killed after taking them from the Sanjak hotel-prison that had been converted into a whorehouse for Serbian troops. And when before the tribunal and the journalists, Herak, with suitable mimicry, told of killing a young woman of twenty—"I ordered her to take off her clothes and she screamed, but I hit her again and she took them off, so I raped her and gave her to my companions, and after we all had raped her we took her in a car to Mount Zuc, where we shot her in the head and threw her into the bushes"—Faulques, who had Herak's head in his viewfinder, an insignificant, common face that in times of peace would have been considered almost pitiful, slowly lowered his camera without pressing the shutter release, with the certainty that no photograph in the world, not even the image and sound that the television cameras were recording, could reflect or interpret that reality. Geological amorality, Olvido had said once in regard to something else, although it may have been about the same thing: impossible to photograph the indolent yawn of the Universe. And that was how Faulques' thirty years as a war photographer came to an end. The inertia of those three decades carried him to other scenes of war for a time, but by then he had lost the last traces of his faith in what the lens showed, the old hope that had animated his fingers on the shutter release and rings for focus and aperture. Later—Olvido would never know how much she had had to do with it all—Faulques spent a lot of time wandering through museums, putting together a collection he was making of battle paintings and of the public viewing them, a strange series, the purpose of which he himself was gradually discovering. After an exhaustive labor of research and documentation, armed with the correct permissions and a Leica without flash or tripod, a 35-mm lens and the proper color film for shooting with natural light and at low speeds, the former war photographer sat for several days in front of each of the sixty-two paintings of battles he had chosen from a long list drawn from nineteen museums in Europe and America, and photographed a painting and the people he found before it, individual visitors and groups, students and guides, at moments when the room was empty or when it was so crowded that he could scarcely see the painting. He worked for four years, selecting, discarding, until he had gathered a last series of twenty-three photographs, ranging from the crazed eyes of a man knifing a Mameluke in *The Second of May,* barely glimpsed among the heads of the people thronging the Goya hall of the Prado museum, to Bruegel's *Mad Meg* in darkness, with the plundering warrior and his sword on one side, and on the other the profile of a scholar studying the painting in a nearly empty room in the Mayer van den Bergh museum in Antwerp. The final result of it all had been the collection entitled *Morituri:* his last published work. The shortest route between two points: from man to horror. A world in which the only logical smile was that of the skulls painted by old masters on canvas and board. And when the twenty-three photographs were ready, he realized that he, too, was ready. So he put down his cameras forever, called on everything he had learned about painting in his youth, and looked for the appropriate site.

The woman from the tourist boat came out of the office and started toward the terrace, on her way to the parking lot. Faulques observed that she stopped to talk with the port watchman, and that she said hello to all the waiters. She seemed talkative, and she had a pretty smile. Her hair, very blond and long, was pulled into a ponytail. Attractive despite being plump, carrying an extra kilo or two of weight. When she walked by the table where he was sitting, the painter of battles looked at her eyes. Blue. Sunny.

"Hello," he said.

The woman stared at him, at first surprised, then curious. About thirty, Faulques calculated. She said "Hello" in return, looked as if she was going to walk on, but hesitated, undecided.

"Do we know each other?" she asked.

"I know you." Faulques had got to his feet. "At least I know your voice. I hear it every day at exactly one o'clock."

She looked at him more closely, confused. She was almost as tall as he. Faulques waved his hand toward the tender and the coast in the direction of Cala del Arráez. After an instant, she smiled a big smile.

"Of course!" she said. "The painter of the tower."

"*A well-known painter who is embellishing an entire interior wall with a large mural.* I would like to thank you especially for the words 'well-known' and 'embellishing.' In any case, you have a pleasant voice."

The woman burst out laughing. She smelled slightly of sweat, Faulques noticed. Clean sweat, from the sea and the sun. Part of her job, he imagined, from entertaining tourists from ten o'clock in the morning.

"I hope I haven't caused you any problems," she said. "I'd be truly sorry if I've bothered you . . . But we don't have many local celebrities we can show off to visitors."

"Don't worry. The road to my place is long, inconvenient, and uphill. Almost no one comes."

He invited her to sit down and she did. She ordered a Coca-Cola from the waiter, lit a cigarette, and told Faulques a few details of her job. She was from a city inland and she took care of the office in Puerto Umbría during the tourist season. In the winter she worked as an interpreter and translator for consulates, embassies, courts, and immigration offices. She was divorced and she had a five-year-old daughter. And her name was Carmen Elsken.

"You're German by birth?"

"Dutch. I've been living in Spain since I was a little girl."

They chatted for fifteen or twenty minutes. A courteous, inconsequential conversation, not overly interesting to Faulques, except for the fact that this woman was the owner of the voice he had been hearing every day for a long time. So he let her talk, maintaining a relative silence from which he emerged only to ask polite questions. At any rate, it was inevitable that their chat would eventually turn to him and to his work in the tower. They say in the village that it's original, Carmen Elsken commented. Very interesting. An enormous painting that covers the whole inside wall and that you've been working on it for nearly a year. It's a shame that it can't be visited, but I understand why you would prefer to be left alone. Even so—she observed him with renewed curiosity—I would really like to see that painting someday.

Faulques hesitated a moment. Well, why not, he said to himself. She was pleasant. Her compatriot Rembrandt would not have hesitated to paint her as a bourgeois woman with warm flesh and promising neckline. Her hair was pulled back tight and smooth at her forehead and temples, in nice contrast with her skin. The painter of battles had nearly forgotten what it felt like to have a woman close by. The image of Ivo Markovic flitted through his head. *There's not much time left,* the Croatian had said. *You should go down to the village.* A time-out to reflect. A truce before the final conversation. The painter of battles studied the blue eyes across the table. It was his nature to be observant, and he noticed a spark of interest in them.

He put his right hand on the table and noticed that she looked at it when he set it down.

"Starting tomorrow, I have things to do, but this afternoon might be possible . . . If you want to make the climb, you'll see the tower. But a car can go only halfway. The rest has to be done on foot."

Carmen Elsken hesitated about four seconds. Yes, she would come up, with great pleasure. Would sometime around five be all right? The tourist office closed then.

"Five is perfect," Faulques replied.

The woman stood, and he stood up as well, shaking the hand she offered. A warm, frank clasp. He noticed that the spark of interest was still in her blue eyes.

"Around five," she repeated.

He studied her as she walked away, the blond hair, the white skirt of her dress swishing over her broad hips and tanned legs. Then he sat back down, ordered another beer, and looked around, suspecting that he might see Ivo Markovic standing somewhere nearby, grinning from ear to ear.

Faulques continued to scan the sea and the distant line of the coast toward Cabo Malo, while Carmen Elsken slowly faded from his thoughts. The sun was beginning to descend in the sky and the intense light gave objects a precise clarity, a special beauty, like a glaze that instead of making colors more dense, clarified them, gave them incomparable transparency. Beauty, he said to himself, returning to his memories; that was one of the possible words, but only one of them. He had also reflected on that once or twice with Olvido, in a different time. Beautiful landscapes didn't always signify light and life, or a future beyond five o'clock in the afternoon—or any other hour humans set with inexplicable optimism. Faulques' thoughts again turned to Ivo Markovic and his lips twisted in a brief, cruel grimace. He and Olvido had had that conversation as they stood before some Turner watercolors in the Tate Gallery in London: Venice at dawn, looking toward San Pietro de Castello or from the Hotel Europa, could be an idyllic scene when viewed through the eyes of a mid-nineteenth-century English painter, but could also be the blurred line—the watercolor with its ambiguous tones was perfect for that—between the beauty of a dawn and the representation in art that the varied palette of the Universe, the fascinating chromatic specter of horror, placed at the disposition of any observer standing in the right spot. Lines of clouds could streak across the sea on the eastern horizon of the morning like the announcement of a perfect new day of light and shapes; but they could also be like the smoke that, blown by an offshore breeze, carried the smell of death from a devastated city—*smell of war,* Olvido used to say, touching her clothing with a horrified smile: I'll carry this scent to my death. In the same vein, the red, orange, and yellow light bathing the campanile of San Marco at the first explosion of day seemed to a retina previously imprinted with other, similar conflagrations closer to the fleeting splendor of cannon fire than to the slow, delicious affirmation—not always exact, in the experience of the now painter of battles—that following night comes the day, and beauty. There were nights without a dawn, the last shadows that were the end of everything, and days painted with a palette of shadows.

Faulques drank another sip of beer, his eyes lost in the thin, distant gray line that disappeared into the sea. Those Venetian watercolors were also related in his memory with different circumstances. Among others, with the cold, diffuse light of an autumn dawn on the outskirts of Dubica, the old Yugoslavia, waiting for the moment to cross the Sava River with a group of soldiers. Olvido and he had spent the night shivering in the storeroom of an abandoned factory with a hundred and ninety-four Croatians on their way to fight, come dawn. At first Olvido was welcomed with the usual male deference—in that day there still was some—toward a woman who, of her own volition, found herself in the midst of a war. In the glare of their flashlights, the soldiers looked her over with curiosity. What are you doing here? you could read in their amazed smiles, in the low-voiced talk among themselves. Olvido and he had looked for a reasonably comfortable place to settle into, and some young men had given them, from their provisions, a can of pineapple packed in syrup. Then, as time went by, the soldiers sank back into their personal isolation, the self-absorbed silence of someone who is approaching a crucial encounter with fate and destiny. Some thirty of them were nearly children; they were fifteen or sixteen years old and they had grouped around a teacher from their school with whom they had enlisted in a block. The teacher was a young man about twenty-eight who'd been promoted to officer status, and who, despite the steel helmets, weapons, and military belting stuffed with ammunition and grenades, moved among them with the look of the teacher he had been until only a few weeks before, a man whom the parents of those same boys had begged to look after them as he had in school. He went from one to the next, talking in a low, calm voice, checking their equipment, giving them cigarettes and, to the older ones, sips from a bottle of *rakia,* or with a felt-tip pen writing on a shirt, a helmet, or the back of a hand the blood type of those who knew it. Faulques and Olvido had spent the night lying very close together to keep warm, not opening their mouths even though the cold kept them from sleeping, sensing on their closed eyelids the beam of some flashlight illuminating them for an instant. The first light of dawn finally filtered through the holes in the roof and the broken windows of the storeroom, and in that ghostly darkness the soldiers began to get to their feet and go outside toward the dirty light that outlined their bodies like the silhouettes in Venetian watercolors, dozens of men and boys looking around like dogs sniffing the air before heading toward a horizontal line of fog, a slightly lighter gray that seemed to float just above the ground; moisture rising from the nearby river was in the indecision of dawn shading into a darker, somber, irregular smudge, a configuration of straight lines and surfaces broken into strange angles: the destroyed bridge over the Sava the soldiers had to cross, making use of its debris, and then climb a long slope between two hills and attack Dubica, invisible on the other side. Rubbing limbs stiff with cold, Faulques and Olvido started toward the river with the others, their cameras inside their camera bags since there wasn't enough light to shoot. It looks like one of those Turners, she'd said. Remember? Shadows in the dawn light. But the damned Englishman had forgotten to paint the cold. She had buttoned up the neck of her knee-length jacket, and after slinging the camera bag over her shoulder had smiled at Faulques. There will never, she said suddenly in the middle of that strange smile—and she said it with melancholy—be another war like this one. She kissed him on the cheek, repeated the word "never" in a lower voice, and set out after the soldiers. From those silhouettes that looked as if they were suspended above the mantle of fog covering the riverbank came, first only one, then two or three, and finally multiplied all around them, the sound of bolts being drawn on weapons, *clic clac.* There was a hint of orange and gold in the sky to the east as they waded into the waist-deep water and, with the help of the rope strung during the night, crossed the river on the twisted remains of the bridge. And on the other side, when they began climbing the slope between the two hills, soaking wet from the waist down, their feet squishing inside their boots, the bluish-gray light grew strong enough that Faulques, with the aperture of one camera open to the maximum—f 1.4 exposure on the lens and 1/60 shutter speed—could photograph the soldiers dividing into two groups, following their officers toward the hill on the right or the one on the left, stubborn, empty, brave, tense, expressionless, distrustful, distorted, cautious, terrified, uneasy, serene, indifferent faces. In sum, every possible variation among men confronting the same test in that light a watercolor painter would have classified as extraordinarily beautiful, light that like an anticipatory shroud wrapped men who were on the verge of death in subtle, delicate tones. Faulques looked for Olvido and saw her among the soldiers, walking four or five meters to his left, with her wet jeans pasted to her legs, the black, military-cut coat buttoned up high, rubber bands holding her braids, and her cameras still in the camera bag over her shoulder, as if shooting photos was the furthest thought from her mind, the excuse she didn't need in that dawn of equivocal and terrible beauty. And when they were farther up the slope and on the other side of the hills they heard the reverberation of shots and explosions, and the soldiers around them clenched their jaws and held the weapons they were carrying more tightly, crouching lower and lower as they neared the top, she began to look around her, to focus on the nearby faces with an intense and pitiless curiosity, as if she were seeking silent answers to questions that could be resolved only in an uncertain dawn like that one, in the medium of a cosmic watercolor in which each silhouette, including her own, was a miserable sketch. Then mortar fire burst from just behind the peak of the hill, and an officer—the last reflex of the male protecting the female before turning his back and crossing his own shadowy line—turned toward Olvido and said *Stop, Stop,* indicating with energetic gestures that she should stay where she was. She obeyed without protesting, kneeling down with her cameras still in her bag, her eyes fixed on the soldiers continuing forward, on the teacher who was climbing the slope with his boys, shoulders hunched and faces pale and contorted in the ambiguous morning light. She stayed where she was, on her knees, while Faulques, who also had halted, had changed his shutter speed and aperture as the sun crowned the hills that smoke from the explosions had encircled with a dusty, golden halo and was beginning to photograph the first men coming back from the peak, or being brought back by comrades, leaving long red streaks on the ground, limping, pressing dressings and bandages to their wounds, spattered with mud and blood and shredded by shrapnel, horrified, blinded men with their hands covering their faces, stumbling down the slope. And Olvido was still kneeling when Faulques got up and ran a little farther up the hill, crouched, and then ran another stretch in order to get a profile shot of the teacher with his arms around the shoulders of two of his boys who were dragging him along, his feet plowing two furrows in the wet grass and half of his chin torn away by shrapnel. And behind them came more of the boys, crying, screaming, or silent, wounded or untouched, some alone, with no weapons, some helping others covered with blood, more scarlet trails crisscrossing in the watercolor some meticulous landscape artist was composing with painstaking care at his Olympian easel. And when Faulques, rewinding his third roll of film, looked toward Olvido again, he saw that she had finally taken out her camera and with her back to the scene was photographing the deserted and destroyed bridge that had sunk to the bed of the lead-colored river, the precarious road they had left behind between the two banks, as if it were there, and not in the shattered men withdrawing from the hills, that she found the key image, the explanation she had come to look for. That was how Faulques knew that she was close to finding it, and that she would not be at his side much longer, because time, too, had its ancient rules. *Arithmós kinesios.* The arithmetic of movement according to the before and after. Especially after. And a photographer—she liked to repeat the phrase she had heard from Faulques' lips—never belongs to the group he appears to belong to. Until then, despite everything, he had held the absurd hope that with time she would become more fully his: sleepy eyes seen every morning, a body declining at his side, in his hands, day after day. A serene old age, remembering. But that morning, when he saw her turn her mud-spattered face toward the bridge and slowly raise the camera, seeking the image of the dangerous road they had left behind—the photograph of the *before* of the arithmetic of movement that had brought them to the riverbank where men were dying—Faulques in turn looked toward the *after,* and saw only his own past. That was how he learned that they would never grow old together, and that she would travel on to other places and other arms. A man, he remembered having heard more than once, believes he is a woman's lover, when in truth he is only her witness. *Arithmós kinesios.* Faulques was fearful when he thought of having to return to the solitude that awaited him in the words "before" and "after," but he was even more fearful that Olvido would survive that last war.

16.

HE DIDN'T SEE IVO MARKOVIC in the village or on the way back to the tower. He left his bike beside the shed and took a look around, suspicious: the small stand of pines, the edge of the cliff, the loose rocks on the slope that led down to the cove and the pebbled beach. Not a sign of the Croatian. The sun, already past its apogee in the early hours of the afternoon, cast on the ground the motionless shadow of the painter of battles, who couldn't decide whether or not to go inside the tower. Something in his old professional instinct, trained to move through hostile territory, told him to be careful where he set his feet. Again he looked all around, alert to signs of danger. He was near—Markovic himself had warned him the day before—the dark line.

The inside of the tower smelled of tobacco. Of snuffed-out butts. That was strange, for the windows were open and before he left Faulques had emptied the mustard jar his visitor used as an ashtray. He was sure of that, he decided, perplexed, looking at the remains of the three cigarettes. He leaned over to sniff them and frowned. Smoked only recently. The alarm sounded louder in his brain. He was moving with caution, slowly, as if Markovic might be hiding there. That wasn't reasonable, he thought as he went up the spiral stairway. It wasn't Markovic's style. Nevertheless, until he was upstairs and certain he was alone in the tower, the painter of battles was not comfortable. He sat down on his cot and looked for further signs of the Croatian. He had been there, no doubt about that, while Faulques was down in the village. A sudden thought made him get up and open the trunk where he kept the shotgun. It wasn't there, nor were the shells. Besides poking around as he pleased, Markovic had taken precautions. And hadn't even taken the trouble to hide it.

The pain came, still slight, with no treachery this time. It affirmed itself gradually, loyal to a certain point, warning him in advance of the stabs that soon would follow. And along with the pain, or its prelude, also came the right dose of indifference. To hell with it, Faulques concluded as he came down the stairs. Everything had its good side and its bad: a street, a ditch, a pain. That, specifically, condemned him to certain things and put him on his guard for others. Markovic was becoming just one more element in the landscape. A question of priorities. Of time and time left. And when the true, the intense pain finally struck with a spasm that numbed his waist, the painter of battles had already shaken two tablets from the box and swallowed them with a glass of water. All that remained was to wait. So he squatted down, back against the wall—the dog chewing on a cadaver, sketched in charcoal and still unpainted, was just behind his head—gritted his teeth, and waited, patient, as the shooting pains reached their climax then grew further apart, and weaker, until they disappeared. And in the meantime, with his gaze absorbed by the part of the mural in front of him—Hector bidding Andromache farewell before the combat, painted at the left side of the door—he remembered something he'd heard Olvido say in Rome: *Taci e riposa: qui se spegne il canto.*

He slowly shook his head as he repeated those words in a low voice, through clenched teeth, never taking his eyes from the mural. Be quiet and rest: the song ends here. It was the first line of a poem by Andrea de Chirico that Olvido liked a lot. She had first mentioned it in an apt place—Andrea was the brother of Giorgio de Chirico—and at that moment Olvido and Faulques had been visiting the painter's home in Rome. They walked through the Piazza di Spagna, a few paces from the steps of the Trinità dei Monti, and at number 31—an old palace converted into apartments—she stopped, looked up toward the windows of the fourth and fifth floors, and said: My father brought me here when I was little to visit the elderly don Giorgio and Isabella. Let's go up. The house, under the direction of a foundation, had not yet been turned into a museum, but the porter showed himself vulnerable to Olvido's smile and a tip, and for half an hour they had the pleasure of exploring: high ceilings with stains of moisture, parquet floor creaking beneath their feet, a little cart with dusty bottles of grappa and Chianti, the dining room with still lifes on the walls—*stilleben,* Olvido murmured, silent lifes—the television where de Chirico had sat for hours watching images with no sound. Beside paintings from the neoclassical period were disturbing, faceless mannequins whose shadows lengthened among melancholy greens, ochres, grays, empty spaces that little by little had been growing smaller, as if over time the painter had begun to fear the shiver of the absurd and the nothingness he himself evoked. And before a 1958 canvas that reproduced the red glove he'd painted forty-four years before in *Enigma of Fatality*—although any question of time was suspect in an artist who sometimes falsified the dates of his own works—Olvido, pensively contemplating the painting, murmured in Italian the line about quiet and rest, and the song ends here. Of your life. Of the ancient lament. Then she looked at Faulques with deeply sad eyes, and in the white, ghostly Roman light illuminating the house, told him that it hadn't looked like that back then, that there had been more furniture and old paintings in the salon, and upstairs in the studio, a kind of automaton or enormous, sinister mannequin like the ones the artist painted in his early period, that had frightened her when she was young. She said that nodding her head, and added, Yes, I'm serious, Faulques. That night after my father brought me here—we usually stayed at the Hassler, near here—I couldn't sleep. Every time I closed my eyes I saw those *manichini*, like someone who discovers a cruel smile on the face of a wooden doll. Maybe that's why I never liked Pinocchio. After she'd said that, Olvido stood back from the canvas and paused to look all about her, deep in thought. There are two of de Chirico's paintings, she suddenly commented, that are special. I'm sure you know them, or you should, because one of them reminds me of your photographs: it's filled with rulers, triangles, and drafting tools, and it's called *Melancholy of Departure*. Do you know the one I mean? Of course you do. It's in the Tate in London. The other one is called *Enigma of Arrival*. Interesting, don't you think? She was very serious as she said that, and she reached up to stroke Faulques' face with affection, but said nothing. Later she'd walked alone through the rooms as he followed behind, watching her, spying on the image of a little girl who had moved through that house holding her father's hand and passing a strange and motionless ancient of days sitting in front of a television with no sound.

When the pain was gone, the sedative, as always, left its residue of gentle lucidity. Faulques got to his feet, eyes still fixed on Hector and Andromache. He went to the table, prepared his brushes and paints, and set to work on that part of the mural. He went from darkness to light; brilliant natural light through the open door—sun illuminating the inside of the tower, reflected from the bright golden rectangle creeping across the floor—was falling on the distant reddish light from the erupting volcano slightly to his left, on the other side and above the battlefield where the caballeros were engaged with their lances or awaiting the moment to enter the fray. Between those two lights, in the upper background, cooled with layers of blue and gray with a whitish glaze that accentuated the effect of distance, rose the steel-and-glass towers of the modern city, the new Troy before which, in the foreground, life-size images—Priam, his son, and his wife—were making their farewells. And you, Andromache, bathed in tears—the painter of battles murmured to himself—you will be carried away by some Achaean in bronze armor. For this scene, Faulques had studied to the point of obsession; first in person in the church of San Francesco de Arezzo, and then in what books he could find the figures of the two young people at one side of the *Death of Adam* painted by Piero della Francesca on the upper right part of the main chapel. Like the paintings of Paolo Uccello, those fifteenth-century frescoes had a direct relation to his work in the tower; especially *Constantine's Dream*—Hector's weapons were to some degree inspired by those of one of the guards—the *Battle of Heraclitus,* and *Constantine's Victory over Maxentius.* Faulques' Andromache was inspired by the young girl in the painting by Piero della Francesca—bared shoulder and breast, the child in her arms, the clothes in geometrical disorder, as if she'd only recently risen from her couch, and especially the sad gaze fixed on something beyond the warrior's shoulder. That expression seemed to run the length of the battlefield to the stream of refugees abandoning the burning city, as if the woman could, before the fact, recognize herself in the other women: the conqueror's booty. And before her, fearsome with gun and an array of ancient and modern armament, steel helmet, segmented gray armor somewhere between medieval and Futurist—what's given, you take; Orozco and Diego Rivera again unmercifully pillaged—Hector was raising a metal gauntlet toward the frightened boy child struggling in his mother's arms. And on the ground, the blending of three imperfect shadows formed a single shadow as dark as a presage.

Faulques took a few steps back with the brush in

his teeth, weighing the result. It would do, he told himself with satisfaction. And the light at that hour of the afternoon did the rest. He washed the brush, set it to dry, chose another, broader one and, mixing his paints directly on the wall, worked on Hector's face, applying white and blue over sienna to intensify the foreshortening in the lower part, darkening the shadow of the helmet on the neck. That reinforced the warrior's air of stoic strength, the cold tones contrasted to the warm, harmonically graduated values of the body and face of the woman, the resigned, rigid, almost military mien of the man constrained by rules. For I say, the painter of battles whispered again, there is no man who has evaded his destiny. Faulques knew that better than anyone. One of his early photographic images of war was in fact related: the son of Priam and his wife transcended the scholarly translations of classical Greek; they had faces, voices, authentic tears, and, with precise symmetry—coincidence was impossible—they also spoke the tongue of Homer. The first time Faulques had heard the true lament of Andromache was when he was twenty-three, in Nicosia. That day, at the beginning of a war, beneath a sky filled with Turkish paratroopers descending over the city as the radio crackled *Report to your barracks,* Faulques had photographed hundreds of men telling their women good-bye before rushing to the recruitment centers. One of those photos was on magazine covers halfway around the world: in violently contrasting tones in the horizontal, early morning, light, a Greek with a tormented face, unshaven, shirt barely tucked into his trousers, was hugging his wife and children while a second man with similar features, perhaps his brother, tugged at his arm, urging him to hurry. In the middle distance was a car with its doors open, a distant column of smoke, and an old man with a large white mustache aiming his hunting gun toward the sky, firing futile shots at the Turkish fighter-bombers.

Carmen Elsken presented herself at five-fifteen. Faulques heard her coming. He washed his hands, put on a shirt, and went out to meet her. She was admiring the view, looking over the cleft in the cliff above the cove to see from there the place the tender passed every day. Her hair was loose on her shoulders, she was wearing an ankle-length dress with spaghetti straps, and the same sandals she'd had on in the morning. Pretty place, she said. Calm and very pretty. Then she smiled. I think I envy you, she added. At least a little. Living here would be unique. The painter of battles considered the nuances of the word. Yes, he replied finally. Maybe so. He looked at the sea, looked at her again, and saw that she was studying him with the same curiosity she had shown on the terrace of the bar. He also noted that she was wearing light makeup on her eyes and lips. He turned toward the pines, pensive, speculating whether Ivo Markovic might be around. Then he took Carmen Elsken inside the tower, to the large mural where, after her eyes adjusted from the light outside, she froze. Overwhelmed.

"I wasn't expecting this."

Faulques didn't ask what she *had* been expecting. He simply waited, patient. The woman crossed her bare arms, rubbing them a little, as if the place, or the painting, made her feel cold. I don't understand it too well, she said after a moment. But I think it's extraordinary. It's impressive, I promise you that. Very. Does it have a name?

"No."

That was all the painter of battles said. She, too, said nothing, and after a while she walked along the circular wall, observing every detail. She stopped a long time before the woman with bloody thighs, and before the men on the ground stabbing each other. The city in flames also caught her attention, for she stood there a long while before turning toward Faulques. She seemed confused.

"Is this what you see?"

"What are you referring to?"

"I don't know. To whatever it is . . . To what you're painting."

"It's just a mural. An old building decorated with history."

"This isn't just historical, it seems to me. It's ancient and modern at the same time. It's . . ."

She interrupted herself, searching for the right word. Faulques waited. He looked at the woman's low neckline. Full, tanned breasts. Unconfined. The straps on her naked shoulders seemed a fragile support for that dress.

"Terrible," she ventured finally.

Faulques smiled gently.

"It isn't terrible," he said. "It's life, that's all. One part of it."

The blue eyes now seemed very vigilant. Carmen Elsken studied his eyes and lips. Looking there for the explanation of the images painted on the wall.

"You must have lived a strange life," she said suddenly.

The painter of battles smiled again, this time inside. In fact he had. The Ivo Markovics and the Faulqueses, their retinas imprinted, could not appreciate that point of view. This was how people who hadn't been there were going to see it. Or more precisely, he rectified, looking at the half-painted cement-and-glass towers—those who thought, mistakenly, that they hadn't.

"No stranger than yours, or anyone's, really."

She reflected on what he'd said, surprised, and shook her head. She seemed to be rejecting an intolerable hypothesis.

"I never saw this."

"The fact that you haven't seen it doesn't mean it isn't there."

Carmen Elsken's lips were parted, her eyes still smiling but a little disconcerted. The full skirted cotton dress, Faulques noticed, favored her too broad hips.

"Have you always been a painter?"

"Not always."

"And what did you do before that?"

"Photographs."

She asked what kind of photographs, and he pointed to *The Eye of War,* which was still on the table among the painting materials. She leafed through a few pages and looked up, surprised.

"Are these yours?"

"Yes."

She turned more pages. Then slowly she closed the book and stood with her head lowered, thinking.

Now I understand, she said. She gestured toward the mural and looked inquisitively at Faulques.

"I'm painting," he said, "the photo I was never able to get."

She had moved to the wall. She stopped in front of the woman at the head of the line of refugees opening her mouth to scream, her face contorted under the icy stare of the soldier.

"You know what? There's something about you I don't like."

Faulques smiled judiciously.

"I think I know what you're referring to."

"That's what I don't like. The fact that you know what I'm referring to."

She was staring at him intently, unblinking, and her eyes didn't look sunny any longer. After a time she turned back to the painting.

"There's something evil here."

She was referring to the scene of the boy crying beside his raped mother. An inverted pietà, Faulques thought suddenly. He'd never caught that before, not even while he was painting it. Maybe it had taken a woman's presence—a real flesh-and-blood woman—for the image to take on its full meaning. Like that time in the Prado when a visitor standing right beside him had had a heart attack in front of van der Weyden's *Deposition,* and with the milling crowd, the doctor, the sanitation workers who came to take away the corpse, the stretcher, and the oxygen apparatus, the room had all of a sudden had a different feel, as if it were a Wolf Vostell *happening*.

"Please understand. It isn't that I don't find you likeable," Carmen Elsken was saying. "Just the opposite. You're an interesting man. A handsome man, besides, if you'll allow me. How old are you . . . ? Fifty?"

Faulques didn't answer. The painted images on the wall were absorbing his attention. Intuited symmetries that were suddenly taking on substance. A precise network on which he had placed each brushstroke, each moment of his memory, each angle of existence. The child's face suggested the features of the soldier-executioner guarding the refugees. The mother lying on the ground was repeated to infinity in the line. Cursed be the fruit of your womb. And Carmen Elsken was right. Evil as landscape. Whoever had called it Horror, with a capital "H"—too much literature on the subject—was merely intellectualizing the simplicity of the obvious.

"Why did you speak to me in the port?"

Faulques came back with difficulty. The woman was right before him. Her shoulders naked beneath the fine straps of her dress. She had a peculiar odor, he was suddenly aware. An intimate, nearly forgotten scent. Of a strong and healthy woman.

"I told you before: I hear your voice every day, at the same hour. Besides, you're a good-looking woman. If you'll allow me."

There was a silence, and she looked away. Again she was surveying the mural, but this time her thoughts seemed to be somewhere else. Then she looked at the painter of battles' hands with an indecisive air, as if awaiting some word or attitude, but Faulques neither spoke nor moved. She shifted a little. She seemed uncomfortable.

"Thank you for showing me your work."

"I'm the one who thanks you for coming."

"May I come back sometime?"

"Of course."

Carmen Elsken walked to the door, stopped at the threshold, and looked around. It's all so strange, she said. Like you. Then she faced him squarely, silhouetted against the light from outdoors, the Prussian blue eyes made slightly less blue by the surrounding white locked with his. And Faulques knew that if he took one step toward her, lifted his hand and slipped those straps from her tan shoulders, the dress would fall to her feet with nothing to stop it, and the external light would gild her naked body. He felt a slight shiver. Fleeting. There is a time for everything, he told himself. And this wasn't it. It couldn't be. He looked away, toward the floor, and lifted his shoulders slightly. Really, he thought with amazement, it wasn't hard at all to leave things as they were. Not now. So he walked past the woman—he could feel her amazement as he brushed past her, went outside, and waited for her to join him. She came slowly, studying him thoughtfully, and when she reached his side, she smiled, and her mouth opened to pronounce words that never passed her lips. Faulques accompanied her to the beginning of the path, shook the hand she held out to him, and watched her walk away. Before she was out of sight among the pines, Carmen Elsken turned twice to look back.

When Faulques returned to the tower, the sun was lower in its slow descent over Cabo Malo, and the light through the doorway was lending a yellow glow to the white plaster on the opposite wall where figures somewhere between Bruegel and Goya—the frontier of atrocity seen through modern eyes—were sketched in charcoal on different planes at the foot of the erupting volcano: the man clubbing the wounded one to death with his harquebus, the one stripping the dead, the dog devouring cadavers, the executions, the torture wheel, the tree with bodies hanging like clusters of fruit. Evil beyond the control of reason and presented as man's natural instinct. The painter of battles stood rooted before the scene, studying it. Evil, Carmen Elsken had said with extraordinary lucidity, or intuition. That was the precise word, and now it was slithering through every twist and turn of Faulques' memory as he picked up his brushes and started working on that area of the mural, glimpsing out of the corner of his eye the Evil incarnate in the gaze of the soldiers, in that of the child sitting on the ground beside his mother. That childish and disturbing face was not the fruit of his imagination. It had an exact locus in space and time, in addition to graphic proof: page 42 of the photography book on the table. It held Faulques' simplest and most terrible photographs. A smiling child, an empty soccer stadium. But there had never been a war disaster as sinister as this.

It had happened on the ill-defined Serbo-Croatian border, a little before Vukovar. The village was called Dragovac; an Orthodox church, another Catholic, a town hall, a sports stadium. A quiet country place. The Balkan conflict had passed through with no apparent noise; the one visible trace was the leveled property where the Catholic church had stood. For the rest, there was no house burned, in ruins, or with traces of combat or shooting. The inhabitants devoted themselves to their chores and seldom saw soldiers. Everything would have been nearly bucolic had one detail not intervened: the Croatians of Dragovac, about a hundred persons, had disappeared overnight. Only Serbians were left. Rumors were circulating of another slaughter, so Faulques and Olvido had provided themselves with Yugoslavian Army safe conducts and driven there by way of the highway that followed the Vrbas River. They reached Dragovac in the morning, when nearly everyone was working in the fields. They parked in front of the town hall and walked around without being bothered by anyone. There was no hostility, and no cooperation; people replied to every question with evasion or silence. No one knew anything about the Croatians, no one had seen Croatians. No one remembered them. The one incident occurred at the open space where the Catholic church had stood, when two militiamen wearing the Serbian eagle on their caps asked to see their papers. No photo, they were told. *Verboten*. Forbidden. At first Faulques was worried because they had said *verbluten,* and that meant to die by bleeding to death—later he considered that there wasn't much difference, and that maybe that's what they'd meant to say. A timely smile from Olvido, some cigarettes, and a little chat had cleared the air. Period, Faulques concluded. Let's go. They went back to the car, and were about to leave town when they passed the stadium. Not a soul in sight. Suddenly Faulques had a strange sensation and stopped the car. They sat there, Faulques with his hands on the wheel, Olvido with the bag of cameras in her lap, looking at each other. Then, without a word, they got out of the car and walked around. No one was there except a boy watching them from beside a dead tree. Something sinister was floating in the air, the absence of sound in the gray cement building, so somber and deserted that not even birds were flying above it. And when they walked beneath the arch of the entrance and came out on the bare soccer field, no grass, raw dirt, and that strange odor, Olvido stopped, shaking. They're here, she said in a low voice. All of them. That was when the boy joined them. He had followed them, and now went to sit close to them on one of the stadium steps. He must have been about eight or ten years old, and he was thin and blond, with very light-colored eyes. A Serbian boy. He had a rough wooden gun stuffed into the belt of his short pants. And then, before either Faulques or Olvido had spoken a word, the boy smiled. You are looking Croatians? he asked in schoolboy English. Then without waiting for an answer, his smile grew broader. In this town you will find none, he said, his voice contemptuous. *Nema nichta.* No Croatians here, never been any. Olvido shivered again, as if struck by a blast of cold air. He knows as well as you and I, she murmured. But Faulques shook his head. He knows better than we do, he said. And he likes it. That was when he raised his camera to focus on the boy; eyes icy as frost, and that merciless, evil smile.

17.

"I HOPE IT WASN'T TOO ANNOYING," said Ivo Markovic.

He was sitting on the steps of the spiral stair, hands crossed in his lap, enveloped in the reddish light coming through the west window. His attitude was peaceful and courteous, as usual. Nearly solicitous.

"I thought, just between you and me, that the gun was a little too much. It tilted the balance of the situation . . . I don't know if you understand what I mean."

Faulques shrugged without answering. In fact, and to his amazement, what Markovic had just told him didn't matter much. He finished cleaning the brushes, sucked the tips, and put them away. He checked to see that all the jars of paint were closed, then looked at the Croatian.

"I thought we were going to play fair," he said.

"Yes, as far as possible." Markovic blinked behind the lenses of his glasses, as if what he had just heard embarrassed him. "Except that I want to be sure that it's fair on both sides."

"I don't imagine myself strangling you with my bare hands. I'm too old for that."

"You're being dramatic, señor Faulques."

The painter of battles couldn't avoid a sneer. Or maybe it was the trace of a smile. He shook his head, busied himself putting his painting utensils in order, and again stopped in front of Markovic. The Croatian had showed up a quarter of an hour before, cleanly shaven and wearing a freshly ironed shirt. He knocked at the door, asking permission to come in, and once inside took a good long look at the mural, and another, no less long, at Faulques. You've done more painting since I was last here, he said. The figures beside the door, the hanged men, and the rest. Really, you've been working hard. And look. This strange couple—pointing at Hector and Andromache—remind me of me telling my wife good-bye. Funny, isn't it? Paradoxes of life. She was crying because she was afraid I'd be killed, and then she was the one who died. With the boy. And here I am. Markovic repeated pensively the *And here I am,* and stood looking at the three cigarette butts Faulques had just put on the table. He seemed completely absorbed, and then he touched his nose. It's true, he said. I took the liberty of coming this morning while you were down in the village. I wanted to take a look. I spent some time admiring your work. There are things I needed to think about, alone, before this painting. And let me tell you this: I don't know if it's good, but it makes you think. It says a lot about you. And about me. Then I was indiscreet, and looked through your things. Upstairs I found the shotgun and shells. I threw all of it over the cliff before I left.

Faulques had finished arranging his things, ending up before Markovic, who was still sitting on the step. With calm, deliberate movements, he went to the table, took a knife from the drawer, and placed it among the painting utensils: a strong, threatening diver's knife, its blade a little rusted. The Croatian followed every movement with his eyes.

"The bad thing about memories," he said finally, "is that they can turn you into a prophet. Don't you agree? Even you yourself."

He said this in an enigmatic tone. He seemed to be awaiting a nod of agreement, a gesture of complicity. After a pause he took out a pack of cigarettes and put one between his lips.

"Have you ever imagined a crazed mole, señor Faulques?"

He bent his head to light the cigarette and then sat staring at the lighter, turning it over and over. Finally he put it back in his pocket.

"When I got out of the concentration camp and learned the news about my wife and son, that's how I felt. Like a crazed mole digging in every direction, with no objective. Until I thought of you. That led me back to sanity. To light."

He contemplated Faulques with a friendly expression. Grateful. Faulques shook his head.

"Your sanity is debatable."

"Don't say that. I'm so sane that I amaze myself. Thanks to what you did to my life, I've become aware of the role we all play in this painting. Truthfully, I'm grateful. Very."

He pulled a few times on his cigarette, reflecting, and then got up and walked toward the mural. Also, he said, I've learned a few things. For example, that once something's done it can never be undone, or remedied. You can only pay the price. The penance. I hope that you've learned that, too.

"And tell me . . . why did you paint that woman with her head shaved? Isn't the rape enough? The blood on her thighs and the little boy seeing it?"

He seemed preoccupied with that. Truly upset. Faulques walked over to him. They stood side by side, studying the painting. Professional distortion, said the painter of battles. I suppose. A photographer's reflexes. Women with shaved heads, women violated.

"Do you know those old photos of the liberation of France? In a photograph it's nearly impossible to tell if the woman was raped. You have to explain it, and then the image doesn't work. And it's the same if you paint it. A woman with a shaved head is more dramatic. It allows the imagination to work better."

Markovic reflected on that, and showed his agreement. You're right, he said. Dramatic. Smoke made him squint as he leaned over to study the image on the wall more closely.

"There's something disturbing about that woman," he commented. "Maybe her . . . I don't know how to say it. Animality? She seems almost inhuman, if I can say it that way. Those naked thighs, the belly. There's something about her that's more animal than human." He looked at the painter with renewed respect. "That isn't accidental, is it? That isn't incompetence on your part."

Faulques made a vague gesture.

"I'm not a talented painter. But maybe what you say is true. Violence, any violence, turns the person subjected to it into a thing, a piece of animal flesh . . . I think you will agree."

"I do. From experience."

Markovic moved along the circular wall that the light from the west was darkening in a few places and turning red in others. He stopped at the man who was clubbing the dying man. The body on the ground, barely sketched, was nothing more than a few gray and ochre lines. A formless face.

"Someone said," commented Markovic, "that the person who hits, who tortures, who kills, becomes an irrational animal himself . . . What's your opinion on that? Do you believe that you can think and beat someone at the same time?"

Faulques meditated on that a moment. Or seemed to be meditating.

"They're compatible," he said. "Killing and thinking."

"Like that sniper of yours? The artist of the rifle."

"As one example."

"Once I read that there is nothing intelligent in the act of killing."

"The person who said or wrote that is not well-informed."

Markovic nodded. I believe that too, the gesture said.

"And how are you doing? Have you thought over the things I've been telling you? I mean whether you feel you're an accomplice or a participant in your painting . . . Do you think someone can think and photograph at the same time?"

"What I think is that you talk too much. I'm beginning to regret not having that shotgun."

"You have the knife."

"That's not the same."

Now Markovic laughed, pleased. A frank, sincere laugh. He drew the last drag on his cigarette, crushed it out in the mustard jar, and laughed again. Then once more he stood looking at the mural, and after that pointed to *The Eye of War,* still on the table. Two of your photos are very well-known, he said. They're in that book. From Africa. A man who's being beaten by several people and then hacked with machetes before your camera. You know the ones I mean?

"Of course. Freetown, in Sierra Leone. The man they killed there. One photo shot before and the other afterward."

Markovic nodded, satisfied. It was interesting, he said, to compare those two photos with images on a TV program he'd seen about war photographs. He didn't know whether Faulques knew, but he, too, appeared in that report, in a sequence recorded at the time of the event. In your first photo you see how the victim was being beaten and hacked with machetes, and in the second you see him lying on the ground, bleeding, badly slashed. However, in the television footage shot from a greater distance, you could see Faulques shooting the first photo, and then on his knees, asking them not to kill the man. In a posture like praying, or pleading.

The painter of battles' mouth twisted.

"I wasn't convincing."

It certainly wasn't among his best memories. If all wars were a road to hell, Africa was the shortcut. *Chac, chac.* That sound of machetes striking flesh and bone was another thing he hadn't been able to photograph, not even paint. Certain sounds were perfect in themselves, and had their own color: the tempered green in the middle and long tones of the violin, the dark blue of the night wind, the gray of rain drumming on the window. But that chopping sound was impossible to compose on the palette. Its features were lost, like planes in Cézanne's colors.

"You didn't, it's true, convince them." Markovic was watching him closely. "Although I confess that I was surprised to see you do it. I'd thought you were an indifferent witness."

"There's your answer. Sometimes photographing and thinking are compatible."

"At any rate, you kept working. You took the second photo after the man was dead at your feet . . . Had it occurred to you in the interim that maybe they killed him because you were there? That they did it so you would photograph it?"

The painter of battles didn't answer. Of course he'd thought of it. He'd even suspected that that's exactly what had happened. Now he knew that no photograph is inert, or passive. They all had an influence on the surroundings, on the people they framed. On each of the infinite Markovics whose lives the camera appropriated. That's why Olvido photographed only places and objects, never persons; she had been the subject of cameras for too long not to know the dangers. The responsibilities. In the time they had traveled together through wars, it was she who succeeded in keeping herself on the margin, not Faulques.

"Do you think that kneeling down for ten seconds redeems you?" Markovic persisted.

Faulques slowly returned to the present: the tower,

the man at his side examining the mural. Those photographs the Croatian had been talking about. After thinking it over for a moment, Faulques gestured with upturned palms.

"There were times my camera prevented things."

Markovic clicked his tongue, doubtful. Then he in turn seemed to reflect, and he made a gesture that rectified his reaction. Maybe, he concluded finally, Faulques wasn't actually proud that he had prevented something. But maybe he wasn't sorry for the times he hadn't, either. He was thinking, for example, of those kids he had photographed in Lebanon, attacking a tank.

The painter of battles looked at the Croatian with surprise. That individual had done his homework.

"I told you, you're my broken razor." Markovic tapped his forehead with one finger. "I've had a lot of time . . . You remember that photo?"

Faulques remembered. On the outskirts of Beirut, four very young Palestinian children had left their cover so he would photograph them attacking an Israeli Merkava tank with a handheld RPG grenade launcher. The tank's turret had swung around like a lazy monster, fired its cannon, and killed three of the boys. Front page on the world's newspapers. David against Goliath, and so on. One child left standing in the dust in front of the tank, grenade launcher on his shoulder, looking with bafflement at his three dead companions. Faulques knew that if he hadn't been there with his cameras, it would never have happened. Or not that way. Apparently, Markovic thought the same thing. The painter of battles wondered how much time the Croatian had dedicated to studying each of his photos.

"You know what I think now?" Markovic asked. "That photographing people is the same as raping them. Beating them. It tips them out of their normal course, or maybe puts them back on it, I'm not sure which . . . It also obliges them to confront things that weren't in their plans. To see themselves, to know themselves in ways they would never have done otherwise. And sometimes it forces them to die."

"Now you're the one who's being dramatic. It's simpler than that."

The gray eyes grew smaller behind the lenses of the spectacles.

"You believe that?"

"Of course. The influence of the camera is minimal. Life and its rules are present. If those boys hadn't been there, if you hadn't been there, it would have been someone else . . . An ant that gives itself too much importance. It's all the same which ants a man steps on. From below it will always appear to be God's shoe, but what kills them is geometry. The footsteps of Fate on a strictly regimented chessboard."

"Oh, now I understand what you're saying." Markovic shot him a malicious look. "That eases your conscience, doesn't it?"

"Of course. There's no way to ask an accounting of anyone. Futile to go there and beat someone's face to a pulp . . . Besides, remember how I got that shot, without a telephoto lens, with a 35-mm lens and from the level of a man's head. That means that I was close to those boys when the tank fired. And I was standing up."

Neither of the two spoke. Markovic was now studying the beached boats and the ones sailing away through the rain. The innumerable little figures heading toward them, leaving the burning city. Fire and rain, the tension of opposites giving vigor to nature and direction to life, warm colors shrouded with polyhedral, steely, cold forms. And that axis of conquerors, ships, and warriors, different from that of the conquered, a question of angles and perspective, the vertex in the city, one diagonal leading to the raped woman and the boy, stabilizing the line of refugees. All so serene. The eye of the observer was drawn first to Hector and Andromache, then slid naturally toward the battlefield, through the horsemen battling below the indifferent volcano, and, after passing through the devastations of war, ended at the dead boy and the living boy, the latter the victim and also the future executioner of himself—only the dead children were not tomorrow's killers. Despite their rawness, the disasters of war were confined to the middle distance, boxed in by the colors and forms that surrounded them, and the eye stopped for a moment on the warriors waiting to join in the combat, on the soldier in iron, on the woman at the head of the line of refugees, on the thighs of the woman lying on the ground. And finally, completing a triangle, on the volcano, equidistant between the city in flames, to the left, and the other city waking in the fog, unaware of living its last day.

The composition was good, Faulques decided. Or at least reasonably good. Like music to the ear, it forced the eye to look unhurriedly where it should look. Leading you by the hand from the evident to the hidden, that framework of lines and shapes upon which the figurative—people, enigmas distilled into physical manifestations—fitted together with somber intensity, kept everything within natural limits. Prevented abuse, the scream. Excess. It refuted the apparent chaos. On Faulques' mental palette, that painting had the weight of a blue circle, the drama of a yellow triangle, the inevitability of a black line. Because—Olvido pointed out once, although surely it was stolen from someone—an apple could be more terrible than a Laocoön. Or a pair of shoes, she had added later, when she saw a man, with his crutches propped against the wall, polishing his one shoe on a street in Maputo, in Mozambique. Remember, she said, Atget's disturbing photographs in Paris: old shoes lined up on shelves, waiting for owners that seem impossible. Or those of the hundreds of shoes piled up in Nazi extermination camps.

"How strange," Markovic commented. "I always thought that painters beautified the world. That they softened ugliness."

Faulques didn't answer. It was all a question, he was thinking at that moment, of what the observer had in his mind as he looked, or of what the artist put in the viewer's head. Shoes or apples. Even the most innocent of these could suggest a labyrinth, with Ariadne's string twisting inside like a worm.

"You know what I think, señor Faulques? That you don't do yourself justice. You may be a very competent painter, after all."

Now Markovic moved, turned in a circle, checking the windows, the door, the upper floor. He seemed to have a mental plan of it all. A last review.

"I'm sure that anyone who comes into this tower, even if he doesn't know what you and I know, will feel a certain uneasiness." He suddenly looked at Faulques with courteous interest. "How did the woman who was here feel?"

For a moment, the two men's eyes locked. Then the painter of battles smiled.

"Uneasy, I suppose. To a certain point. She said this was evil, and terrible."

"See? That's what I mean. Then you're not as bad a painter as you say you are. Despite all the angles and so many straight lines and so many long shadows . . ."

He lifted his arms, his gesture taking in the totality of the mural. Finally he dropped his hands to his sides.

"Circular, like a trap," he frowned. "A trap for crazed moles."

He looked at Faulques with affection. An affection that the light gray eyes, behind the glasses, made ironic, or cold. The painter of battles shuffled the words "cold" and "affection," attempting to reconcile them in his mind, as he would on a palette. He gave it up, but Markovic was still staring at him, and that was exactly the look. Somehow, the Croatian murmured, I'm proud of you.

"Sorry?"

"I say I'm proud of you."

Silence. Markovic's gaze still hadn't changed.

"And I, señor Faulques, am waiting for you to be proud of me."

The painter of battles rubbed the back of his neck. Perplexed was not the exact word. In fact he understood perfectly what the other man wanted to say. What stunned him were his own sentiments.

"It's been a long road," he conceded.

"As long as yours."

Now Markovic was observing the mural. I believe, he added, that there isn't much more to say. Except that you may want to tell me about that last photo.

"What photo?"

"The one you took of the dead woman on the Borovo Naselje road."

Faulques looked at him, impassive.

"Let's call this off now," he said. "It's time for you to go."

The Croatian tilted his head slightly, as if to assure himself that he'd heard correctly and that everything was in order. That everything was as it should be. Then he nodded slowly, took off his glasses to clean them with his shirttail, and put them back on.

"You're right. That's enough."

It sounded like anticipated nostalgia, the painter of battles thought. Two men accustomed to each other, on the verge of parting. To his deep surprise, he felt extremely calm. Things were going along as they should. At their own time and rhythm. For a moment he wondered what Markovic would do afterward, without him. Without the broken straight razor buried in his brain. At any rate, it wasn't going to be Faulques' problem.

The Croatian took his time going to the door. He did it almost as if he didn't want to go. He stopped there and lifted his hands to light another cigarette with Faulques' lighter, then nodded toward the mural.

"Take your time, señor painter. You may still be

able . . . I don't know. Some of it isn't finished." He turned toward the stand of pines near the edge of the cliff. "I'll be out there, waiting. Take the whole night. Does that seem all right? Till dawn."

"Sounds all right to me."

The late afternoon light was shining, very low, through the pines, surrounding Markovic with a reddish atmosphere that seemed to blend with the painted light of the scenes on the wall. Faulques saw him smile, sadly, cigarette between his lips, saying good-bye to the mural with one last, long look.

"What a shame you can't finish it. Although, if I've understood correctly, that may be the point."

18.

ALL THE COLORS OF A shadow could be transmuted into the color of that shadow, and this one was red: yellow and carmine and a little more yellow, adding a touch of blue to suggest the color of blood, of the gummy mud on the bottom of boots, of crumbled bricks, of the glass covering the ground and reflecting nearby conflagrations, of horizons with blazing petroleum wells, of cities black against explosions of light, the background of impossible paintings that nonetheless seemed extremely realistic. It was, in sum, the shadow of the volcano, or rather, of the objects it illuminated, both its irregular sides foreshortened in the splendor of the crater lording over all from its lethal, Olympian apex, from the upper vertex of the triangle, tinting everything around it with red symmetry.

Inside the tower there was no sound but the droning of the generator outdoors and brushes rasping against the wall. The painter of battles was working feverishly by the light of halogen bulbs. He stopped for an instant, mixed a brownish carmine, burnt sienna, and a little Prussian blue to obtain a warm black, and immediately applied that to emphasize the edges of the zigzagging wounds, like red and ochre lightning flashes, opened in the sides of the volcano. He backed up—when he touched his face he left paint on the stubble on his chin—observed the result, and turned with anxiety toward the part of the mural in the shadows. The bodies hanging in the trees, one of the two armies battling on the plain, some ships to the right of the door, and a section of the modern city were still charcoal sketches on the white plaster. Trying not to think of that—one night didn't give him much time—Faulques went back to his work. The volcano was finished, or nearly so. That completed three parts of the planned mural.

He chose a medium round brush and on a clean corner of the tray quickly mixed white, yellow, a little carmine, and a dot of blue. Then, again approaching the wall, with the resulting color he prolonged one of the cracks on the side of the volcano, giving it the look of a road, a path, and edged it on both sides by mixing grays and blues directly onto the wall. The long, thick stroke—he hadn't time to work it in detail—gave the road an odd appearance. It was a road that in truth led nowhere; it emerged from the crack in the volcano and died here where it met white plaster. It had not figured in Faulques' plans, nor was it sketched on the wall. The effect, nonetheless, was good. It introduced a new axis, an unexpected variant, an exceptional line running from that volcano to the one hanging on the wall of the Museo Nacional de Arte in Mexico, to the green eyes that had met Faulques' when he was looking at that painting for the first time. To Faulques himself, standing there observing Olvido Ferrara walk into his life. A menacing road that ran ahead as straight as the line of a shot, passing through the landscape on the wall to a certain place in the Balkans.

What the hell. Surprised, the painter of battles paused and drank a sip of the cold coffee remaining in the cup sitting atop *The Eye of War.* Reflecting on volcanoes and roads. There wasn't time for anything new, he told himself. Every area of the mural had been meticulously planned before being transferred to the wall, and he'd not foreseen that particular variant; he did, however, see that it fit as if the space had been reserved for it from the beginning. The painter of battles drained the coffee, confirming that in his head, in the eyes contemplating the mural, in the paint-stained hands and the wet brush, unexpected possibilities emerged. Hidden nuances that may always have been there. Paradoxically, those new strokes venturing into the part as yet unpainted—or the bare space itself—seemed to materialize and confirm what had been painted on the rest, in the same way that a handful of sand sifting through your fingers until it disappeared would perhaps be a suitable artistic concept for the word "sand."

The pain sent its warning again, issuing from his gut. The painter of battles didn't move for a couple of seconds, lying in wait for it, and when the warning was confirmed he barely smiled to himself, with the perverse malice of knowing things the pain didn't know. In any case, Faulques was not disposed that night to concede anything to it; he didn't have time. So he cut it off immediately, almost precipitously: two tablets, a sip of cognac from a glass. He set the bottle on the table among the jars and brushes and after a moment's hesitation picked it up again and drank directly from the bottle. Then he went outdoors and propped himself against the exterior wall, feeling the coolness of the night breeze as he waited for the medication to take effect. He watched the stars and the distant reflection from the lighthouse slashing across the cliff. At some moment, among the luminous dots of the fireflies flitting beneath the dark mass of the pines, he thought he saw the red glow of a cigarette.

When the last thrusts of pain faded, Faulques went back inside the tower, feeling the gentle chemical lucidity of the sedative dissolved in his stomach. Prepared to renew his work, he again reviewed the part of the mural that wasn't finished. Suddenly he saw something he'd not seen before. A different, more heterodox and daring work had slipped in there, he discovered with great surprise. A white space in which what was incomplete, absent, was a confirmation of its very presence. Motivated by this intuition, he put down the brush—without rinsing or drying it, just as it was—and worked at obtaining the effect he wanted by coating the thumb of his right hand with the mixture on the palette. Then he rubbed the paint the length of the recently created road, making it into an inexorable river of long meanderings, of streambeds and tiny offshoots difficult to perceive at a glance. He kept working with his hands, without brushes. Now he was applying paint with his fingers—white, blue, yellow, white—obtaining unique greens similar to the morning light on a meadow, grays like the asphalt of a highway plowed up by shrapnel, dirty blues of a sky clouded by the smoke from burning houses. And a green as liquid as the eyes of the woman he remembered in that landscape, jeans tight over her long legs, khaki safari jacket, blond hair combed into two braids held by rubber bands, the bag with her cameras over her shoulder and one across her chest. Olvido Ferrara walking along the Borovo Naselje road.

She had said something that very morning. She said it as they were checking the equipment after spending the night curled up together under an archway on a patio near the main street of Vukovar that seemed to be sheltered from Serbian mortars. They'd been bombing the immediate areas: several times flashes illuminated the broken roof tiles of nearby buildings, but three hours of silence had followed. The two photographers got up at dawn, when the first light was creating a chiaroscuro-like glaze over everything, and it was then that Olvido had looked around—fronts of deserted houses, bits of brick and glass scattered everywhere—and she had spoken without looking at Faulques, as if expressing aloud a thought that was deep inside her. It's more a matter of imagination than of optics, she'd said. Then she fell silent, glancing around that somber place, the camera body open in her hands, the film half loaded. She closed the camera back with a *clic*, started the winding motor, and smiled at Faulques, distracted, as if everything that was in her head at that moment was somewhere far away. Those guys, she added suddenly, that Géricault and Rodin, were right: only the artist is truthful. Photography is what lies.

Later that morning, Faulques could hear Olvido's white sneakers crunching on gravel—the road was pocked with holes from artillery—as he walked along the other side, the two loaded cameras in his hands, eyes on the terrain and on the crossroad ahead, an open area they would have to pass through to get to Borovo Naselje. A group of Croatian soldiers preceded them and another group followed. Shots from automatic weapons rattled in the distance: a muffled crackle chorused by beams of the burning roof of a nearby house. There was also a dead Serbian soldier in the middle of the road, killed the day before by one of the mortars that had left star-shaped depressions in the road. The Serb was on his back, his clothing shredded by shrapnel, covered by the same gray dust caked on his closed eyes and open mouth, his pockets turned inside out, and his boots missing. Beside him were things disdained by the pillagers: a green steel helmet with a red star, an empty wallet, a few documents scattered about him, a key ring, a ballpoint pen, a wrinkled handkerchief. As he drew near the corpse, Faulques considered the possibility of a shot with the burning house in the background. So he calculated the light at 1/125 shutter speed and the aperture at 5.6, and readied the Nikon F3, and as he drew near he paused an instant, knee on the ground, and framed the body: legs spread open in a V, shoeless feet with one toe poking through a hole in a sock, arms outspread with his rejected belongings scattered nearby, the burning house to the left making another angle with the road. What there was no way to photograph was the buzzing of flies—they won all the battles—or the odor, evocative of so many other odors and buzzings, flies and stench among bloated bodies in Sabra and Shatila; hands bound with wire in the dumping grounds of San Salvador; in Kolwezi, trucks offloading cadavers pushed out by mechanical blades: *zumzumzum.* A clever photographer, someone had once said, could photograph anything well. But Faulques knew that whoever said that had never been in a war zone. It was impossible to photograph the danger, or the guilt. The sound of a bullet as it bursts a skull. The laugh of a man who has just won seven cigarettes by betting on whether the fetus of a woman he just disemboweled with his bayonet is male or female. As for the corpse of the shoeless Serb, maybe a writer could have found a few words. For the flies, for example. *Zumzumzumzumzumzum.* The smell was another thing. Or the unrelieved loneliness of the dead, dust-covered body: no one brushed the dust off a cadaver. Only the artist is truthful, Faulques remembered. And told himself that maybe it was true, that photography could have been truthful when it was naïve and imperfect, in its beginnings, when the camera could capture only static objects, and cities on old plates appeared as deserted scenes in which humans and animals were merely glimpsed, hazy, phantasmal traces very like those of a later photograph taken in Hiroshima on August 6, 1945: on a wall the hint of a human silhouette, and a stairway dissolved in the deflagration of the bomb.

When he lowered his camera, Faulques saw that Olvido had stopped on the other side of the road in order not to interfere with his shot, and that she was watching him. He got up and crossed the road toward her, and as he did so noticed that she did not take her eyes off him, as if she were studying his every movement, his every gesture, his every expression. In recent days he had caught her several times looking at him like that, first it had been furtively, then openly, as if she were trying to engrave in her memory everything about him, all the images of that stage of a long and strange journey she was about to end. A journey for which she already had a return ticket in her pocket. Faulques was feeling infinitely sad and cold. To hide this he looked around: the soldiers moving toward the crossroad, the burning house. Overhead was a cloudless sky, and a sun that hadn't as yet reached a height that made it difficult to shoot photographs and was casting Olvido's shadow on the loose gravel of the road, its roughness deforming her silhouette. For an instant, Faulques thought of trying a shot of that flawed shadow, but he didn't do it. It was then that Olvido saw a torn, faded notebook on the ground. A school notebook with blue covers, missing some pages, lying open on the grass. She raised her camera, took two steps forward, looking for the frame, took another step to the left, and stepped on the mine.

Faulques looked at his hands stained with red paint, and then studied the mural encircling him. Forms changed when touched with color. The white spaces, the charcoal sketch on the white plaster, no longer seemed empty to him. Under the intense light of the halogen bulbs, everything fused in his brain the way Impressionist paintings do: colors, spaces, volumes that blended into the desired representation only on the viewer's retina. The completed figures and landscapes were as real, as true—*only the artist is truthful* came to mind—as those barely hinted at, forms foreshadowed on the wall, the meticulous brushwork and heavy lines, still-wet paint applied with his fingers over figures already painted or over white spaces. A long road. There was an underlying schema, a perspective as fabulous and endless as a Möbius strip that ran around the circle of the mural without ever stopping, integrating each of the elements, weaving together the ships sailing away in the rain, the burning city on the hill, the refugees, the soldiers, the raped woman and boy executioner, the man about to die, the woods with hanged men like clusters of fruit, the battle on the plain, the struggling men slashing at each other in the foreground, the caballeros about to join the combat, the confident, sleeping city amid its steel, concrete, and glass towers. The visible universe and the conceivable immensity of nature. Everything he had wanted to paint was there: Bruegel, Goya, Uccello, Dr. Atl, everything that had prepared Faulques' eyes and hands to express the things that during his life had penetrated the viewfinder of his camera and been imprinted on the Plato's cave of his retina—the photographic film and paper played only secondary roles—explained at last, combined in the geometric formula whose beginning and final result converged in the triangle presiding over everything: the black, brown, gray, red volcano. The symbol of the cryptogram, stripped of sentiments and implacable in its symmetries, its cracks of lava spreading out like a spider web whose net encompassed the cipher of the universe, the fissures in the wall of the old tower serving to sustain it all, the dawn of the day that soon would be seeping through the windows, the man waiting outside while the painter of battles completed his work.

Only one thing was left to do. Suddenly it seemed

so obvious that his lips twisted in a smile. Olvido Ferrara, were she there, would have laughed herself sick: he imagined her throwing back her head of wheat-colored hair, mocking him with her liquid, green eyes. *It's more a question of imagination than of optics, Faulques.* The photograph lies, and only the artist . . . and so on and so on.

He went to the table and picked up the magazine cover with the photo of Ivo Markovic: a blond young man with drops of sweat on his face, eyes vacant and expression weary, very different from the man waiting out by the cliff. Lorenz butterflies and broken razors were active in that image, which at the moment of being imprinted on the negative was still unaware of its consequences, and which had lasted into the present: Faulques looking at that photo in the old tower above the sea. *Truth is in things, not in people,* he remembered. *But it needs us to be manifest.* Olvido would still have been laughing, he thought, if she could see him at that moment, magazine cover in his hand, scrabbling among the painting materials, the empty and filled tubes and jars, brushes, books piled on the table. He remembered her lying on the floor for hours trimming photos in which the only living thing was a blurry smear of humans fading like fleeting ghosts. Collages and *trouvés*. Of course. At last he found a large, nearly full pot of acrylic medium. With a thick, clean brush he soaked the back of the page and then turned to the wall, looking for a good place to put it. He chose a white space situated between the volcano and the confident modern city and pasted it there, smoothing it onto the slightly irregular surface of the wall. Then as he studied what he'd done, never taking his eyes off it, he felt for the bottle of cognac. He grasped it in fingers growing stiff from the acrylic beginning to dry on his hands, lifted the bottle to his mouth, and took such a long swig that it brought tears to his eyes. I have it now, he said to himself. Now everything is where it should be. Then with various tubes of pure color in his left hand, he went back to the mural and began to apply paint in thick strokes, first curves and then both straight and spontaneous lines, wet over wet, using his fingers as palette knives until the photo of Ivo Markovic was integrated into the whole, joined to the wall and to the rest of the mural with a polyhedral frame of ochres, yellows, and reds that he finished with a slash as dark and long and phantasmal as a shadow, destined to remain there when the deteriorating wall had eaten the pasted-on page.

The painter of battles left his tubes of paint on the floor and washed his hands in the basin. He felt strangely relaxed. Empty as a nutshell, he thought suddenly. Slowly he dried his hands, reflecting on his thoughts and feelings. It was strange to see himself as if he were painted into the mural, almost at the end of the journey. He dropped the rag on the table, looked for the box of tablets, put two in his mouth and swallowed them with another sip of cognac. That would prevent the pain from reappearing at an inappropriate moment. Then he picked up the knife and slid it in the back of his belt. Equipped for combat, he thought suddenly, and smiled slightly. Olvido liked that: she enjoyed the moment of preparing to leave, the tension of waiting, as she silently reviewed her equipment in some hotel room before they started off to some difficult place. Checking cameras and film, filling her pack and pockets with necessities: medicine kit, maps, water, notepad, pens. Only what she could carry and would not impede walking, running, surviving, before she closed the door on everything superfluous. I look like a little girl playing dress up, she'd said once. Ready to be someone else. Don't you think, Faulques? Or not to be anyone. In any case, each time I leave behind an old skin, like a weary serpent.

Before he turned out the spotlights and went outside into the night, the painter of battles took one last look at his work. It would look better, he thought, when the natural light fell through the east window and, as it did every day, lent its characteristic golden tone to the effects of light painted in the mural. Then, as the rays of the sun moved along the wall, the fire in the city would be redder, the volcano more somber, and the rain more gray. Even though it wasn't a masterpiece, he said serenely. He tipped his head, reflecting. Absolutely not. Strange, Ivo Markovic and Carmen Elsken had called it. All those angles, and on and on. With an absorbed smile, Faulques wondered what Olvido Ferrara would have said. What would people in the future who came to see his mural think . . . as long as the tower was standing?

It wasn't a good painting, he concluded. But it was perfect.

19.

HE CLOSED AND LOCKED THE DOOR and slowly walked toward the black outlines of the pines, which the distant flashes from the lighthouse revealed at intervals beneath a star-filled sky. The calm was absolute; even the soft breeze had died down. Faulques heard only his own footsteps, the shrilling of crickets in the undergrowth, and the long, muffled, almost human death rattle of pebbles being dragged by the tide. As he neared the woods, he stopped a moment, surrounded by the luminous dots of the fireflies. He was tranquil, his mind clear. Serene in memory and intentions. He felt no apprehension or fear. With the effects of the sedative, his heart was beating regularly. Precisely. It didn't change when a shadow emerged from the trees and the beam from the lighthouse shone for an instant on Ivo Markovic's shirt.

"You've moved fast," the Croatian said. "It's still an hour till dawn."

"I had all the time I needed. You were right."

"I don't understand."

"My work was almost finished, and I didn't know it."

They were silent. After a while, Markovic's dark

silhouette moved a little. The next flash from the lighthouse revealed him sitting on a boulder. The painter of battles squatted down near him.

"Have you come armed, señor Faulques?"

"To a point."

"Then don't come too close."

There was another long pause. It seemed as if the Croatian was laughing to himself, quietly, but it may have been the sound of the sea below.

"Am I to believe that you are satisfied with your painting?"

Faulques shrugged his shoulders in the darkness.

"I think so." He shook his head. "No, I'm sure. It's the way it should be."

Markovic said nothing. The tiny dots of the fireflies danced between the two motionless shadows.

"Without you I would never have been capable of seeing it," the painter of battles continued. "I would have kept working for days and weeks, until the entire wall was covered. Moving away from the moment . . . from the exact stopping point."

"I'm pleased that I've been useful."

"You've been more than that. You made me see things I hadn't seen before."

A pause. Maybe Markovic was mulling over the words he'd just heard. Faulques shifted a little until he was sitting against the trunk of a pine. From there he admired the flashes from the lighthouse, the luminous tapestry of the housing developments creeping up the side of the mountains beyond Puerto Umbría, and, toward the horizon, the black dome riddled with stars.

"Tell me the truth, am I in the painting?" the Croatian asked abruptly.

His interest seemed real. Sincere. Faulques smiled to himself.

"I already told you. You, me . . . we're all in it."

Markovic was slow to speak again.

"Symmetries, no?"

"That's it."

"All those painted lines and angles."

"Yes."

Markovic lighted a cigarette. In the glow of the match reflected on the lens of his spectacles, Faulques could see the lowered head, the eyes closed against the glare of the flame. It was a good time, he thought. Five seconds of blindness would be enough to use the knife and finish the whole thing. His skilled instinct calculated angles, volumes, distance. He considered, dispassionately, the most convenient approach, the move that would put things in their place. At that point in his story, Faulques knew too well that between the act of taking a photograph—that mechanical ballet on the chessboard that brought the hunter closer to the prey, or the prey to the hunter—and the act of killing a human being stood only minimal technical differences. But he had to douse that thought. He sat indolently propped against the tree, his back sticky with resin. He was soiling, he thought absurdly, his last clean shirt.

"Is there a conclusion, señor Faulques? In the movies there is always someone who sums things up before the dénouement."

The painter of battles focused on the motionless tip of the cigarette. Fireflies flitted around them, fleeting, golden. Their larvae, he thought, fed in the viscera of living snails. Objective cruelty: fireflies, whales. Human beings. In millions of years, few things had changed.

"The conclusion is there," he pointed toward the dark mass of the tower, aware that Markovic couldn't see his gesture. "Painted on the wall."

"As well as your feeling about what you did to me?"

That irritated Faulques.

"I didn't do anything to you," he rebutted harshly. "I have nothing to be sorry for. I thought you'd understood that."

"I do understand. The wings of the butterfly aren't guilty, right? No one is."

"Just the opposite. We are. You and I. Your wife and your son. We are all a part of the monster that moves us around the chessboard."

Again silence. Then came Markovic's quiet laugh. This time it wasn't the murmur of the sea on the rocks below.

"Crazed moles," the Croatian prompted.

"That's it." Faulques grimaced. "You expressed it well the other day . . . The more obvious everything is, the less sense it seems to make."

"There's no way out, then?"

"There are consolations. The prisoner running as they shoot at him believes he's free . . . Do you know what I mean?"

"I think I do."

"At times that's enough. The simple effort to understand things. To get a glimpse of the strange cryptogram . . . In a certain way, a quiet tragedy more than a farce, don't you think? There are always temporary analgesics. With luck, they're enough to keep you going. And used wisely, they're good to the end."

"For example?"

"Lucidity, pride, culture . . . Laughter . . . I don't know. Things like that."

"Broken straight razors?"

"That, too."

The tip of the cigarette glowed.

"And love?"

"Including love."

"Even though it ends or is lost, like everything else?"

"Yes."

The cigarette glowed three times before Markovic spoke again.

"I think I understand it all now, señor Faulques."

To the east, where Ahorcados Island raised its dark peak then faded into the sea, the faint line of dawn began to show, intensifying the contrast between the still black water and the sky. The painter of battles was cold. Mechanically, he touched the handle of the knife in his belt, at his back.

"We need to finish things," he said softly.

Markovic gave no sign that he had heard. He had put out his cigarette and lighted another. In the flame of the lighter the Croatian's cheeks looked sunken and the shadows beneath his eyes more dark.

"Why did you photograph the dead woman?"

More irritation was the first thing Faulques felt when he heard that. A restrained anger that coursed through his veins like a supplementary heartbeat. It was the second time Markovic had asked that question.

"That isn't your affair."

Markovic seemed to reflect on whether it was or it wasn't.

"In a certain way it is," he concluded. "Think it over and maybe you'll agree with me."

Faulques thought. Maybe, he said to himself finally, I do agree with him.

"Because I need to tell you," Markovic persisted, "that it was a real surprise . . . I was walking down the road with my companions, we heard the explosion, and some of us went to take a closer look. But we were in a zone with a lot of activity and our officer ordered us to keep going. A dead woman, someone said. Then I recognized the two of you. You'd photographed me three days before, when we were fleeing Petrovci . . . I couldn't see the woman very well, but I knew it was the same one. And as we passed by I saw you take up your camera and shoot the picture."

There was a silence and the tip of the cigarette glowed. Faulques focused on that red dot similar to the countless red dots, darker and more liquid, that had spattered Olvido's body; she was motionless, unusually pale—her skin suddenly white, as if overexposed—on her back in the ditch, her right hand beside the camera at the level of her stomach, her left arm bent, the one with the wristwatch, palm turned upward and near her face, the earring in the shape of a little gold ball in the lobe of the ear from which a thread of red blood trickled, staining a braid and running down her cheek to her neck and mouth and around half-open eyes staring at the grass and the clumps of overturned dirt where a pool of blood was collecting. Kneeling beside her, with his cameras hanging loose, deafened and confused by the closeness of the explosion, Faulques, as Olvido's safari jacket and jeans grew dark with blood on the part of her body in contact with the ground, had reached out, first to look for a place where he might stanch the bleeding, and then to touch her neck, seeking a pulse already impossible to discern.

"Did you love her?" Markovic asked.

Faulques looked toward the east. There was not a breath of air and the horizon was noticeably lighter, showing blue and gray tones as the light of the stars dimmed.

"Maybe that was why you took the picture . . . Right? To make things seem normal."

Even then, the painter of battles didn't speak. Before his eyes he saw, in the developing tray in his darkroom, the outlines and shadows of a photographic image emerging, the way the subtle line of the horizon in the distance was becoming more pronounced. *The house where you are living is dark,* he remembered. He had looked at Olvido, dead, through the viewfinder, first blurred and then clearer as he turned the focus ring from infinity to 1.6 meters. The image in the viewfinder appeared in color, but the thing Faulques remembered above all others, the one that time and memory preserved—he had destroyed the only copy on paper and the negative lay buried among kilometers of archived film—was the gamut of grays as the fixative slowly brought out an image on the photographic paper, a slow materialization revealed in the red light of the darkroom. The little gold earring in Olvido's earlobe was the last thing to appear in the tray. Charon must have been satisfied with her offering.

"I saw the mine," he said.

His eyes were still on the blue-gray line of the horizon. When at last he turned toward Markovic, the spark of the lighthouse outlined the Croatian for an instant.

"Do you mean," he asked, "that you saw the mine before she stepped on it?"

"Yes. Or, to be more precise, I divined it."

"And you didn't say anything?"

"I hesitated three seconds. That was all. Three. She was leaving, do you understand? She was already leaving me. Suddenly I wanted to know how far . . . I don't know. How she was leaving didn't depend on me. Maybe geometry had something to say on that subject."

Markovic listened very quietly. If it weren't for the red tip of his cigarette, or the periodic flashes from the lighthouse that silhouetted the Croatian, Faulques would have thought he wasn't there.

"She took two steps forward," he continued. "Exactly two. She wanted to shoot something there on the ground, a school notebook . . . I saw that the grass in the ditch was standing straight up. Tall, and untouched. No one had stepped on it."

At that, Markovic clicked his tongue. Familiar with grass trodden and untrodden.

"I get it now," he murmured. "You always have to be suspicious of that."

"I thought . . . Well. She could stop where she was. You understand."

Markovic seemed to understand very well.

"But she moved," he said.

She moved. Faulques nodded. The way a piece moves on a chessboard. She'd taken one more step, this time to the left. Just one.

"And you were looking at all those lines and squares . . . Quiet, and fascinated."

That was the exact word, the painter of battles conceded. Fascinated. Before she took that last step, she had raised the camera to take the photo. Only three seconds: a nearly imperceptible instant. Chaos and its rules, to put it that way, had had its chance. Then Faulques had thought that was enough, and had opened his mouth to tell her to stop. At that instant there was a flash, and Olvido collapsed.

"Do you remember the last thing she said? Didn't she look at you before or say anything to you?"

"No. She was walking along; she was going to shoot the picture and she stepped on the mine. That's it. She died without me, without any sense I was watching her. Without realizing she was dying."

The glowing tip of Markovic's cigarette disappeared. The fireflies, too, had disappeared and the compact mass of the tower was slowly emerging where the sky was shaded from black to dark blue.

"She was leaving," Faulques insisted.

He heard the Croatian. A quiet shuffling on the ground, a stirring in the bushes. The painter of battles touched the shaft of his knife but left it where it was, his fingers brushing over it but not pulling it out. Suddenly he was so tired that he could have dropped off to sleep right there. After all, he thought, what was going to happen had been happening for a hundred and fifty million years. Something as ordinary as life and the universe itself. Also, it was very late for everyone, he thought. Especially him.

Markovic's voice sounded quiet, brooding. Instead of conversing, he seemed to be expressing a thought aloud. Once again he stood out against the flare from the lighthouse. He stood taller than usual.

"When I came to look for you, señor Faulques, I thought I was going to kill a living man."

The painter of battles rested his head against the tree trunk and waited calmly, his eyes open in the darkness. He was remembering other dawns, early mornings when he was readying equipment, following a precise routine, pausing at the threshold before closing the door to take a last look around and be sure that everything left behind was orderly and clean. Sitting in the taxi on the way to the airport, traveling through the deserted streets of a sleeping city, not sure whether or not he would be back.

"Well," he said in a low voice, "you will have to make do with what there is."

He didn't change his position or move his head from the support of the trunk as gray, then gold and orange light spread across the horizon. The black silhouette of the tower was backlighted against the first flush of dawn, then everything around it, trees, bushes, rocks, slowly took form. The distant flash of the lighthouse was extinguished just as a soft land breeze blew toward the cliff, where the sea was calm and he no longer heard the sound of pebbles moved by the undertow. Finally, Faulques looked toward the place Ivo Markovic had been, and saw only a half dozen cigarette butts on the ground.

The painter of battles sat where he was for a long

time, never shifting position until the red disk of the sun had risen above the line of the sea near Los Ahorcados Island and its first horizontal rays warmed his skin and made him shut his eyes. Then he got to his feet, brushing pine needles from his trousers, and took a slow, three-hundred-and-sixty-degrees look around him. The gulls screeched as they swooped around the tower, its stone golden in the reddish light from the east. On the side opposite the horizon, the irregular coastline stood out in the soft morning mist, its points given perspective by varied shades of gray, from the darkest and nearest to the most hazy and distant. Like you see in old paintings.

It was, he decided serenely, a beautiful day.

He went down the narrow, steep path, and when he reached the beach, which was still in shadow, he looked out over the sea, quiet, immense, an enormous sheet of mercury the growing light was beginning to turn blue in the distance. He took off his sneakers and shirt and waded a little way into the water, carefully placing his bare feet among the rounded stones on the shore. The water was cold, as it was each morning before his usual one hundred and fifty strokes out and one hundred and fifty strokes back. Its coolness invigorated his muscles and cleared his head. He went back to the dead trunk, to leave, along with his shoes and shirt, the keys to the tower, the few coins from his pockets, and the knife still stuffed in the back of his belt. Then he looked up and smiled, bedazzled: the sun was peering above the cut in the cliff through the branches of the pines, its rays obliquely illuminating the small beach. At that instant Faulques felt a discomfort in his side, the notice of imminent pain returning once more, claiming its rights. The certainty made him shake his head, totally absorbed in the moment. This time, he told himself, it's too late.

Before he went back to the water, he picked up one of the coins he'd set on the dead trunk and put it in his mouth beneath his tongue. Then, now in water up to his waist, he noticed how his track through the pebbles was being erased, just like the sketches disappearing on the finally completed mural drying in the morning sun.

When the pain stabbed again, the painter of battles scarcely noticed. He was swimming with pure concentration, vigorous, moving out with good rhythm and precise geometry, in a straight line that cut exactly in two the semicircle of the cove. In his mouth, along with the savor of salt, he tasted the copper of his coin for Charon. He wondered what he would find beyond the three hundred strokes.

La Navata, December 2005

ABOUT THE AUTHOR

ARTURO PÉREZ-REVERTE's bestselling books, including *The Club Dumas, The Flanders Panel, The Seville Communion,* and the Captain Alatriste series, have been translated into thirty-four languages in fifty countries and have sold millions of copies. Pérez-Reverte was born in 1951 in Cartagena, Spain, and now lives in Madrid, where he was recently elected to the Spanish Royal Academy. A retired war journalist, he covered conflicts in Angola, Bosnia, Croatia, El Salvador, Lebanon, Libya, Nicaragua, Romania, the Persian Gulf, and Sudan, among others. He now writes fiction full-time.